The Cabochon Emerald

The Cabochon Emerald

ELIZABETH HAWKSLEY

Elizabeth Hawksley

ROBERT HALE · LONDON

ISBN 0 7090 6069 6

Robert Hale Limited
Clerkenwell House
Clerkenwell Green
London EC1R 0HT

Photoset in North Wales by
Derek Doyle & Associates, Mold, Flintshire.
Printed in Great Britain by
St Edmundsbury Press Ltd, Bury St Edmunds, Suffolk.
Bound by WBC Book Manufacturers Limited,
Bridgend, Mid-Glamorgan.

*To my son
Gabriel,
with love*

Chapter One

The Prison de Carmes, Rue de Vaugirard, in December 1793: a bitter day and the child shivered, huddled under her grey woollen cloak. Her name was Anna de Cardonnel and she had just celebrated her seventh birthday. A week earlier her mother, the Vicomtesse Anne-Louise de Cardonnel, had been arrested on the charge of suspicion of anti-government activities and was now in the Carmes awaiting trial.

Anna was a thin child with narrow hands and feet and serious brown eyes. She was very simply dressed in a blue woollen dress under the grey cloak and she wore the obligatory Revolutionary cockade pinned onto the collar. She looked younger than her seven years and when she arrived at the prison gates she was let in without much demur.

'Oh, it's you again,' muttered the guard. 'More like a skinned rabbit than ever.' He glanced in a cursory way at the basket Anna carried. 'Some wine for Citoyen Roblâtre, no doubt?' He turned and spat onto the cobblestones. 'I wish someone would bring me something to drink.'

'You may have a pâtisserie, if you wish,' offered Anna. 'Tante Marie made them. They're very good.'

The guard hesitated and then shook his head. He had children of his own and he felt sorry for the child. 'Doubtless they need them more than I do, poor wretches.' He jerked his head towards the prison behind him. 'Go on, get in before I change my mind.'

The Carmes had once belonged to the Carmelites, but was now inexpertly turned over to the keeping of Revolutionary prisoners. It was dark, gloomy and overcrowded and the smell of dirt and the overpowering odour of latrines and unwashed humanity hit you the moment you entered. Citoyen Roblâtre, the gaoler Anna had come to see, sat with one of the turnkeys in a small guard room, a half empty bottle on a small table beside him. A guttering candle on the window ledge only served to emphasize the fact that daylight barely penetrated, certainly not on this damp December day.

Roblâtre grunted when he saw Anna. 'Well?'

Anna tried to stop her voice from trembling. 'If you please, Citoyen Roblâtre, may I see my mother?'

'You know that prisoners aren't allowed visitors.'

Anna took out the bottle and placed it on the table, the label turned towards him.

Roblâtre picked it up and studied it carefully. Then he stumbled to his feet. 'Maybe just this once.' He lurched off down one of the darkened corridors and Anna, basket on her arm, trotted after him.

She was shown into one of the larger cells. The heavy bolts of the oak door creaked open and Anna was pushed in. There were six truckle beds on the bare stone floor, each with a straw mattress and a couple of blankets. The windows had been blocked up for two thirds of their height and the cold winter's daylight came in through the small gap left at the top, which was heavily barred. The newly formed Republic was evidently taking no chances.

Madame de Cardonnel, heavily pregnant, was sitting on one of the beds, her hand on her stomach and some sewing lying neglected on her lap. She had once been a pretty woman, but now there were lines etched into her brow and she looked pale and drawn. In La Conciergerie there was a fountain in the women's courtyard and the inmates were able to keep up some standards of cleanliness. Here in the Carmes there was only the occasional bucket of cold water – if you had the money – and Madame de Cardonnel, who had once been so fastidious, was forced to wear her underlinen for several weeks and was unable to wash her hair.

'Half an hour, *citoyenne*.' Roblâtre waited while the vicomtesse expressed her thanks – he liked to hear aristocrats thank him – and then hurried back to his bottle of wine.

Anna moved across, stood in front of her mother and curtseyed dutifully. A sempstress, who had been sitting next to Madame de Cardonnel, muttered. 'Curtseying indeed. We're all equal now.' But she moved away slightly.

The vicomtesse unfastened Anna's cloak and laid it on the bed. She flashed a warning glance at her daughter. She knew very well that the sempstress was one of the *moutons*, hoping to buy her own safety by selling information, and the vicomtesse had something very important to give to Anna. She needed to smuggle out her last remaining jewel, the most important one of all – the cabochon emerald. She had whispered its existence to nobody, not even to Madame de Custine who shared her cell. Not that she doubted Delphine's integrity, but too much hung on this jewel and silence was the best option.

Anna must take it. A child would not be suspected and she had been to the prison several times before and was known. The vicomtesse had been in Italy with her husband, who was on a diplomatic mission for King Louis, during her pregnancy with Anna. Those nine months had been anything but easy and the birth long and difficult, even with all the comforts of their little palazzo in Rome and the skill and attention of the nursing sisters who had attended her. She was under no illusions about the possible outcome this time.

She held out her arms to her daughter – rather stiffly, for the vicomtesse had not been brought up to caress children – and made room for her on the bed. Anna, equally awkwardly, snuggled up. Gone was her pretty *maman* with her porcelain skin who used to smell so nice, but, just for a while, Anna could be close to her.

'How is your father?' asked the vicomtesse in a low voice.

'He is well. He came to see us yesterday and he was in good health.'

Madame de Cardonnel sank her voice still lower. 'Did he say anything about the passports?'

'No, *madame*.' Together with wearing the Revolutionary cockade, Anna had had to learn to call her father 'Papa' and use the familiar '*tu*', but somehow she couldn't manage it with her mother.

Madame de Cardonnel sighed. Getting permission to leave Paris was a tricky business nowadays and even if her husband had got them all passports, how was she to be got out? Bribery was a possibility, she knew, but the cabochon emerald was their last piece and it could so easily be discovered ....

The vicomtesse glanced round to see whether they were observed. The sempstress was supposedly reading a book, but she was sitting at an angle where she could watch every movement. 'Anna,' she said in a louder voice. 'We have forgotten the cakes. Pray, offer them round.' The sempstress, who had a sweet tooth, took her time about her choice and did not notice that the vicomtesse had taken up her daughter's cloak and had gently pushed something into a special pouch underneath the Revolutionary cockade. Long before Anna had moved off to offer a cake to Madame de Custine the job was done. All the vicomtesse could do now was pray that Anna was not frisked and that the secret pouch held on to its treasure.

When Roblâtre came to escort Anna out, mother and daughter clung together for a moment. The vicomtesse hugged the thin little body to her with the eyes that held too many grown-up secrets and knew too much. She dropped a kiss on the smooth brown head. 'Goodbye, *chérie*.' One last kiss and she pushed Anna gently from her. Anna, half-blinded by tears, stumbled from the room.

Outside the Carmes a plump woman stood chatting to one of the guards. Marie Bonnieux was a pretty woman of about thirty-five with fluffy fair hair and sparkling blue eyes who had originally worked in a village on the Vicomte de Cardonnel's estate. For some years she had been the vicomte's mistress and just before the Revolution he had brought her to Paris and set her up in a little shop of her own. Madame Bonnieux ran a pâtisserie in the Rue Cadanet. Not a fashionable part of Paris but 'poor folks have as much right to good things as the rich, eh, citoyen?' She nudged one of the guards and winked.

'Right, *chérie*.' He glanced up at the clock. 'Your niece should be out soon.'

'She'd better hurry,' said Madame Bonnieux. 'It looks like rain. Still, I don't begrudge poor Citoyenne Cardonnel a pastry or two.'

'It's very good of you,' said the guard good-humouredly. He knew that the child was no niece of Madame Bonnieux and she knew that he knew, but so long as there were bribes and cakes everyone was happy and the fiction was maintained.

The prison door opened and Anna came out. She was looking pale and drained. Madame Bonnieux looked at her and Anna gave a tight little nod.

That evening, in Madame Bonnieux' kitchen, Anna's father unpicked the pouch and gently tipped the cabochon emerald onto the kitchen table. The shutters had been fastened and the doors locked. A small pool of candlelight was the only light. The cabochon emerald, so dull in daylight, now held a fiery glow deep within it. The setting, too, was marvellous, a gold filigree sprinkled wih minute diamonds and rubies which twinkled in the candlelight.

'It's beautiful, Papa,' breathed Anna.

'Must you let it go, Victor?' asked Marie.

'For the moment, yes.' The vicomte sighed. 'Père Ignace holds out good hope of getting the passports, but he needs security. I have some money in London. Not a lot, but enough to redeem this. And you know we have family there, my wife's father being English.' He touched the emerald gently, then turned to Anna. 'Time you went to bed, *petite*.'

When Anna had gone he said, 'I shall miss you, Marie. I wish to God you could come too.'

'Come Victor, be sensible. Your wife wouldn't like that – and I shouldn't blame her. I shall do well enough if I keep my head down.'

The vicomte put his arms around her. 'Yes, I think you'll be safe enough,' he said. 'At least as safe as anyone can be now. But I'll miss you. Of course I have a deep regard for my wife, but it was an arranged marriage and our interests are very different. With you, I can be myself.'

'I think you should go,' said Marie, after a moment's silence.

The vicomte picked up the emerald and slid it into an inside pocket. Madame Bonnieux went to check the road outside through a crack in the shutters. 'All's clear,' she said.

At the door the vicomte turned. 'If anything happens ....'

'Nothing will happen,' said Marie. But when he had gone she leaned back against the door and crossed herself slowly.

London 1800. Ludgate Street, part of one of the main thoroughfares in the City of London which ran from Temple Bar to St Paul's Cathedral, consisted of a row of shops, each with a bow-fronted window, and the occasional smaller house with no shop window. Such a house was number 7 which had an ordinary sash window with an attractively arched top and a signboard over the portico which read *L. Redbourn and Sons*,

Commodities Merchant. Through the sash window one could glimpse a well-polished mahogany desk with a Windsor chair and behind it, against the back wall, a high clerk's desk with two high-legged stools, and above them several rows of shelves. In the middle of the room lay a handsome Turkey rug, the reds and blues of which gave a pleasant touch of warmth to what was otherwise a somewhat austere room. On it was a small round oak table, around which sat Luke, Hester and Laurence Redbourn. They were all dressed in black for their father had died but ten days before. Hester, the eldest, looked older than her thirty-one years. Her cheeks were drawn and her black silk dress with a neat mourning brooch at the neck made her look pale and washed out. Beside her was an ivory-headed cane, for a bad fall in childhood had left her lame. Her gentle brown eyes were full of concern as she looked across at Luke, her elder brother. Luke Redbourn was twenty-five and now head of the family business which dealt in everything from tallow to rope, anything that the ships in the burgeoning dockyards might need. It was not, perhaps, a glamorous business, but it was a profitable one and old Mr Redbourn had recently embarked on a small insurance business which Luke was pledged to carry on. Luke was slightly taller than middle height, being about five foot ten inches, and he had inherited his father's somewhat stocky, build. His arms and legs were strongly muscled and he had considerable breadth of shoulder. His mother, who had much preferred her younger son, used to sigh and complain that he didn't look so much like a gentleman as a prize fighter.

'I have no pretensions to being a "gentleman", mother,' Luke said impatiently. 'I am content to be a plain, honest businessman.'

Mrs Redbourn would sigh and rest her eyes on her younger son, Laurence, whose willowy grace and good looks certainly fitted him for the role of gentleman, should he choose to play it.

Mrs Redbourn had died two years before, when Laurence was sixteen, and so far as looks went he had turned out very well. He was several inches taller than Luke and had a slim elegant figure. Whereas Luke was dark and with looks that could only be described as moderate, Laurence's eyes were blue, his mouth well sculpted and his features classically moulded.

But it was Laurence who was the problem.

Luke turned slightly in his chair to face his brother. 'Father warned you that if this ever happened again it would be serious.'

Laurence shrugged.

'Laurence! Embezzling is not a schoolboy's misdemeanour, you know. If this ever came to light – if Mr Carr should choose to prosecute, which he has every right to do – you would be in prison, make no mistake about it.'

'I needed the money,' said Laurence sulkily. 'Old Carr only paid me thirty shillings a week. What am I supposed to do? Father wouldn't have me here after that other business. How the deuce was I to live on such a sum?'

'Most clerks would be delighted with such a sum,' retorted Luke. 'Our clerks here start on eighteen shillings. Good God, Laurence, our father started me on eighteen shillings!'

'And Mr Carr promised to take you into junior partnership later on,' put in Hester. 'Oh, Laurence, how could you disappoint us all so?'

'Oh, stop preaching,' shouted Laurence. 'I don't consider a dried-up old maid has anything to say in all this. All you do is stay here and live off us. What do *you* do?'

Hester went white. She groped for her handkerchief.

Luke put his hand over hers for a brief moment. 'Apologize to your sister, Laurence,' he said sternly. 'I won't have her insulted. She keeps house here, organizes the servants, the shopping, the cooking, washing and I don't know what else.'

Laurence flashed Luke a baleful glance and muttered

something that might have been an apology. Whilst his mother was alive he had been the spoilt younger son, allowed to want for nothing. If he ran up a few debts his mother had paid them. She'd cried a little, but she'd found the money, and Laurence never wasted time thinking about what personal economies she might have made for his sake. He'd thoroughly resented his father's view that he must start at the bottom as his brother had done. Shortly after his mother died, Laurence was put to work in this very room. His father had great hopes of him, for he was a bright young man, but things went wrong. First, small sums disappeared; then some accounts were found to be inaccurate and the business was twenty pounds down here, ten pounds there. Lastly, one evening, returning unexpectedly to the office, old Mr Redbourn caught Laurence with his hand in the cash box. He had promised to reform, but his stunned and disappointed father decided that a clean start was preferable. There were fervent promises of amendment from Laurence. Mr Redbourn had found him a job at Carr's. Two years later the shock of Laurence being found embezzling the company funds at Carr's had given Mr Redbourn a heart attack from which he never recovered.

'You must leave the country,' said Luke after a moment's pause. 'I've had a letter from Mr Carr which makes that inevitable.' He picked up a piece of paper and read: '*As the money has been returned I'll agree, for the sake of your respected father, to drop proceedings. But I should warn you that if Laurence attempts to take any post within my sphere of influence I shall not hesitate to inform his employers of his true character.*'

Laurence bit his lip and kicked moodily at the table leg.

'Very well then,' said Luke as Laurence said nothing further. 'I have arranged a passage to New York on the *Antigua* sailing from Liverpool a week from today. Child's Bank is arranging with the Bank of New York for a quarterly fifteen pounds to be credited to your account in New York – or any other city convenient to you – providing that you stay there. If you call in at Child's they are expecting you and can finalize the details. They will also give you twenty pounds in dollars. That should be more than enough to preserve you from want while you look around. And I hope to God that America can control you where we, so obviously, cannot.'

'Am I supposed to thank you?' snarled Laurence.

'No,' said Luke wearily.

'Luke has been more than generous,' said Hester, unable to bear it any longer. 'What has he done – what have we done – to deserve this enmity?'

'Do you think I don't know that dear Luke is delighted to see me go?' retorted Laurence. 'He's been waiting to get his own back ever since that business over Caroline.'

'Caroline has nothing to do with it,' Luke said shortly.

'No? Well let me tell you one thing: Caroline found your goody-goody ways a bore. "I didn't know he'd be so respectable" she once said. "I want a bit of life".'

Hester reached over to put a restraining hand on Luke's arm. The colour had drained from his face and she could see he was making an effort not to speak. Six months ago Luke had been engaged to Caroline, the enchantingly pretty seventeen-year-old daughter of one of their father's business friends. You couldn't dislike Caroline, but she was one of those girls who seem constantly to need attention, and neither Hester nor Mr Redbourn could see her settling down to the humdrum realities of married life. Luke, however, was passionately in love, and they could only hope for the best.

Caroline had been by turns capricious, wilful and enchanting and Luke had lived in a sort of emotional turmoil, half beguiled, half exasperated. Then one evening he had surprised Caroline and Laurence entwined on the sofa.

Caroline had gone home weeping. Laurence had attempted to brazen it out saying that if Luke couldn't keep a girl interested then he deserved to lose her and anyway Caroline was a baggage. And Luke had closed his heart down.

'Get out,' said Luke quietly. 'Get out, Laurence, before I say or do something that we would all regret.'

Laurence got to his feet and went to the door with an affected swagger. 'I hope I shan't see either of you again,' he said. 'Believe me, it's a pleasure to go.'

'Oh, Laurence,' wept Hester. 'You will write, won't you?' He had been her darling little brother and she could not bear to see him go with such hatred in his heart.

For a moment Laurence hesitated, then he said, 'You're a silly goose, Hester.' He left the room and a moment later they heard the front door bang behind him.

Madame de Cardonnel had handed over the cabochon emerald just in time. Within a week of seeing her daughter she went into labour and was transferred to the infirmary. There, four days later, she died and the baby with her. Their bodies were thrown into an unmarked grave along with several others and covered with lime. By a cruel irony twenty-four hours later the vicomte received the passports on which he had almost ceased to hope and he, Marie Bonnieux and Anna, travelling as American citizens from Louisiana, left Paris and headed for London.

The choice of England was not a haphazard one for the de Cardonnels had long had a British connection. In 1517, David Cardonnell, who was in the train of John Stewart, fourth Duke of Albany and uncle to the ill-fated James IV of Scotland, left his homeland with his wife, Anna, and followed the Duke of Albany to France. He found favour with the French court, not only for his good looks, but also for his facility with languages.

Over the succeeding centuries the Cardonnells, now de Cardonnel, were granted an estate in Provence and rose to the dignity of vicomte. They always retained their Stuart connection. A later de Cardonnel had been on hand to welcome the exiled Charles Stuart to St Germain and had taken himself an English wife. The present vicomte's grandfather had accompanied Bonnie Prince Charlie on his disastrous expedition to recover his throne in 1745.

When the vicomte's aunt, Jeanne de Cardonnel, had married Sir John Broxhead as his second wife, it was merely a continuation of a family tradition. But Sir John had died barely two years after the marriage and Jeanne had returned to Paris, bringing with her her infant daughter, Anne-Louise. It was this half-English Anne-Louise Broxhead who married her cousin, the vicomte, in 1785 and their daughter, Anna, was named after Anna Cardonnell, who first came over from Scotland with her husband in 1517.

When, therefore, it came to exile, it seemed only natural to the vicomte to reverse the direction of his ancestors and return to Britain. He spoke the language, he had some money deposited in Child's Bank in Fleet Street and his wife's half-brother, Sir Robert Broxhead, old Sir John's son by his first marriage, would doubtless help them.

On a cold January morning in 1794 in their house in Brook Street, Sir Robert Broxhead and his lady were in the small breakfast parlour at the back of the house. Sir Robert, a bluff, robust man in his early forties with light-brown eyes under beetling brows and wearing an old-fashioned wig, was reading a letter which had just arrived and wondering how best to explain it to his wife. Sir Robert, society said, lived under the cat's foot and would rarely risk Lady Broxhead's wrath. Any hint of trouble and he retreated to his club where he gambled more than was good for him.

Lady Broxhead was sitting opposite to her husband and reading her own correspondence, most of which concerned the various charities she supported. She was a woman in her late thirties and, having married rather late, still seemed to retain something of a spinsterish air. She had not been a pretty girl, being too sallow with lank brown hair and a somewhat prudish manner. Her dowry was barely moderate and she had suffered all the agonies of being a debutante who did not 'take'.

Then, when she was turned thirty and resigned to being on the shelf, everything changed. A great-aunt died and left her £10,000 and her prospects were suddenly transformed. Sir Robert Broxhead was only one of a number of suitors who had presented themselves and, with a mixture of relief and resentment, she had chosen him. They had but the one daughter, Julia, now five years old.

Lady Broxhead was actually, though she could not know it, in advance of her time. Her particular brand of moral earnestness and prudery were to be very much part of the coming century. In 1794, however, they were out of place.

She glanced up from her correspondence. 'Sir Robert? You seem worried.' She was aware that her husband gambled and was constantly concerned that his debts would outrun his means. Could the letter he was holding be a debt of honour?

But the reply, though reassuring on that score, brought another concern. 'This is a letter from my brother-in-law, Lady Broxhead. It appears that he and his daughter – little Anna, you remember – are in England. My poor little sister ...' – he paused and blew his nose firmly – 'is dead. She was arrested and died in the Prison de Carmes giving birth to a stillborn son. Dear Anne-Louise, she was such a delightful baby. And she was very fond of me, you know. I was so upset when, after m'father died, she went back to France with her mother.'

'God rest her,' said Lady Broxhead piously. She had never met the Vicomtesse de Cardonnel, but she regarded the very fact that her husband had a half-French half-sister with the deepest forebodings. 'What does he want?' she asked. Money, she thought. London was full of destitute French aristocrats. God forbid that he wanted them to take them in.

Sir Robert looked at her over his cup of coffee. He knew well enough what she was thinking but, whilst he deplored it, equally he did not want to upset her. 'The vicomte is family, my dear,' he reminded her mildly. 'His parents were always very kind to me when I went over there and I was very fond of dear little Anne-Louise.'

Lady Broxhead remembered her Christian duty. 'Of course we must offer them help,' she said.

A couple of days later the vicomte and Anna were sitting in the Broxheads' drawing-room, an austere room with chairs arranged formally round the edge and ice-blue silk on the walls. Stern ancestors gazed down from their frames. The vicomte had spent the previous few weeks realizing that the world does not welcome a man with very little money and that English acquaintances who had been glad to partake of the de Cardonnel hospitality in Paris, now greeted him with reserve.

Lady Broxhead, he saw, was one of those. She was sitting rigidly upright on her chair and, though she offered him every courtesy, it was plain that she feared his demands.

'Have you any plans, my lord?' she asked.

'Certainly,' said the vicomte, with an ironic gleam in his eye. 'I have taken on the lease of a pâtisserie in Somers Town. I had enough money in Child's Bank to do that and I hope it will prove to be an investment.'

Lady Broxhead shuddered. A pâtisserie! Heavens, the man was proposing to become a tradesman!

'But why not?' The vicomte spread his hands. 'I have too much pride to live off my relatives.' He bowed courteously towards Sir Robert. 'It is an honest job and there are others who are far worse off than I am. The Comtesse de Saisseval is making straw hats and I understand the Duchess de Contaut has taken up painting for a living. Doubtless there are many more. But what is one to do, madame?'

Lady Broxhead had no answer.

The de Cardonnels' new home was in Phoenix Street, just off the Polygon in Somers Town, a recent development to the north of Marylebone and much favoured by the French émigrés, for it was cheap. The vicomte had been able to acquire a ten-year lease on a small shop with living accommodation above for £250. That sadly depleted his funds but he had hopes that it would pay. The emerald had disappeared: Père Ignace had never turned up, or, if he had, he had never got in touch with the vicomte through Child's Bank as he had promised. The vicomte had made enquiries. There was no news of Père Ignace having been arrested. Indeed, one of the émigrés had actually seen him on the northbound *diligence*. He had simply vanished, together with the emerald. There was nothing the vicomte could do. He made an arrangement with the bank that if Père Ignace turned up with the cabochon emerald then Child's would advance him the money to redeem the emerald with the emerald itself as security. If not, then the remainder of the money would remain in the bank against a rainy day.

The shop had been built as a baker's shop. In the basement were the ovens and a huge coal store. On the ground floor was the shop with its large bow-fronted window and shelves with a smaller kitchen behind. Upstairs were two rooms on each of two floors. Out the back was the laundry, a necessary house and a small garden. There was also a well with a heavy wooden cover.

Anna, who in France had been confined to the nursery, was fascinated. Gone was the old formality where a child might be seen but never heard. She ran all over the house shouting, 'Look Papa! look at this little cupboard.' And 'Tante Marie, what's this for?'

'Calm down, *petite*,' said Marie good-naturedly. 'Here, come and help me with these carrots. Careful with that knife.'

Later, when Anna had gone to bed, Marie asked, 'How did you get on with your brother-in-law, Victor?'

'Sir Robert was very kind and his lady very grudging. However, I cannot complain. Their daughter, Julia, who is a couple of years younger than Anna, will be getting a governess soon, and they have kindly offered to educate Anna with her cousin.'

Marie shrugged. 'That costs them nothing.'

'True, but it will give Anna the entrée, which may be useful when she grows up – especially if she gets on with Julia, who seems a nice enough child. It will ensure that her English is good at any rate.'

'And that is all? One does not want to be mercenary, but we have very little to spare, Victor, and I don't know if the English will *like* my cakes.'

'They'd be mad not to,' said the vicomte, kissing her. 'Just before I left, Sir Robert took me into his study and offered me a hundred pounds a year, which I have accepted with grateful thanks.'

Marie did some rapid calculations in her head. 'Ah now, that was kind,' she said. 'That will help.'

'I doubt whether Lady Broxhead knows of his generosity, though,' said the vicomte sceptically.

Anna grew up not unhappily. She got on well with her cousin Julia, a well-grown, plump little girl whose placid nature hid a romantic soul. From the age of about eight Julia was always in love with somebody and Anna was the recipient of all her artless confidences. Lady Broxhead would have been horrified had she known that her precious daughter was sighing over one of the footmen or staring worshipfully at a stripling curate in church on Sunday. It was probably just as well for Anna's acceptance by her aunt that Julia was the more conventionally pretty, with hair that curled naturally and a rosebud mouth.

Anna remained skinny. She was not as outgoing as her cousin, those serious brown eyes had seen too much, and she was always aware that she was in the Broxhead house on sufferance only. The feeling of things that must not be told, which she had learnt so early in her visits to the Carmes prison, remained with her. She worked hard, she enjoyed her lessons, she was happy to play with Julia, but she never referred to her home in Phoenix Street, nor to her father setting out in the morning pushing a hand-cart with cakes and pastries for Gunter's Tea Rooms, nor to Marie Bonnieux. Instinctively she realized that it would be best if she kept silent about these things.

Sir Robert and Lady Broxhead became Uncle Robert and Aunt Susan. She even won a measure of approval from her aunt.

'I must admit, Sir Robert,' Lady Broxhead said on more than one occasion, 'Anna's application does encourage Julia to work.'

'Julia's a lazy little puss,' said Sir Robert. He didn't set much store by female intelligence anyway and couldn't really see much point in Julia slaving over the globes and French grammar.

When Anna was twelve and Julia ten, Lady Broxhead remarked complacently, 'Dear Julia is quite as well grown as Anna. I declare they could be the same age!' Anna was almost as undeveloped and skinny as she had been at seven and Julia was now the taller.

Sir Robert grunted. In fact, he found Anna a taking little thing. She had a poise and elegance beyond her years and, unlike Julia, who tended to bounce, Anna was graceful in everything she did. But then Sir Robert had inherited his father's predilection for petite Frenchwomen. He was even indulgent towards his niece's desire to learn Italian and good-naturedly arranged for Signor Puglietti, who taught the girls singing, to come and teach her. Signor Puglietti was a dapper little man with expressive black eyes. Julia was already in love with him and now she demanded Italian lessons as well. To Lady Broxhead's annoyance, within six months Anna was able to hold a reasonable conversation in Italian whilst Julia was still struggling.

'The de Cardonnels are good at languages,' said Anna apologetically. 'Besides, I was born there. Perhaps that helps?' She didn't really think it made any difference, but she could see that her aunt was put out by her linguistic ability.

'Most unladylike,' sniffed Lady Broxhead. 'But if your uncle will encourage you ....'

When Anna was fourteen the vicomte removed her from the Broxhead governess and sent her to Abbé Carron's school. This had been set up in Somers Town to give French girls a proper convent education, such as they might have had at Madame de Maintenon's royal foundation at St Cyr.

'You need some polish,' he told Anna, when she protested. 'Your written French is deplorable! Accents missed out, endings don't agree and I don't know what else. I want you to have all the advantages of a good French education.' He sighed. 'I admire the English in many ways, their political stability, for example, but one cannot admire their indifference to the intellect! I want you to think clearly and to be able to use the brain God gave you.'

'Uncle Robert thinks education is wasted on girls,' said Anna. 'He says, what's the point, when they're only going to get married?'

'The unexpected can happen, Anna,' said her father quietly. 'You and I know that. Sir Robert is fortunate that he does not.'

The vicomte, who realized that his health was beginning to fail, took care to keep his affairs in order. When the shop lease expired in 1805 he renewed it for a further ten years and made it over to Marie Bonnieux. It was now a flourishing concern and, whatever happened, she would be safe. The remaining money, about £500, was put in trust for Anna until her twenty-first birthday, with Sir Robert Broxhead as trustee and guardian.

The vicomte was sure he could rely on his brother-in-law to see that Anna made a suitable marriage. What he did not know was that Sir Robert's gambling debts were making things increasingly difficult in Brook Street. There might come a time when Sir Robert would shut his eyes to a young man of dubious credentials paying his addresses to his niece if it meant that his financial problems were eased.

In January 1806 the vicomte, accompanied by Marie and Anna, went to see Lord Nelson's funeral cortège wind its slow way up from the docks to its final resting place in St Paul's Cathedral. It was a cold day, with a bitter wind and the vicomte's weak chest grew tight. He began to wheeze and then gasp for breath. Anna and Marie got him into a hackney cab and some-how got him home. They piled blankets on him. Marie rushed around with mustard footbaths and brandy and water, but it was in vain. He died three days later, holding on to Anna's hand and with Marie's arm supporting him.

He was buried in old St Pancras Churchyard beside so many of his compatriots and Anna and Marie Bonnieux tried desper-ately to comfort each other. Anna wrote to Child's Bank about her father's will and then, as she was sure her father would have wanted, to his old friend Cardinal York in Rome.

Anna knew that her father had made Sir Robert Broxhead her legal guardian until she was twenty-one. But it was a shock to learn that she was to go and live with her uncle and aunt.

'I don't want to live in Brook Street and I'm sure Aunt Susan doesn't want me there,' wept Anna. 'Why did Papa do it? He knew how I felt.'

'He wanted you to take your rightful place in society,' said Marie. She was wearing a hastily dyed black dress and now wiped her eyes with a corner of the hem.

'Papa was much happier here, with you, than he ever was in Paris,' said Anna. 'He once told me that it was because he had a proper job to do. Why couldn't he see that I might feel the same?'

'In less than two years' time you will be twenty-one,' said Marie encouragingly. 'What you do then will be up to you.' Privately, she expected Anna would be married and settled long before that date. She might have virtually no dowry, but she had a piquancy and charm that Marie couldn't help thinking many gentlemen would appreciate.

1806 was one of those years that Lady Broxhead preferred to erase from her memory. First of all, Anna de Cardonnel was living with them, seemingly permanently, unless they could find her a husband. Lady Broxhead liked Anna well enough and acknowledged her good points; nevertheless, an indigent niece in mourning was not what she wanted.

Then Julia, on the verge of her come-out, had gone down with measles. She had had it badly too, and in the end, Lady Broxhead cancelled any hopes of Julia's season and sent both girls down to Ramsgate with Julia's old nurse to get some sea air.

Her husband, too, was causing her some anxiety. She knew he was gambling more than was good for him, for several times he had asked her if she could retrench. His man of business came and was closeted with Sir Robert in his study and talked of mortgages and loans. Then there was the unfortunate affair with that actress. Lady Broxhead realized that husbands often wandered from the path of virtue, she just wished she didn't have to know about it. The female in question positively flaunted her conquest and Lady Broxhead was forced to remonstrate. The actress was duly dismissed, but it was a humiliating experience.

However, by the beginning of 1807 things had improved.

Some accommodation had been reached with Sir Robert's creditors; Julia's health had recovered; Anna was now out of mourning; and Lady Broxhead planned to bring both girls out in a modest season. She had every intention of marrying them both off by the end of it.

On a bitter January day in a tavern just off the dockside in New York, Laurence Redbourn sat talking to one Raymond le Vivier, a small man with a nut-cracker face who always sported a red and white spotted neckerchief. Le Vivier had come to London from France as a young man at the beginning of the Revolution and had been fortunate enough to find a job as a clerk to a City lawyer, Hargreaves by name. He had worked there for some fifteen years, gradually becoming a trusted confidant. Unfortunately, an unlucky run of dice had led him to sell information which he knew to be confidential. He got out of the country just in time and fled to America.

Laurence plied le Vivier with as much porter as he could hold. He was particularly interested in extracting information about a certain will. It appeared that one of Mr Hargreaves' clients had left a young lady, an Anna de Cardonnel by name, a large sum of money to be held in trust for her until she was twenty-one, which would be on October 4, 1807. The young lady in question did not know of this happy state of affairs.

' 'Course,' said le Vivier, 'if I was a handsome cove, I might have a shot at her myself. Besides, I can't go back to England, not with a charge laid against me.'

Indeed he couldn't. Laurence fingered the knife he always carried and wondered whether it would be safest to slide it in between his companion's ribs in some dark alley. He decided it wasn't worth the risk. As le Vivier himself said, he couldn't go back to England anyway. But Laurence could. He knew himself to be a personable young man. Why shouldn't he have a touch at this female himself?

A couple of months later in London Dock a slim young man made his way down the gangplank and looked about him. He had not been in London for seven years and things had changed. The docks themselves seemed to be under constant construction. Business was obviously booming.

Good! Laurence Redbourn was looking for opportunities and where there was money there was opportunity – for a confidence trickster. And Laurence knew himself to be one of the best. At the moment he was penniless (a matter of a miscalculation in a business fraud) but he knew where money was to be found.

A couple of evenings in a gambling den would set him up financially. After that he needed a female accomplice. Somebody who could provide him with impeccable credentials. If he were going to pay court to this girl – when he discovered where she lived – then he would need a respectable background. Now, who did he know who owed him a favour?

Chapter Two

'I've accepted him, Anna! Please say I was right!' Julia, in a state of some excitement, was seated on the window seat in her bedroom, her legs curled up underneath her.

Anna was sitting beside her cousin. She had been staring wistfully out of the window wondering what Tante Marie was doing and whether her new puppy was settling in. She now turned and looked at Julia.

'Mr Wellesborough? Oh yes, I think you were right.' Anna summoned up the Honourable Bertram Wellesborough in her mind's eye with an effort. He was a perfectly innocuous man, but there was nothing to be said about him. He was rather short and plump, with thin, fair hair that flopped down over his forehead. He didn't have a lot to say for himself, thought Anna, but then Julia would doubtless chatter enough for both of them. Mr Wellesborough was kind, he didn't outrun his income, his gambling was moderate and he was quite as rich as the Broxheads had the right to expect.

'But I don't love him,' confessed Julia. 'I *like* him very well, but that's it.'

'Do you have to love him?' enquired Anna, slightly puzzled. Surely marriage needed to be based on something less ephemeral? Her parents had been courteous, even mildly affectionate towards each other – but love?

29

'I so hoped to marry for love,' sighed Julia. She was passionately addicted to novels, particularly those by Mrs Radcliffe, and she was well aware that after two and three-quarter volumes of trials and tribulations the heroine could expect to find that the romantic stranger, dressed in humble peasant's garb, who had spent several hundred pages rescuing her from earthquakes, villains and the supernatural would turn out to be, at the very least, the son of an earl, fabulously rich and passionately in love with the heroine.

Anna leant over and kissed her cousin's cheek. 'I'm sure you'll become very fond of him.'

Julia sighed. 'I couldn't disappoint Mama. She has scrimped and saved so for this season.' It was supposed to be a secret, but both girls were well aware that Sir Robert was in financial deep water. 'But oh, Anna! I did so want to be *passionately* in love!'

Anna couldn't help laughing and after a while Julia joined in. 'I shall just have to take a lover,' said Julia despondently.

In Lady Broxhead's boudoir another conversation was taking place. It too concerned marriage. Lady Broxhead had presented her husband with an ultimatum.

'Anna,' she announced, 'must go!'

'Come, come, my dear,' said Sir Robert, placatingly. 'We cannot just throw her out. And you know she has no dowry to speak of, unless we count the cabochon emerald.'

'The cabochon emerald!' snorted his wife. 'I, for one, do not believe it ever existed. As for Anna smuggling it out of the prison when she was seven years old, I hope I am not so credulous. And where is it, pray? Certainly the vicomte never had a feather to fly with.'

'Anna is my niece,' Sir Robert reminded her. 'Her father left her in my charge.'

Lady Broxhead forced herself to remain calm. 'I do not deny that Anna has always behaved very properly and has proved herself very useful on several occasions.' In fact, Lady Broxhead had made the fullest use of Anna as a sort of unpaid secretary to answer her letters and help her with the organization of the dance she gave for Julia.

'Exactly so,' Sir Robert's frown lifted. 'I cannot just send her back to that dreadful cake-woman, or whoever she was.'

Lady Broxhead shuddered. The existence of Marie Bonnieux had come as a shock to Lady Broxhead. Anna had actually been living with her father and his mistress! Thank goodness the girl had had the sense to keep quiet about it. If it ever got out all chance of marrying her off would be gone.

'She is a taking little thing,' said Sir Robert. Anna, he thought, had something special. She was not tall, her figure was slight with long thin hands and feet, but she held herself well. She had a straight nose, finely arched eyebrows and clear brown eyes whose gaze could be disconcertingly candid. Her hair was like her mother's, brown and straight, and instead of having it curled every night, she twisted it up in an elegant knot.

Somehow – and Lady Broxhead could not forgive her for this – in spite of possessing no jewellery save a pearl cross Sir Robert had given her, and wearing clothes of the simplest cut, she managed to outclass Julia. Men noticed Anna and were attracted by her charm.

But she had no money and it was Julia, who had inherited a respectable sum of money from a great aunt, who had found herself a husband. Lady Broxhead was reluctant for her husband to settle any money on Anna in their present financial state (a thousand or so had been mentioned) but she was even more reluctant to have Anna still with them once Julia was married.

'She ought to be able to find herself a husband with the thousand you want to settle on her,' said Lady Broxhead (with an inward sigh). A country parson perhaps with £150 a year would be about right for a girl with only a thousand. If Anna must have the money then Lady Broxhead certainly didn't want her outshining her own daughter.

'Oh, I think she can manage something better than that,' said Sir Robert.

'My dear Sir Robert!' cried his wife. 'You have had an offer for Anna?'

'Not an offer precisely, let us say, a nibble.'

'And who is it from?' Lady Broxhead became quite animated.

Sir Robert reached into his waistcoat pocket and handed her a card *L Redbourn and Company, Commodities Merchant* read the legend. There was an address in the City.

Lady Broxhead's mind worked swiftly. A City merchant! It couldn't be better. A merchant in her book was barely above a tradesman and of no social standing whatsoever. Doubtless he was successful enough to satisfy Sir Robert's concerns for Anna's financial security, but they would never meet them in society. Anna would marry this L Redbourn and quietly and permanently drop out of sight.

'My dear Sir Robert!' Her ladyship was all smiles. 'This *is* good news. Tell me more.'

'He's a tall, good-looking fellow. About twenty-five, I should guess. A bit on the smooth side, but pleasant enough. Has social ambitions, anxious to marry well. He lives with his widowed mother.'

'He sounds delightful.'

'I have suggested that they both pay us a visit so you may judge for yourself.'

Luke and Hester Redbourn had been having their usual quiet breakfast together before the business of the day. Luke was reading the newspaper and absent-mindedly stroking Ben, a fine black and grey tabby cat sitting on his knee. Business had prospered over the last seven years, in particular the insurance.

Luke had a group of highly skilled men, ex-sailors many of them, whose job it was to inspect personally any ship whose owners wanted it insured. And his conditions were stringent: tonnage was carefully measured, caulking was checked, even the crew had to be vetted. The result was that L Redbourn and Co rarely lost a ship and ships that were registered with the company were known to be reliable.

Hester was sipping her coffee. Her eyes rested on her brother affectionately, but with concern too. That business with Caroline had hit him hard. Not that he eschewed the company of the fair sex. He was a sociable man and liked Hester to invite friends over for a convivial meal and perhaps some music afterwards. He often enjoyed a rousing debate with her particular friend, the rather alarmingly named Miss Minerva Leatherbarrow, whose views on the subjection of woman Hester found shockingly radical. Minerva had little time for men, but she tolerated and even liked Luke, and put up with him calling her the Athena of Islington.

But although several of Luke's business colleagues had sisters or daughters who would love to become Mrs Luke Redbourn, so far he had taken to none of them. He would allow them to be charming girls, but his heart remained untouched. If he ever took a purposeful walk down towards Covent Garden in search of less reputable female company, he never embarrassed Hester with the knowledge of it.

He had an affectionate heart, Hester knew, but at the moment his caresses were reserved for the cat.

There was a knock at the door and Walter entered with a letter. Walter had been with the family ever since Hester could remember. He was now well over sixty, thin and spare, but his grey eyes were still bright and he was remarkably agile. Hester had once seen him sprint down the hill to catch up with Luke who had left the house forgetting something. Walter returned seemingly unpuffed.

Luke thanked him and slit open the letter. Walter left.

'It's from Laurence,' he said.

'Laurence!' echoed his sister. They had only heard from him once and that was several years ago, when an oil-skin parcel, containing a fine beaver wrap arrived, addressed to Hester. It had contained no note, but Hester knew that it had come from Laurence. 'What does he say?' she asked eagerly. She allowed herself a brief dream of a reformed Laurence coming home with a delightful American wife on his arm.

'He's found a job with prospects in Boston, apparently. He doesn't say what. He will write when he's more settled. Fond love to both of us.' He looked across at her downcast face.

'Hester,' he said gently. 'You must face it. Laurence is up to his old tricks. I doubt whether he's in Boston at all.'

'I know.' Hester blew her nose with determination. 'But I can't help hoping .... But I'm sure you're right. I'd be more inclined to believe him without that last bit.'

'So I think. I wonder what he's up to?'

Hester toyed with her toast and then said, 'I didn't like to say so before, in case I sounded like a hysterical female, but I thought I saw Laurence a few days ago.'

Luke looked up sharply. 'Oh? Where?'

'Leicester Square. I was in Newton's looking over some muslins and standing by the window. I just happened to look up and there he was – if it was him – on the other side of the road. Of course I ran outside, but he had gone. Afterwards I decided I was being foolish.'

'If it is him, then doubtless he will call if he wants to see us. If not, I suggest, my dear Hester, that we leave him alone.' Luke was anxious not to worry his sister, but he found her news disquieting.

The moment his sister had left the room, Luke rang the bell. Walter appeared. 'It's possible my brother is back,' said Luke without preamble.

'I'd best keep an eye open then,' said Walter imperturbably. 'No point in being taken unawares.'

It was the Sunday following and Anna, escorted by the footman, Charles, had gone to the French church in Phoenix Street. Charles was a fellow Frenchman. His father had been a watchmaker who had died during the Terror, leaving Charles and his mother in very distressed circumstances. The vicomte had recommended Charles to Sir Robert initially as a boot boy and, as he had grown up into a tall young man with a splendid pair of calves (much admired by Julia), he had attained the dizzy heights of footman and was now well able to support his widowed mother.

Part of his job was to escort Anna or Julia if they should wish to go shopping or on some outing, for it was unthinkable that a lady should go anywhere unescorted. Most Sundays he accompanied Anna to church and then spent some time with his mother before escorting Anna home. The last thing Lady Broxhead wanted was a confrontation with Anna about her seeing 'that dreadful cake-woman' as she mentally called Marie, so she took the line of least resistance and allowed herself to believe that Anna was visiting the Comtesse de Saisseval or one of the other aristocratic French families living in Somers Town.

Anna greeted Madame Bonnieux with affection. 'Tante Marie! How good it is to see you.'

The service over they walked the few steps to the pâtisserie. There was a kitchen behind the shop, with a small oven the family used for everyday and Anna sank down thankfully on one of the Windsor chairs and looked around as she did every week. Everything was reassuringly familiar; the herbs hanging up by the window and the strings of garlic and onions, the clothes'-horse by the fire and the old much-scrubbed pine table. Under the table, his head on his paws, lay Hercule, a fast-growing young puppy of doubtful parentage, that Marie had just acquired for comfort and security. Anna held out her hand to the puppy and allowed him to sniff it before bending down to pat him.

Unlike Julia, who would have liked nothing better than a life of adventure, Anna found that she needed stable points of reference. Her early experiences had left her feeling that nothing was to be counted on and, even though she had known the house in Phoenix Street since she was seven, part of her still felt insecure.

Madame Bonnieux, older now and greyer, but with the same bright blue eyes and plump figure, went to stir the potage and to adjust the seasoning. Anna rose to set the table and lay the familiar earthenware bowls. There was a baguette and a bottle of red wine.

'How are things at the Broxheads?' asked Marie.

Anna laughed. 'Full of wedding plans. Aunt Susan is driving poor Julia mad with calls for fittings and shopping for the trousseau and answering letters. Julia says she wishes she'd gone for an elopement.'

'And your Aunt Susan?'

Anna raised her eyes to the ceiling. 'She can't wait to get rid of me. *I* would be more than willing to come back here, but of course "what would people think?". That seems to weigh heavily with Aunt Susan.'

'There is no young man on the horizon?'

'Not as far as I know. I have no dowry, you see. Uncle Robert would never allow me to come back here, so poor Aunt Susan has no option but to put up with me.'

Marie sniffed. 'If that good-for-nothing Père Ignace hadn't scuttled off with the cabochon emerald ....'

'I don't believe it was particularly valuable,' said Anna thoughtfully. 'I don't think uncut stones are, though it was in a very fine setting, of course. And we cannot be sure that Père

Ignace did run off with it. Nothing was ever heard from him. He may have been caught in France for all we know.'

'Your dear father always said we'd make our lives miserable if we continually dwelt on what might have been,' said Marie, gesturing to Anna to hand her the bowls. 'All the same, I have my doubts about Père Ignace. The clergy usually have their eye out for the main chance.' Madame Bonnieux was deeply cynical about priests.

'Aunt Susan doesn't believe that the cabochon emerald ever existed,' said Anna, taking her bowl and sniffing the potage appreciatively.

'It might just as well not have done,' retorted Marie. 'At least it would have been a sort of dowry for you, Anna.'

Anna didn't reply, but dipped her spoon into the potage. 'Mm. Delicious.' She paused to savour it, then said, 'I'm bored, Tante Marie. It's all paying calls, receiving calls, rides in the Park and the endless evening parties, dinners, evenings at the opera, balls. No one seems to have a serious thought at all. They don't know what life is like out there.' She gestured with her hand. 'Often I find myself talking to somebody and I think, "You just don't know what the world can be like".

'You know, Tante Marie, the night my mother was arrested I was having tea upstairs with Alphonsine, my *bonne*. It was all just as usual when suddenly one of the footmen burst in shouting that soldiers had come and we were to get away. Alphonsine dragged me upstairs and we hid in a little cupboard at the top of the house. We could hear cries and screams and the sound of things being broken. It seemed to go on for ages. I could hear Alphonsine's terrified breathing. I just didn't know what was going on. I couldn't understand it, that's what made it worse. Eventually all was quiet and we came out. The house had been ransacked. The silk on the walls had been ripped to pieces, ornaments smashed.

'I have never forgotten it, that understanding that just

underneath was all this, a sort of senseless savagery. And what upset me most of all was that someone had smashed a musket butt into the face of Princesse Clothilde, my doll. She'd been a birthday present and was quite new. I thought she was the most beautiful thing I'd ever seen. It's silly, I know, to weep over a doll, when there were far worse things that had happened in the house. It's so difficult to explain ....'

'I know,' said Marie, quietly. 'Sometimes I feel it too, when I remember Paris during the bad times. The fear when you went out. Oh God, the smell of blood after the guillotine had done its work. You don't forget those things however hard you try.'

'And going to see Maman,' said Anna. She put down her spoon. 'I was so frightened and I knew I couldn't show it. She was so different, thin and drawn with this huge stomach. God forgive me, but sometimes I used to wonder if she really was my mother at all. I used to have nightmares afterwards about being shut in the Carmes and them coming to cut my head off.' She shuddered.

'I know, *petite*,' said Marie gently. 'I used to get you up and give you some hot chocolate. Do you remember?'

'Yes, yes, of course,' said Anna, trying to smile. 'You were very good to me. And when we got to London you made me my rag doll. I haven't forgotten. I don't know what's brought it back now. Perhaps because with Julia's wedding I know that everything's going to change yet again and, coward that I am, I still have this feeling that change means disaster.'

'You're not a coward, Anna. Never think that. A brave person is not one who never feels fear, but one who feels fear but still does what has to be done. That is what you did. Your father could not have got us those passports without the cabochon emerald and it was you who brought it out of the prison. That took courage.'

Anna picked up her spoon again and took another sip. 'I wish now I'd been more open with Papa about Uncle Robert's

financial difficulties, but at the time it seemed disloyal when
Uncle Robert had been so kind. If Papa had known, he might
have left things differently.'

'Perhaps, once your cousin is married, your aunt will
concentrate on finding you a suitable husband,' suggested
Marie encouragingly.

'God. I hope not! I don't think I'd like a husband of Aunt
Susan's choosing.'

In his rooms in Charles Street, just off Drury Lane, Laurence
watched critically as the woman at the dressing-table dusted
her face with a light powder and carefully darkened her
eyelashes with burnt cork. Her light-brown hair was twisted up
into a becoming, but modest chignon. From the neck up the
woman looked like a lady – not one in the first flush of youth,
perhaps, but a sober, respectable woman in her middle years,
possibly a widow.

From the neck down, however, the view was very different.
Her black lace corset, which pushed up her breasts
provocatively was anything but decorous, and her pink frilled
garters could only be described as scandalous.

'Pass me the bodice, darling.'

The demure black garment was lying on the bed. Laurence
handed it over. 'Shall I do you up?'

'If you please.'

The neckline was modest, the sleeves long. Instantly she
looked like a lady from the waist up. 'Now the petticoats and
the skirt and I'm nearly done.' She whisked herself into the rest
of the clothes with a speed born of long practice in the theatre
dressing-room. 'Now, how do I look? Will I do?' She composed
her features and assumed the slightly mournful mien of a
widow of the first respectability.

Laurence couldn't help laughing at so sudden a transform-
ation. 'Helen, you're wonderful.'

39

'Mama,' she corrected. 'I hope it works,' she added doubtfully.

'Mama?' he laughed. 'Of course it'll work! It couldn't fail.'

Helen turned round, suddenly sober. 'Laurence, are you sure you want to go through with this imposture?'

'Of course I'm sure,' he said impatiently. 'I need the money and, from what I've discovered, she has it.'

'You're sure about that? It's not just an indiscreet clerk's gossip?'

'I'll take a chance,' said Laurence. He surveyed himself critically in the cheval glass. He saw a tall young man, good-looking, though with rather small features, light-blue eyes and hair carefully cut *à la Titus*. His suit was well made without being ostentatious and he looked exactly like what he was not – a solid, well-to-do businessman, probably second or third generation, who had acquired a little polish and was anxious to marry well.

Helen, too, surveyed the figure in the glass. He was at this moment, as she knew very well, almost penniless, but he had a nose for where the money was. She had first met Laurence when he was a stage-struck sixteen, always hanging round the Theatre Royal, where she was in the chorus. She had treated him playfully, rather enjoying his admiration, for she was then in her late thirties and admiring young men were no longer so thick on the ground as they had once been. She had become fond of him and eventually let him into her bed and, more disastrously, into one or two secrets. She had lived to regret it.

This fresh-faced schoolboy, as she discovered to her cost, was not at all averse to blackmail, and she had several times been obliged to give him what money she had. She had greeted news of his going to America with relief.

Now, seven years later, Laurence had returned to London and Helen was clinging on to her job by her fingertips. Fortunately, she had kept her figure and her hair had not lost its colour, but she did not know how many more seasons she could count on work. Laurence had offered her ten guineas for her part in the deception, and she needed the money.

Laurence had turned out very good-looking, she decided, with just that touch of ruthlessness that many women would find exciting. She did not doubt that the young lady in question would probably be only too happy to find so handsome a husband. Helen herself was more than a little afraid of him; a fact she strove to conceal.

'How have you been living, over there?' she asked curiously.

'In America? Gambling, my dear. New York is much like London, full of greenhorns from the country. They play cards with me – and I see to it that they lose.'

'Did you never have any trouble?' Helen had not met any Americans, but she always imagined them to be a tough race, and surely a strong country lad would be capable of roughing Laurence up, if he suspected he'd been fleeced?

Laurence laughed. And suddenly, there in his hand, was a small, sharp knife. With one swift movement he jerked Helen's head back and held the knife to her throat. The blade was razor sharp. She swallowed hard, trying to stifle her terrified heart-beats. Laurence allowed the knife to press slightly and then, abruptly, he let her go.

'I'm convinced!' Helen tried to sound nonchalant.

'Good' He saw the fear in he eyes and was satisfied. She would do as he asked. 'Let's go over it one last time.'

'I am a widow of irreproachable virtue,' said Helen obediently. She clasped her hands in front of her in an attitude of prayer.

'I am this L Redbourn, rich merchant of the City of London.' He held up a visiting card. 'I want to move up in the world. I know I can't expect too much, but marriage with Sir Robert's niece will give me the status I'm after.'

'I shall stress that to Lady Broxhead,' promised Helen. 'To be allied with the family must be an honour.'

'According to the scullery maid she's a woman who thinks very highly of herself. I understand Miss de Cardonnel is not looked on with much favour by Lady Broxhead.'

'Oh, why not?' Laurence had done his homework thoroughly, Helen noted.

Laurence shrugged. 'She's a Frenchy. A usurper.'

'So not too much flattery of the niece?'

'Better not.'

'What's she like? This prospective betrothed of yours?'

'I don't know. Never clapped eyes on her. What does it matter? According to my source she will have lots of money. Why should I care what she looks like?'

'But you're going to marry her!'

'My dear Helen!' Laurence laughed at her naivety. If this Miss de Cardonnel proved clever and quick he could probably use her. If not, once he'd got his hands on her money, he intended to put the Atlantic between them. What she did then would be of no concern whatsoever.

Laurence had met Sir Robert at a discreet gambling club in King Street, St James's, where the play was deep. He had gone there as a guest of a young blood with more money than sense and had set himself to charm. There were no furred cards or loaded dice in this establishment, no carefully placed mirrors to show your opponent's hand. Laurence was not dismayed, he had his own tricks. And he knew that to play in the right setting was half the success. Here, all was quiet good taste. The lighting was subdued except for oil lamps on the green baize-covered tables. There were plenty of drinks to be had, and there was an air of solemnity about the place, the quiet hum of concentrated gambling.

Laurence took care to keep the young blood's glass well filled and kept himself sober. He taught him a few (perfectly legitimate) tricks for improving his game. The blood in return lost some money to Laurence – not enough to raise suspicions, but enough to keep Laurence's affairs ticking over. He bided his time.

It was several days before Sir Robert Broxhead visited the club. Laurence spotted at once that the man was a gambler: the slightly feverish way he dealt the cards, the impatience with which he waved away the drinks, both spoke of a man obsessed. Laurence observed him carefully. Sir Robert wore an olive-green evening coat, but preferred knee-breeches to the more fashionable trousers. He looked like what he was, a middle-aged man of rank and property with no desire to 'cut a dash'.

Laurence rose from the table that evening enriched by 200 of Sir Robert's guineas. After a second unlucky evening, Sir Robert said, 'That's it for this evening, Redbourn. If I can't pay I won't play.' He was well aware that his man of business would make a long face about the last two evenings' play.

'I'm sorry to hear that, Sir Robert.' Laurence raised a finger at a hovering waiter. 'What'll you have, sir? I know the brandy's very tolerable.'

Sir Robert nodded. They moved to a quiet alcove by the window and sat down. Laurence swilled the brandy in his glass and said, 'I, fortunately, am wealthy enough to enjoy my taste for gambling without worrying. However, there are other things ....'

Sir Robert, scenting a reprieve, moved his chair a little closer. 'If there were any way I could be of help ...?' There was no need to say that they might come to some arrangement, that was understood. He hoped to God that Redbourn was not hoping for membership of his club, White's. He would certainly be blackballed and it would be embarrassing to say the least.

'My dear father was ambitious for me, his only son.' Laurence gave a sad smile and preserved a moment's respectful silence. 'He always hoped that I would marry well. Of course, I know the limitations, but I feel I owe it to his memory ....'

'Of course,' murmured Sir Robert. 'What sort of dowry did you have in mind?'

'The dowry isn't important,' said Laurence, waving away such vulgar considerations. 'A small settlement is all I ask. No, I am looking for birth, above all. And good connections ....'

Sir Robert leaned forward. 'I believe I may be able to help you ....'

Lady Broxhead had taken steps to see that both Anna and Julia would be out of the way during the Redbourns' visit. She felt that so delicate a meeting needed her full concentration. In the event, she was very well pleased with her guests. While her husband talked to Laurence in his study, Lady Broxhead decided to grill his mother in her boudoir. Helen saw at once that the boudoir was meant to intimidate; the silver coffee pot and delicate china cups, the expensive knick-knacks on various occasional tables, a flattering portrait of Lady Broxhead by Sir Thomas Lawrence, all told the same story. Helen sat down on the chair indicated and tried to assume an appropriate expression; modest, impressed, and mildly intimidated.

'Tell me about your son,' commanded Lady Broxhead, when refreshments had been handed round by a bewigged footman. 'He certainly seems a very pretty-behaved young man.' She had looked at Laurence with a mixture of approval – his manners were good and his air and address that of a gentleman – and a faint feeling of digruntlement; he was really much too good-looking for Anna. She found herself thinking that the Honourable Bertram Wellesborough, now officially engaged to Julia, who was short, rather stout and had little conversation, should somehow have swapped his looks and address for Mr Redbourn's. It would have been more fitting. If the truth were known Mr Redbourn would have no difficulty in being taken for a gentleman and Mr Wellesborough none at all in being taken for a tradesman.

Helen put down her coffee cup and clasped her hands together. 'He is the sweetest-natured boy in the world,' she declared. 'Just like his dear father.' She paused and dabbed delicately at her eyes, careful not to remove any of the burnt cork. 'My only complaint is that I don't see enough of him. He works so hard, Lady Broxhead, not like so many young men, nowadays.' She then gave her hostess a brief run down of all the points that Laurence had impressed upon her; his respectable income, his desire to better himself, his reliable nature. 'He is even thinking of moving to Birmingham where he says the business opportunities are better.'

Birmingham! Lady Broxhead's eyes lit up. What could be better? Anna would be very happy with a respectable, well-to-do young man, of more than passable good looks, and she would live a hundred miles away.

Helen leaned forward confidentially, 'I hope I am not speaking out of turn,' she said, 'but my son said in the carriage on the way here that he would count the blessing of being allied with *your* family, Lady Broxhead, to be one of the greatest benefits of the match.' Had she said too much, she wondered? She saw Lady Broxhead pull herself up and, yes, the silly woman had swallowed it! She was positively preening!

'I believe the Broxheads to be one of the oldest baronetcies in the kingdom,' she announced. 'And I, myself, was a Selborne!'

'Mrs Redbourn' was duly overcome. A Selborne! Gracious!

What a sensible woman, thought Lady Broxhead. Quiet, lady-like and properly honoured by the connection. She would do her best to promote the match. She rose to her feet. 'Shall we join Sir Robert and your son?' she said graciously.

In Sir Robert's library Laurence took careful note of what he saw, and his quick eye spotted at once that this was a family in somewhat straitened circumstances. The rugs on the floor were fine Persian ones, but they had been darned. The wallpaper was slightly faded and the mirror over the mantelpiece could have done with regilding. It was nothing to signify, but Sir Robert and his lady had probably decided that it would have to do for one more season.

All the better, they would be more likely to accept him as a husband for their niece. Sir Robert was all joviality. He made a few general enquiries about Laurence's income and said that his niece was a good girl and deserved a good home. And that was it. Sir Robert lacked either the will or the desire to cross-question his prospective nephew-in-law. He was a good fellow, he was sure of it. Anna would be a lucky young lady.

'Well, well,' he ended. 'I believe we may have a match, eh? I shall give my niece a thousand. Always meant to do that. And her father left her five hundred. She's not entirely penniless! Pretty little thing too. French, y'know. *Petite*, that's the word.'

'In that case,' Laurence reached into his pocket and took out a fistful of vowels. 'I believe we may dispose of these.' He held them up one by one to the candle flame. 'I don't believe in gambling in the family.'

He watched Sir Robert's face as he did so. There was shame, but relief too. A man's gambling debts must at all costs be honoured and he, Laurence, had just burnt several hundred pounds' worth of gaming vowels. It was an expensive gesture, but Laurence guessed that Sir Robert would now feel that he had no option but to promote the marriage.

'That's good of you, Redbourn,' Sir Robert grunted.

'This is a special occasion, is it not? Next time I shall not be so lenient.' Laurence laughed pleasantly.

Unfortunately, Sir Robert didn't believe him.

There was a knock at the door and the footman announced Lady Broxhead and Mrs Redbourn. Both gentlemen rose to their feet. The usual courtesies were exchanged. Laurence, catching Helen's eye, raised an eyebrow. Helen gave him a suspicion of a wink.

'But come, Redbourn,' said Sir Robert heartily, 'you have not yet met my niece. We cannot proceed so precipitately. This is not the Middle Ages where a couple can be married off without having even met!'

'Miss de Cardonnel is *French*, Sir Robert,' put in Lady Broxhead, hastily. 'The French understand arranged marriages. Your sister's marriage with the vicomte was arranged, was it not?'

Laurence saw that Lady Broxhead wished to expedite the marriage. He really must congratulate Helen, who seemed to have done her job faultlessly.

Helen sat quietly in the background, but she was not as unattentive as she appeared. She had said nothing of it to Laurence (she had learnt her lesson and would never confide in him again) but she, too, had done her homework. She had got her dresser, Peggy, to make discreet enquiries about Sir Robert, and Peggy had told her about his affair with the actress which had been stopped by his wife. Helen knew the actress in question; a rather loud, brassy female, with a certain flashy allure – if you liked that type – but one who would always cause problems.

Helen surveyed Sir Robert covertly. Not a bad-looking man, she thought, if a little old-fashioned. She had noticed that his eyes had held an appreciative twinkle when he looked at her, and his figure was still good. So he was susceptible to feminine charm, was he?

Perhaps sensing her scrutiny, Sir Robert turned his head and caught her eye. Helen gave him a tiny smile, demure, yes, but there was just a hint of mischief.

Chapter Three

Julia had been packed off to visit her godmother during the Redbourns' visit and Anna had been sent to Bond Street, accompanied by Charles, to collect her ladyship's new Capote bonnet. 'And be sure to see that the ribbons match my brown mantle, Anna,' was Lady Broxhead's parting instruction.

Anna did her aunt's numerous errands, slightly puzzled as to why she and not Martha, her aunt's maid, should be asked to do these things. She duly collected the bonnet, matched some embroidery silks and failed to find the second volume of Fordyce's Sermons in Bell's Circulating Library. She returned slightly earlier than she'd expected and thus saw Laurence and Helen leaving the house. A cab was drawn up and she was in time to see the whisk of black skirts as Helen climbed in. But it was Laurence who caught her attention. A tall, good-looking gentleman, whoever was he? He stood for a few seconds at the top of the steps after the front door closed behind him. Then suddenly he spun round and spat at the door with all his force, before running down the steps and jumping into the cab.

Anna turned to look at Charles, who was a step or two behind her, carrying the parcels, but his view was blocked by a coal cart and he appeared to have seen nothing.

They went into the house. Anna directed Charles to see that Martha got the parcels and, when he had gone downstairs, moved over to the Sèvres bowl, which stood on a marble-topped table in the hall and was used to hold visiting cards. There were only two cards in it: Mr L Redbourn, Commodities Merchant, with an address in Ludgate Street and a Mrs L Redbourn. Anna looked at them in astonishment. A City tradesman and his wife – or possibly mother – to visit? Surely not? She turned to the maid who had opened the door.

'The gentleman who left just now,' she said, 'who was he?'

'A Mr Redbourn, Miss Anna. Came with his mother and they called on Sir Robert and Lady Broxhead, they did. And he didn't tip neither,' she added, *sotto voce*.

'Thank you, Sarah.'

Anna went upstairs slowly, her mind most unpleasantly jolted into awareness. A sudden intimation of danger went through her like iced water. Without realizing how she knew, she understood that this had something to do with her. No mere tradesman would enter by the front door – and bring his mother with him. These were visitors with privileged access. And they saw both her uncle and her aunt. For a purely domestic matter Sir Robert would not be involved. For a matter of male concern, Lady Broxhead would not be needed. No, this was strictly family business.

Mr L Redbourn, Commodities Merchant: Anna had the most unnerving feeling that *she* was the commodity.

Lady Broxhead had turned the matter over in her mind and decided to strike while the iron was hot. Mr Redbourn must be secured at any price. Her daughter's wedding was now only a few weeks away and immediately after that she could announce the engagement of her niece – perhaps a small dress party? – and a quick and quiet marriage. It would then be well into July. Most of the *ton* would have left for their country estates, but that would not matter. Mr Redbourn could not expect more than a small gathering to celebrate the event.

It was now about two o'clock and luncheon would be laid out in the small breakfast parlour for those who wanted it. Julia would still be at her godmother's. Now would be the perfect time to settle things with Anna.

'Ah, Anna dear,' she exclaimed as she entered the breakfast parlour to find her niece carving the ham. 'Just the person I wish to see.'

'Oh?' said Anna. 'Ham, Aunt Susan?'

'Ham?' echoed Lady Broxhead, slightly disconcerted. 'No, thank you.'

'I found the embroidery silk you were after, but not the library book,' said Anna. She was anxious to divert her aunt's mind. They both sat down, but Anna noticed with dismay that her aunt was only toying with her food. She forced herself to appear unconcerned.

'Sir Robert and I have had some visitors today of special concern to you.'

'Oh?' said Anna politely. She had long ago realized that 'Oh' was a most useful comment.

Lady Broxhead continued. 'A Mr Redbourn has been smitten with your charms and wishes to get to know you better. You have made a most desirable conquest – clever girl,' she added with unaccustomed archness.

Anna could not help laughing. 'He can hardly be a sensible man, Aunt Susan, for I have never even met him!'

Lady Broxhead saw that she had made a tactical error. Anna, unlike Julia, did not have her head full of romantic notions.

'You mistake him, Anna. Mr Redbourn *is* a sensible man, almost a gentleman, in a very respectable line of business in the City. He wishes to raise himself – a most worthy ambition – and, having seen you in the park and at the opera, he wants to pursue the acquaintance with the most honourable of intentions. He has an income of nearly a thousand a year, not to be sneezed at by a portionless girl, and, of course, a well-respected name in the City.'

Anna said nothing for a moment. Her instinctive reaction was to repudiate this gentleman immediately and forcefully. But that, she saw, was impossible. She had no wish to upset her aunt and create ill-feeling just before Julia's wedding. She stared down at her plate thoughtfully. 'Does Sir Robert agree?' she asked at last.

'He does indeed.' Anna was being sensible, thank God. 'He thinks it would be a most fortunate match – for both of you,' she added graciously.

'And have this Mr Redbourn's credentials been checked independently?' asked Anna. 'Or is he recommended only by himself?'

Lady Broxhead reddened. Anna, she thought crossly, had a most unendearing habit of picking on the very thing one least wanted to look at. She doubted whether Sir Robert had been anywhere near Ludgate Street. 'Naturally, your uncle has checked him thoroughly.'

The door opened and Sir Robert entered.

'I am just telling Anna of her good fortune, Sir Robert,' said his wife.

'A very proper young man,' said Sir Robert, with forced jocularity. 'Good-looking too. And I know the ladies like that, eh?'

'So it has your blessing?' said Anna. She had lost all her colour and was feeling the walls closing in. Suddenly, she was back in the Carmes, walking along the icy corridor to her mother's cell. The food turned to ashes in her mouth. Her hands felt cold.

'He has money and you have rank,' said Sir Robert. 'What could be better?'

'I had not thought to marry yet,' said Anna desperately.

'Come, come,' said her uncle. 'All girls want to marry.' He gave a false hearty laugh.

Anna saw that under the jocularity was an unease. Now why?

'Besides, Anna, you will be of age in October, you know,' said Lady Broxhead. 'Sir Robert will no longer be responsible for you. And what will you do then? A female needs a man to look after her affairs. And a respectable businessman can be relied upon to look after things properly for you.'

Anna thought of saying that the mere fact of being male was hardly sufficient guarantee of financial probity. Sir Robert's own affairs were in such disarray that he was scarcely the right person to have control of hers, but she held her tongue. She was thinking fast. It was now June. Four months before her majority. Could she possibly hold this off until then? What would Sir Robert do if she fled back to Tante Marie? She would create a scandal, and whilst she did not care for herself, it might be awkward for Tante Marie, and would put a slight on her uncle and aunt which they did not deserve. They were, after all, doing the best they could for her.

'Well, I confess this has all come as a surprise to me,' she managed at last. 'I should like some time to think about it, if you please.'

'Good girl,' said Sir Robert, leaning over and patting her shoulder. 'Knew you'd be sensible. Your aunt will give a party for you after Julia has gone. That will be best, eh?'

Anna saw that it was all arranged.

That evening Anna paced up and down her room in an agony of indecision. She had won a grudging consent that nothing should be done until after her cousin's wedding.

But the more she thought about it, the more suspicious the whole thing looked. This Mr Redbourn surely had some hold over Sir Robert? Her uncle was trying to disguise it, but it was obvious that he was anxious that the marriage should take place: there was something else on his mind. As for her aunt, Anna knew that she had not particularly wanted her niece to come and live with them, but she was not aware of any pointed dislike. They had certainly always been on courteous terms. Anna knew herself to be useful to Lady Broxhead and had won a grudging approval.

Why did she want to be rid of her so suddenly?

It could only be money. The household in Brook Street was not a happy one. Wages were in arrears and most of the servants knew that after the wedding the house would be closed and the majority of them paid off. Sir Robert and Lady Broxhead would then retire to their run-down estate in Worcestershire with no loss of face. If they came up to London for the season they would naturally stay with their daughter. The town house could be let. Thirty guineas a week was not too much to ask for a house during the season, provided the location was good.

No, thought Anna, an appeal to her uncle or aunt would be pointless. She had but two options: she could flee back to Tante Marie, which would create a scandal and cast a blight over Julia's wedding, or she could tell this unknown Mr Redbourn that the match would not do.

The more she thought about it the more she felt that the second option was the only way. She would take a cab to Ludgate Street – perhaps Charles could escort her – seek out this Mr Redbourn, and put a stop to the whole thing. She dithered for most of the afternoon. A host of objections occurred to her: the boldness of it – no lady would even think of doing such a thing; the embarrassment; the awkwardness of explaining why she had come. Then she scolded herself. What possible use were ladylike qualms? So far as she could see they would only serve to expedite this appalling marriage.

One of the things that had irked Anna most on coming to live in Brook Street was the curtailment of her liberty. She had never been chaperoned in Somers Town. There she was treated as a sensible person. In Brook Street she discovered there were certain places ladies must never go. Shopping in Bond Street during the afternoon was out – she might meet women of a most disreputable sort. She must not go out without the escort of either a maid or a footman. And she must never, ever go down St James's Street where gentlemen looked out of their club windows and might expose a lady to insult.

No, she would not allow these petty shibboleths to stand in her way. She would go and visit this L Redbourn in Ludgate Street and tell him what she thought of his idea.

Anna dressed carefully for the occasion. She realized, to her amusement, that one needed quite as much care in dressing to turn down an offer of marriage as one would in the hopes of eliciting one. Whereas her cousin dressed in girlish blues and pinks, Anna invariably went for darker colours, and her redingote of twilled sarcenet was in a warm dark brown which set off her pansy dark eyes. Her bonnet, a leghorn (made by the Comtesse de Saisseval), had a high crown and a couple of deep pink ostrich feathers which curled enticingly over the brim. Anna drew on her gloves and checked in her reticule that she had her cardcase which contained, besides her own cards, the card that Mr Redbourn had left in the Sèvres bowl.

Perhaps it was having something she could do about this proposed marriage, but she felt better. She would take a cab. Charles had agreed to accompany her and she was confident that he would keep his mouth shut.

The house in Ludgate Street was more modest than Anna had expected. It was a tall narrow house with an attractive Georgian portico and steps leading up to the front door. Anna had half expected a large shop, perhaps even an emporium, and was somewhat disconcerted. She had a moment's wish to turn tail and run.

But there was no help for it. 'I do not know how long I shall be, Charles,' she said, more steadily than she felt. 'I shall try to be quick.'

'I can wait, Miss Anna.' He preceded her up the steps and

made an imperious rat-tat-tat on the brass door knocker. An elderly, dusty-looking servant appeared. Charles allowed himself to be seen in all his bewigged splendour and waited until Anna was ushered inside before returning to the cab.

The servant took Anna's card gingerly and bade her follow him. Anna did so, increasingly puzzled and not a little alarmed. She had only caught a glimpse of this Mr Redbourn, but somehow the impression of studied elegance didn't seem to fit with the house, which was well maintained, but had obviously not been altered for a hundred years or more. For example, the oak panelling was highly polished wood rather than being painted a more modern light green or blue. The room she was shown into had a fine turkey rug on the floor, a couple of Windsor chairs and a good mahogany table. A brass carriage clock ticked monotonously on the mantelpiece.

Time passed. Anna paced up and down the carpet and tried to quell her nerves. Had she been mad to come? To inform a completely unknown young man of whom she had had barely a glimpse that she could not marry him? Perhaps she should leave? Maybe a letter ....?

The door opened. The man who came in was tall – he was about 5ft 10 inches – and of much stockier build than Anna had expected, with a broadness of shoulder that was plainly visible underneath his sober corbeau-coloured morning coat. He favoured the modern trousers rather than knee breeches, but there was nothing remotely of the dandy about him. His brown hair, which held the faintest russet tinge, was cut short, and dark eyes looked out of a strong, but not particularly good-looking, face.

Anna stared. Two pairs of brown eyes locked. Her colour rose. He was so different from her imaginings, from the glimpse she had had of the immaculate figure spitting at her uncle's door, that she could hardly take it in.

The man held her card in his hand. 'Miss de Cardonnel?'

Anna brushed this aside. 'You are this Monsieur Redbourn of whom my card speaks?' Her English had completely deserted her.

He glanced down at the card Anna was holding. 'I am Mr Redbourn, yes.' A look of amusement creased the lines around his eyes. 'To what do I owe the honour?'

Anna found herself unexpectedly warming to that smile. Then she shook herself. Her nerves were obviously jangled. She must be misinterpreting things. Doubtless he was flattered that she had sought him out. She must put a stop to her foolish feeling that perhaps .... 'Of course, you know why I am here,' she informed him.

'Indeed, I do not, Miss de Cardonnel.' The smile had vanished and a slight frown took its place. He appeared to be considering her carefully.

'It won't do, Mr Redbourn,' she said crisply. 'I don't know what you have bamboozled my uncle and aunt into believing, but I have more sense. You have no more fallen in love with me than I with the man in the moon. It is a fabrication of the most stupid!'

'I am certainly not in love with you.'

'Ha! You admit it! This marriage will not take place, you understand? I am told you want rank. It is true that I am the daughter of the Vicomte de Cardonnel, but I have learnt that French titles are poorly regarded over here. It might be different if I had money, but I have none. You are wasting your time, Mr Redbourn. So will you please inform Sir Robert that you have changed your mind. Good day, sir!' Anna picked up her parasol, gave him a curt nod and swept out of the room.

Her footsteps were heard running down the stairs, the front door banged and she was gone.

Luke was left contemplating her card, turning it over and over in his hands. After a few moments' thought he tugged at the bell pull. The dusty servant came in.

'Walter, ask my sister to come here, would you?'

As Anna had done he began pacing up and down the carpet, hands clasped behind his back. The door opened.

'Luke! What on earth is it?'

'Sit down, Hester. Unless I'm much mistaken, Laurence is indeed in London and up to his old tricks. It seems he is using my business cards on some nefarious business of his own.' He gave her a brief account of Anna's visit.

Hester was shocked. 'A completely strange woman to come here and accuse you of wanting to marry her!' she exclaimed. 'I never heard of such a thing! What's she like?'

'Thin, pale and cross.' It was not the whole truth, he realized. The girl who had stormed into his life was as slender as a wand, with huge, expressive dark eyes, which flashed as she spoke, and there was something about her which made him sorry she had left so precipitately.

Hester gave an unwilling laugh. 'As well she might be. What's going to happen when she realizes that Laurence is not you?'

Luke looked at Anne's card again and then he flung it down on the table. 'I daresay she'll fall in love with him,' he said, his voice suddenly harsh.

'But Laurence would never marry a girl with no money,' said Hester.

'I can't be sure, but I am almost certain that Laurence has found out that she has money somewhere.'

'But what are you going to do? You cannot let a defenceless girl be drawn into marriage with such a man as Laurence.'

'From what I've seen, Miss de Cardonnel is hardly defenceless!' retorted Luke.

Lady Broxhead had decided that Julia must be warned of this new element in her cousin's affairs. She summoned her daughter to her boudoir and relayed the news in measured tones. She was particularly anxious, she informed her daughter, that every encouragement be given towards promoting so unexceptionable a match. Julia could hardly speak for excitement.

'Oh, Mama! It's just like a fairy story,' she exclaimed. 'Lucky, lucky Anna!'

'Julia! Where you get these vulgar ideas from I don't know. Please do not let Mr Wellesborough hear them.'

Julia became sober at once. 'I'm sorry, Mama. But surely Mr Wellesborough will meet this Mr Redbourn? Why, they will be almost related!'

'No, Julia,' said her mother firmly. 'I do not want Mr Redbourn mentioned while things are at so delicate a stage. Perhaps after your honeymoon.'

'But that's ages away,' said Julia indignantly. She met her mother's eye and quailed. Why must it all be so secretive? If this man were so eligible, why may she not meet him now? But there was no use in questioning her mother. 'I shall say nothing,' she promised.

Once freed from her mother's presence, Julia sped to her cousin's room, and knocked excitedly. 'It's Julia. May I come in?'

Anna was sitting by the window, her mind in a turmoil. Try as she might she had not been able to stop thinking about Mr Redbourn. There was something about the strength of those shoulders, the expression in his dark eyes .... She shook herself. Was she mad? He had admitted to not being in love with her. She did not know him. His character might be despicable. Naturally she wanted nothing to do with such a match. She scolded her thoughts back into some sort of rationality.

It was two days since her meeting with Mr Redbourn and she had good hopes, she told herself, that they had seen the last of him. Her uncle had said nothing to her, but perhaps that was due to a slight feeling of embarrassment. Maybe Mr Redbourn had written and her uncle didn't like to mention anything in case Anna felt insulted or upset. Julia's first words demolished that theory.

'Oh, Anna! Mama has just told me!'

'Told you what?' Anna's heart gave a sudden lurch.

'Why, about this Mr Redbourn, of course! Oh, Anna, how *romantic* it is! And Mama says that he's very good-looking too!' She flopped down beside her cousin on the window seat and kissed her affectionately.

So he hadn't written, was Anna's first thought. If he had, Lady Broxhead would know of it. Perhaps he was just going to fade out of the picture. 'Julia, aren't you being a little previous?' said Anna crossly. 'I haven't even met him yet, nor he me.' Whatever would she do if they met in company? How embarrassing such a meeting would be.

'But he's seen you in the park, Mama told me!' exclaimed Julia. 'How can you be so cold, Anna? Why, it's the most romantic thing I ever heard of.' She had met Mr Welles-borough, very properly, at an evening party given by her godmother. She'd been introduced to this plump and somewhat perspiring young man by a friend of her mother's, and if Mr Wellesborough had spotted her across the room and been instantly smitten by her charms, she had never heard of it. She said as much to Anna.

'I'd rather meet a possible future husband as you met Mr Wellesborough,' said Anna firmly. 'That way, everybody knows about him. But what do we know about this Mr Redbourn? Only what he tells us himself.' And whatever her aunt said, she thought, Mr Redbourn was not handsome.

'But Mama says that Papa thinks he's eligible,' protested Julia, dashed.

With praiseworthy restraint Anna stifled the retort that rose to her lips.

The following morning Sir Robert announced to his

asembled family over the breakfast-table that he had received a charmingly worded missive from Mr Redbourn. He had taken a box at the Theatre Royal to see Kemble act in *The Revenge* on Monday June 15. It was the last time that Mr Kemble was performing that season. Might he persuade Sir Robert, Lady Broxhead and Miss de Cardonnel to accompany himself and his mother?

Julia was jealous but resigned. 'But I want to meet him too!' she exclaimed.

'Another time, Julia,' said her mother firmly.

Anna told herself that she was outraged. She had made it perfectly plain that she did not wish to pursue the acquaintance and *this* was the result! He sought to make her change her mind, doubtless. And why? She had told him that she had no money, did not wish to marry him. There were surely other, better-dowered girls in London, who would be willing to listen to his addresses?

She dressed for the evening with extreme care and in a mood of towering resentment.

Helen was worried. This deception was going on longer than she wanted. Already she had had to meet the Broxheads twice and now she had to take an evening off work in order to go to the theatre that employed her to see one of the understudies take her part in the chorus. It was not what she wanted and it was dangerous as well.

She mentioned her fears to Peggy, who was a dresser at the Theatre Royal, and had been a friend ever since Helen had started work there over twenty years ago. Peggy knew all her secrets and would understand.

'I don't like it, Peggy,' she said. 'Supposing somebody recognizes me? And then, what will Mr Kemble think? I don't want him to label me as unreliable. Oh, Peggy, I need the work here. I can't risk not turning up! What shall I do?'

'It's a bad day you ever took up with that Laurence Redbourn,' said the Job's comforter.

'Don't!' cried Helen. 'If you knew how much I've regretted I ever set eyes on him.'

Peggy relented. 'You haven't missed a performance for ever so long,' she said. 'And the understudy is that Maria Dodds, clumsy thing. You needn't worry that she'll be taking your place. But look, Helen, you need something more permanent, like. What about this Sir Robert? Any hopes here?'

Helen considered. 'Possibly. He has that certain look, know what I mean, Peg? But what can I do as this blessed widow?'

'And with Mr Redbourn watching your every move, too,' added Peggy gloomily.

Helen shuddered. She had not told Peggy about the episode with the knife. But it was there at the back of her mind.

Mr and Mrs Redbourn were waiting in the foyer of the Theatre Royal to greet their guests. Introductions were made. The gentlemen bowed, the ladies curtseyed. Anna, suddenly confronted by a total stranger, could only be glad that the crowded room hid her dismay. *This* was Mr Redbourn? He was taller than the other man, less stocky. His eyes were blue, not brown and his hair fairer. Yet, now she saw him again, he was undoubtedly the man she had seen leaving the house in Brook Street. Was his name really Redbourn? How had he got the other Mr Redbourn's card? And, above all, what was going on?

She sat next to Laurence in the box and heard not a word of the first act. Her first coherent thought was that one of these Redbourns must be an impostor. She did not know what she felt most, embarrassment at having accused a total stranger of wanting to marry her, or anxiety and worry as to what game this Mr Redbourn might be playing.

A sudden memory flashed into her mind of the Carmes prison. She had had to dissemble then. She knew, as did her elders, that the cabochon emerald would be hidden in a special pouch behind the Revolutionary cockade: that it would be death to be found out, not only for her parents and Tante Marie, but it would be goodbye to all their hopes of getting out of Paris. Nobody had explained it to her, but she knew.

The interval arrived. Laurence had ordered refreshments for his guests.

'Miss de Cardonnel,' he said, 'may I offer you a little wine?'

'Thank you.' Anna inclined her head graciously and waited to see what he would do. He brought her the wine, set his chair closer to hers – just on the boundary between politeness and intrusion, and started to compliment her on her looks.

Anna resisted the temptation to edge her chair away and looked covertly at him. He was undoubtedly good-looking, though his eyes were too small, but he had a slim, elegant figure, well set off by the dark-blue evening coat, with fawn knee breeches, white stockings and flat black evening pumps. So far as looks went, thought Anna, he did very well.

His conversation was another matter, and Anna couldn't help feeling as if he were probing. 'I understand you came from France as a child, Miss de Cardonnel,' he began. 'That must have been very frightening for you. Did you come with your parents?'

'My mother had died,' replied Anna, shortly. 'I came over with my father.'

'And you both went to live with your uncle?' As Anna didn't reply, he added, 'You were fortunate to have some English relatives.'

'Indeed. Sir Robert has been kindness iself.' Could he really be trying for information? Or was this just politeness?

'One has heard unfortunate cases of people arriving with only the clothes they stood up in. I do trust that you were more fortunate?'

'I was only seven, Mr Redbourn,' said Anna. 'I really

remember very little about it.' She was now almost sure that he was trying to pump her. 'Forgive me, I should like to talk to your mother, if I may. My aunt has been telling me how charming she is.'

'But, of course, how remiss of me.' Laurence was all politeness, but Anna sensed that he was not pleased. His mouth had clamped down to a thin line, those small eyes had narrowed. Anna quashed a feeling of unease and turned her chair slightly so as to talk to Mrs Redbourn.

Mrs Redbourn was delighted to talk to Miss de Cardonnel. Helen saw from Laurence's warning glance that his courtship had not gone too successfully. She now pushed up her veil and hoped that she was enough in the shadows to remain unnoticed.

'Miss de Cardonnel, I was so sorry to miss you when I called with my son on your respected uncle and aunt.' She put a light affectionate hand on Laurence's sleeve. 'I always think it's quite impossible to talk in the theatre. So much noise all the time.'

'Oh,' said Anna. 'Do you go to the theatre often?'

Damn, thought Helen. She recovered herself quickly. 'Only while my husband was alive.' She raised a wisp of handkerchief to her eyes. 'But you, Miss de Cardonnel. May I ask how you rate Kemble's acting? I do not think, myself, that Zaiga is one of his best parts. Or perhaps you prefer Mr Charles Kemble's Don Alonzo?' Helen was aware that she was gabbling.

'Mr Charles Kemble's voice is rather too light for melodrama, in my view. I prefer his brother's performance,' said Anna, with a smile. 'Though I shall have to wait until the end for a proper assessment.' The woman was frightened, she thought. She could see it in her eyes, which every now and then darted uneasily towards her son. Her hands were lying relaxed in her lap, idly playing with her fan, but her throat was tense. Anna had seen people frightened and determined not to show it; her mother; Madame de Custine, who shared a cell with her; Tante Marie, when she opened the door in Paris and knew it might be an agent of the Revolutionary police.

Sir Robert, who had been talking with his wife, now leaned forward. 'Splendid evening, eh?' he said to Anna. 'I like to see a bit of sparkle.' He gestured expansively toward the audience and the thousands of oil lamps and candles which lit the auditorium. In fact, he had slept soundly throughout the first act, but he felt that he should do his bit to encourage the match along. Besides, this Mrs Redbourn was really a most attractive woman.

Helen glanced at Laurence who was now talking to Lady Broxhead. 'I always think it's the *company* that makes for a good evening, Sir Robert,' she said. She allowed him to see a dimple. 'Don't you agree?'

Anna listened to her uncle and Mrs Redbourn talking with only half an ear. She was looking at Mrs Redbourn covertly and had noticed, incredulously, that the lady seemed to be wearing make-up! Could it be possible? No lady *ever* wore make-up, except perhaps the faintest touch of papier-poudré, discreetly applied if it were hot. And yet there was a touch of burnt cork on Mrs Redbourn's upper eyelid and she was almost sure that there was a line, undeneath her chin, as of some sort of foundation not quite blending in.

No, she must be mistaken. She did not like Mr Redbourn, but that was no reason to condemn his mother, who seemed a pleasant person, as well.

If she *were* his mother.

Suddenly the theatre seemed to be full of deception. And not just on the stage. It was a deception that Anna was going to have to join. 'You are a de Cardonnel,' her mother had told her that last time. 'You can deceive this *canaille*.'

During her years in Somers Town Anna had lived among the

canaille and had learnt not to judge people by their class. Some were good and some were bad, just like everywhere else. But all at once she saw what her mother had meant. For this Mr Redbourn, whatever he might pretend, was one of the *canaille*; the woman with him was probably not his mother and she, Anna, would deceive him.

She would pretend to accept his flatteries until she had time to think. She thought of the other Mr Redbourn, of his warm brown eyes resting on her with amusement, and blushed.

Behind her Lady Broxhead, under cover of her fan, said to Mrs Redbourn, 'My niece colours up very prettily. I believe we may have a match!'

The season was drawing to a close and the knockers were off many of the town houses, chandeliers tied up in brown holland and dust covers swathed over furniture. In Brook Street the Broxheads were organizing the final touches for Julia's wedding, now barely two weeks away. The spare bedroom was full of presents and Julia and Anna were constantly needed to answer letters, go to the dressmaker's – for both girls were having new dresses – and helping the maids sew monograms on Julia's new sheets and pillowcases.

Somehow or other Anna never had the time to go and visit Tante Marie and she couldn't help wondering how far this was deliberate policy on Lady Broxhead's part.

Julia had now met Mr Redbourn and was full of admiration. 'I wish *my* betrothed were as good-looking as yours,' she exclaimed one morning, while sitting with Anna hemming pillowcases.

'He's not my betrothed,' said Anna crossly.

'Anna!' exclaimed Julia, putting down her sewing to stare at her cousin. 'I despair of you! He's obviously nuts on you. He's handsome, quite rich and perfectly charming. What more do you want?'

Integrity, thought Anna. 'I don't want to marry him,' was all she said.

'I daresay you will, though,' said Julia pragmatically. 'When Mama determines on something, it usually happens.'

'Not with me,' retorted Anna. But she was worried. Mr Redbourn's acceptance in the house in Brook Street, his inclusion in many small outings as a family friend meant that every day the match seemed to have an increasing inevitability. Lady Broxhead listened to Anna's protests with a smile.

'You can surely be polite to him for a week or so? Sir Robert and I understand your scruples. But why not get to know him a little? Where's the harm in that?'

Anna was made to feel that she was being unreasonable. All the same, to meet an eligible young man almost daily, to have his visits allowed by the family did, as Julia said, give Mr Redbourn's addresses a certain acceptability. Even Lady Clermont, who had been a friend of Marie Antoinette's, was approving, when Anna and Julia went with Lady Broxhead to pay a call in Berkeley Square.

'Lady Broxhead has been telling me about a certain young man who is paying his addresses to you. Miss de Cardonnel,' she said in her majestic way, summoning Anna to a chair next to hers.

'I barely know him, Lady Clermont,' said Anna. 'I understand he is a merchant with a business somewhere in the City.'

Lady Clermont laid an understanding hand on Anna's arm for a brief moment. 'My dear Miss de Cardonnel, I knew your father well, and you may be sure that I have your best interests at heart. Let us be practical, if you were in Paris, and everything as it was then this young man would not be acceptable for a moment. But alas, we have to live in the real world. You are dowerless and your uncle and aunt are not rich. What else would you do?'

'Work,' said Anna. 'There are plenty of émigrés in a worse position than myself. Many too, of far higher rank. Madame de Gontaut and Madame de Saisseval both support themselves.'

'Ah, you are worried about rank,' said Lady Clermont, nodding as though she now understood it all. 'But you must realize that in England we view these things differently. Why, even this Mr Brummell whom everyone talks about, has a grandfather who was a mere *valet-de-chambre*! I could name many members of the aristocracy with even more humble origins.'

Anna was not concerned about rank, but in the face of Lady Clermont's obvious approval for Mr Redbourn, felt unable to voice her true worries. How could she say that she suspected that Mr Redbourn had some hold over her uncle? That Sir Robert might be using her as a pawn in his dealings with Mr Redbourn. It would be the basest ingratitude.

It seemed, from the remarks made to her, that the general agreement would be with her aunt as to the suitability of the match.

But the more she met Mr Redbourn, the less she trusted him. She had cultivated a policy of deliberate vagueness when he tried to ask her about her life before coming to live with the Broxheads, and she noticed that he did the same when she questioned him.

He had learnt, from something Julia had let drop, that they had shared a governess. 'But wasn't that difficult, Miss de Cardonnel, if you were living with your father as I gather you were? I hope you didn't have far to come every day?'

'I enjoyed my lessons with my cousin,' replied Anna evasively. 'But what about you, Mr Redbourn? Where did you go to school? One of the City schools I have heard about, perhaps?'

It was Laurence's turn to be evasive. 'My schooldays are not worthy of your interest, Miss de Cardonnel,' he replied, giving her arm a squeeze.

They were walking in the Park, discreetly followed by

Charles. Anna dropped her hand.

Laurence gave a short laugh and said appreciatively, 'Pretty prude.'

How dare he! thought Anna. How dare he assume that she liked his squeezes and his innuendoes? Whenever she had attempted to reprove him, he merely took it for some sort of encouragement. 'I find I have the headache,' she said coldly. She turned round and beckoned to Charles.

'You cannot deny me the pleasure of escorting you back to Brook Street,' said Laurence. He took her arm and placed it in his. There was a look in his eye that Anna had not noticed before. A steely resolve to have his own way, together with a ruthlessness about doing it. Her fingers were resting lightly on his arm. Suddenly, Laurence gave her arm a pinch. It was not a playful nip, but a real pinch and Anna stifled a cry. 'I am a very determined man,' he continued, as if nothing had happened. 'I am sure, my dear Miss de Cardonnel, that you would not wish to disappoint your good uncle and aunt. What a pity your uncle gambles, it can lead one into such unpleasant situations.'

'I understand you, I believe,' said Anna tonelessly.

Chapter Four

By Saturday Anna was feeling desperate. She would go and see Tante Marie, she decided, whether Lady Broxhead found it convenient or not. She had begun to suspect that Mr Laurence Redbourn was far more ruthless than she had at first supposed. It was only right to warn Tante Marie that she might find her niece suddenly restored to her. Or perhaps she should pay another visit to Ludgate Street? The very idea alarmed her so much that she felt quite sick. What? Approach that Mr Redbourn again after having accused him of wanting to marry her? She would rather die.

Anna worried at the problem all over breakfast. She scarcely noticed Charles entering. He carried several letters on a silver salver which he presented to the ladies. Lady Broxhead had several from the various charities she supported, Julia one and there was one for Anna. Anna turned it over curiously, she had few correspondents and invitations were usually joint ones addressed to either her aunt or her cousin.

'Charles,' Julia looked up from her correpondence. 'More coffee, please.'

'Certainly, Miss Julia.'

Anna put her nail under the seal, broke it and spread open the letter. The writing was in a firm black hand and unfamiliar to her.

Dear Miss de Cardonnel,
If you would do me the honour of calling as soon as may be
convenient, I have some information which concerns you. My
sister will be present.

yours etc.
Luke Redbourn

Anna stared at it and read it several times before she could
take it in. This must be the Mr Redbourn she had met. The
address at the top of the letter was the one she had visited. The
other Mr Redbourn she knew was named Laurence, for she
had heard his mother call him so. Had this Mr Redbourn
signed his full name so that she should know who he was? Or
was it just coincidence?

He had indicated, too, that his sister would be there. That
was kind and surely meant to reassure her. But was she really
his sister? Anna had already met one Mr Redbourn with his
spurious mother, why should she believe another? Such had
been her state when she left the house in Ludgate Street that
she had retained only a confused impression of a tall man with
a certain aura of strength about him.

All feelings of dying of humiliation vanished. Luke
Redbourn's letter was courteously expressed and contained no
hint of their previous unfortunate contretemps. She had
mistrusted Laurence from the moment she had met him: her
instinct told her that Mr Luke Redbourn was to be trusted. She
would go and see him.

'And who is your letter from, Julia?' asked Lady Broxhead. In
her day she had never been allowed to open her own
correspondence, and whilst she allowed Julia to open hers, she
nevertheless felt she had the right to know all the details.

'Theresa Tottenham, Mama. She wants me to go to one of her
mother's insipid musical soirées.'

'Miss Tottenham?' said Lady Broxhead. 'I believe that Mrs Tottenham is a friend of Mr Wellesborough's mother. Naturally you will go.'

Julia made a face at Anna across the table.

'And may I ask who your correspondent is, Anna?' asked Lady Broxhead. 'It seems to be a very absorbing letter.' Perhaps that nice Mr Redbourn had written a proposal, she thought.

Anna thought quickly. 'It is from the Duchesse de Gontaut, Aunt Susan. She begs me for a visit.' The duchesse spoke very little English and it was doubtful whether Lady Broxhead would feel that either she or Julia must accompany her.

'Oh.' Lady Broxhead was disappointed. 'Madame de Gontaut? Where does she live?' It was somewhere outlandish, she remembered. Hampstead possibly.

'In the City, Aunt Susan.' In fact, Madame de Gontaut rented a couple of depressing rooms overlooking old St Pancras Churchyard, but Anna hoped that her aunt would not remember this.

'The City? Well, I daresay I can let you have the carriage this morning.' Lady Broxhead spoke grudgingly, but she was not too displeased. 'My niece is visiting the poor dear Duchesse de Gontaut', she would say to her friends when she paid her afternoon calls. That always sounded well.

Anna accepted with becoming gratitude.

When Anna had left the room Lady Broxhead remarked to Julia, 'How pleasant it will be to have you both settled so well.'

'I'm not sure that Anna likes Mr Redbourn, though,' said Julia dubiously.

'My dear Julia, pray what has that to say to anything?'

Anna spent the half-hour that the Broxheads' carriage slowly wound its way up to Ludgate Street racking her brains to remember something more of Mr Luke Redbourn, but all in vain. She was let in by the same dusty servant and again shown upstairs, but this time to a pleasant room at the back of the house which overlooked a small garden. The window was open and Anna could see a few climbing roses. A gentleman and a lady were sitting there. The moment she saw Luke again she remembered him. He had, she thought with a sense of shock, a *nice* face, a good face. There were laughter lines that crinkled his eyes and his smile was singularly sweet. He was smiling now.

Luke came forward and shook Anna's hand. 'I am grateful to you for coming so promptly, Miss de Cardonnel,' he said. 'May I introduce my sister, Miss Redbourn? Hester, this is Miss de Cardonnel.' Anna, glancing up at him, wondered whether he bore her any grudge for that last disastrous meeting.

Anna saw a thin, worn lady, whose left hand rested heavily on an ivory-handled cane. She had the same colouring as her brother, Anna noted, and they shared the same high-bridged noses. Whoever else this Miss Redbourn might be, it seemed certain that she was related to the gentleman.

'I ... I must apologize,' began Anna, the colour mounting to her cheeks, 'for my previous intrusion. I ....'

Luke began to smile. 'Please,' he raised a hand. 'Explanations are unnecessary. Spare my blushes I beg you.'

Anna, glancing up at him, could barely meet those amused brown eyes. 'But ...' she began.

'You made a mistake. And as our brother, Laurence, appears to have stolen my cards. I do not think that it was your fault.'

'Your brother!' Anna looked at Luke, trying to trace a resemblance. Laurence was tall, fair and willowy with blue eyes. He was undoubtedly the better-looking. Luke was a few inches shorter, dark and well muscled. His features were stronger, less effeminate perhaps?

'You are still doubtful, I see,' said Luke. 'May I ask if you have met my brother yet?'

'Yes,' said Anna shortly.

'Ah,' Luke's smile faded.

'Miss de Cardonnel,' put in Hester. 'Won't you sit down? I'm sure we can all discuss this better in more comfort. Pray allow Mr Redbourn to take your cloak and bonnet. Luke, ring the bell for some refreshments. What will you have, Miss de Cardonnel? Tea, coffee, a little wine?'

'Some coffee, please.'

While the Redbourns busied themselves, Anna looked round. The room was well kept and comfortable without being too formal. The oak panelling was well polished and the furniture old-fashioned. Some late June roses, deep pink and sweet-smelling, sat in a pretty china bowl on a table by the window. There were some books in a little pile on the club fender. Two Staffordshire dogs stood on the mantelpiece with a mirror between them, and a fine black and grey tabby cat lay curled on a rug in front of Miss Redbourn's chair.

Anna began to relax. The room, like its owners, was unpretentious and reassuring.

'As you have now met our brother,' began Luke in a voice which was pleasant enough but quite distant, 'may I ask if you have changed your mind about the marriage?' Like Caroline, she would have succumbed to Laurence's charm, and what could either he or Hester hope to say to influence her?

'Changed my mind!' echoed Anna, astonished.

Hester looked across at her guest. Why, she's so pretty she thought. Hester still retained a soft spot for Laurence. Perhaps Laurence has found in Miss de Cardonnel somebody who truly loves him. He will change. Things will be different. 'Forgive me, my dear,' she said, leaning forward. 'Do you *love* Laurence?'

'*Love* him!' cried Anna. 'Of course not!' She remembered suddenly that she was talking to his sister. 'I ... I'm sorry, Miss Redbourn. I should not have spoken so of your brother.'

Luke had turned to look at her. There was an arrested look on his face. 'I am relieved to hear it,' he said. But there was a note of doubt in his voice. A maid came in with the coffee and placed it on a small table near Hester. When she had gone and they all had their coffee, Luke continued, 'My sister and I have discussed it and we both feel that we must be open with you. But it is a painful family business and we must ask for your confidence.'

'Of course.'

Luke gave her a brief, unvarnished run-down of Laurence's career. 'We had no idea that he was back in England, Miss de Cardonnel. Frankly, we do not know what he is up to, but, believe me, it can be nothing good.'

'He was such a beautiful little boy,' said Hester sadly. 'Perhaps that was the trouble.'

'He was a very spoilt little boy,' retorted Luke. 'However, this is beside the point. We hoped, Miss de Cardonnel, that you would be so good as to tell us what you know and together we may be able to get to the bottom of this.'

Anna related her story. 'I cannot see why he should be pursuing me,' she ended.

'My dear ...' began Hester.

'No, I am not looking for compliments,' went on Anna. 'I am speaking the truth as I see it. From what you say his story of wanting to marry for rank is untrue and I certainly have no money. I am dependent entirely on the generosity of my uncle. He has promised me one thousand pounds when I marry, but as his financial affairs are ....' She turned her hands down expressively and shrugged.

'Who is this lady he calls his mother?' wondered Hester. 'You must know, Miss de Cardonnel, our mother died some eight years ago.'

'Are you sure you have no money, perhaps when you come of age?' asked Luke. He was frowning down at his coffee.

'Only five hundred pounds from my father, unless the cabochon emerald turns up.'

Luke looked enquiringly at her.

Anna told them the story of the cabochon emerald 'My father was in hiding and my mother in prison,' she ended. 'When we got to England and were in a position to redeem the emerald, Père Ignace was not to be found.'

'Was the emerald very valuable?' asked Hester, fascinated. Her own world had been so respectable and circumscribed that it seemed like a tale out of the Arabian Nights to be talking of prisons and being in hiding and lost emeralds.

'In itself, no,' said Anna. 'Of course it was worth some hundreds. The setting, which was Indian, was fine, but scarcely enough to tempt your brother, I should have thought.'

'Are you sure that Laurence is not in love with you?' asked Hester, a little wistfully. 'I've always thought that a good marriage would be the making of him.'

'Your brother has no feelings whatsoever for me, whatever he might pretend to the contrary,' said Anna firmly. She would have liked to have added that he was concerned only for himself, but felt that this would be unkind.

Luke had been making notes and now looked up. 'Miss de Cardonnel, I confess I am bewildered. Like you, I cannot believe that the emerald, even if he has tracked it down, and the uncertain thousand from your uncle and your own five hundred pounds, is enough to explain Laurence's sudden desire for matrimony.'

Anna raised an eyebrow.

Luke smiled. 'You have already said that you are not looking for compliments,' he reminded her.

Anna laughed, and Luke, looking at her, felt a small knot, somewhere behind his heart, begin to loosen.

'Laurence has gone to some trouble and expense over this,' he continued. 'He has acquired a respectable mother. You have been his guest at the theatre and in the Park. He will expect some considerable financial return for such an investment.'

'Perhaps we should talk to Sir Robert Broxhead?' worried Hester. 'I don't like all this hanging over Miss de Cardonnel.'

'My uncle is very eager for the match,' said Anna. 'I don't know why. It's almost as if ... but no, that's impossible.'

'Nothing's impossible where Laurence is concerned,' said Luke. It sounded, from his guest's hesitation, as if she feared some sort of blackmail and Luke could not rule that out. He thought for a moment. 'How imminent is this threat of marriage?'

'I haven't even been *asked* yet!' said Anna indignantly. The Redbourns laughed and after a moment Anna joined in. 'My cousin Julia is getting married in about two weeks' time. Nothing will be done before then.'

'Could I ask you to wait, Miss de Cardonnel?' asked Luke. 'I should like a little time to try to find out what Laurence is up to. He once forged my name on a bill, so I am anxious to put a stop to whatever he's doing for all our sakes. And then, with your permission, I shall come and see Sir Robert and lay all the facts before him.'

'But isn't that leaving Miss de Cardonnel in an awkward position?' asked Hester. 'I am sure we ought to go to Sir Robert now.'

Anna sat up. 'Of course you must find out what he is up to,' she said. 'I am not to be intimidated by such as he!'

'Bravo!' said Luke. 'But if things become really difficult, you must feel free to tell Sir Robert what you know of Laurence and I shall, of course, back you up.' He reached out for the bell-pull. The dusty servant appeared.

'Walter, would you show Miss de Cardonnel to her carriage, please?'

When Anna had gone Hester said archly, 'You didn't tell me she was so pretty, Luke.' There had been a softened expression in his eyes that she hadn't seen since the happier days of his engagement to Caroline.

Luke was staring down at the bowl of roses on the table. He touched one pink bloom gently with his finger and didn't reply.

The remaining days before Julia's wedding passed in the usual pre-wedding bustle and nobody, least of all Lady Broxhead, who considered it her duty to pry, had much time for talking. It was just as well for Anna had much to think about. She had liked Luke and Hester Redbourn she decided. Whatever their brother had turned out to be, they were both plainly good people. It might not be very romantic, and would certainly not satisfy Julia, but Anna had learnt to value simple human decency.

Laurence called only once. 'I shall not inflict my company on you for too long,' he told Lady Broxhead with a smile. 'I know you have much to do just now.'

'You are too thoughtful, Mr Redbourn. I assure you that after the wedding we shall be delighted to see you. Shall we not, Anna?'

'I am sure Mr Redbourn is well aware of my sentiments,' replied Anna. She had barely looked at him during his visit and soon excused herself from the room.

Laurence flashed her a malevolent glance. The little bitch, he thought. When they were married he would have great pleasure in teaching her a lesson or two. Laurence was not too particular about how he treated women and had discovered that a constant fairly low level of physical violence soon sapped any tendency to 'uppishness'.

But Anna had more to think about than Laurence. Julia was suffering from pre-wedding nerves and inclined to burst into tears at inconvenient moments.

'I know I *ought* to want to marry Mr Wellesborough,' she wailed. 'I just wish he were different. More, well, good-looking, like your Mr Redbourn.'

Anna controlled herself with an effort. 'Mr Wellesborough is a very kind, good-natured man, Julia. He is plainly very fond of you and has been most generous about the marriage settlements.'

'I know,' sobbed Julia.

'I like him,' said Anna, offering her cousin her handkerchief. 'You know where you are with him. He's steady.'

Julia blew her nose firmly. 'I'm being silly,' she said. 'I know I'm lucky, really. And I quite like him, too.'

'Well then,' said Anna. She had been brought up to think of love matches as impractical and probably doomed to disappointment. Julia was far better off, she reckoned, in marrying Mr Wellesborough and reserving her romantic adoration for the heroes of Mrs Radcliffe's Gothic novels.

As for herself, love had never yet entered her life and she didn't think it ever would. Anna prided herself on the fact that such foolishness was just not in her nature. She liked to think that it was part of her French inheritance; a practical outlook on things. And yet, though it was scarcely acknowledged, Anna was dimly aware that some vital ingredient was missing: that certain something which had induced her father to bring Marie Bonnieux to London with him, to brave the whispered condemnation of his fellow-exiles and have her live with him openly, instead of keeping her in discreet obscurity.

The vicomte had never discussed his affair with his daughter, possibly out of loyalty to her mother. Even after his death Marie didn't speak of it. It seemed to be an embargoed subject. Anna had learned early on that love was not a topic for discussion.

With Mr Redbourn mercifully absent, Anna began to relax. She even managed a quick visit to Madame Bonnieux the Sunday before the wedding. She was not in time for church, but went straight to her old home in Phoenix Street.

'Anna, *chérie*,' Tante Marie embraced her affectionately. 'Luncheon is just ready. Come in.'

Anna took off her cloak and bonnet, hung them carefully on the peg behind the kitchen door, and sank thankfully down on one of the Windsor chairs. There was the usual delicious smell from an earthenware casserole on the hob.

'I haven't seen you for weeks,' said Marie reproachfully.

'I know. I wanted to come but somehow there was always so much to do and Aunt Susan made coming here seem impossible and terribly selfish. She's very good at that.' Anna looked round. There was a new pot of basil on the window sill, otherwise everything seemed blessedly familiar. 'Good God! How Hercule's grown!'

Hercule was frisking round the table, tail lashing wildly in excitement. He finally calmed down enough to sit at Anna's feet, panting wildly, and allow her to tickle his ears.

There was much to catch up on and Anna, with a sense of relief, poured the Redbourn saga into Marie's sympathetic ears. For some reason, though, she found she could not bring herself to be open about Mr Luke Redbourn; she was aware as she was speaking that it sounded as though he were quite twenty years older than he obviously was. She didn't stop to analyse why.

'I don't like this, Anna,' said Marie at last. 'It sounds a nasty business to me and I don't like you mixed up in it. I think you should tell Sir Robert.'

'What can I tell him?' countered Anna. 'I really don't want to mention my visit to the other Redbourns. I am well aware of how unladylike it was of me.'

'He should have visited them himself,' retorted Marie. 'It's a great neglect of his duty as a guardian.'

'I may be making a mountain out of a molehill,' said Anna. Surely the story she had been relating belonged more to the Gothic romances Julia was so fond of reading? Here, in Tante Marie's kitchen, with its whitewashed walls and brass pans hanging up, it all seemed a world away. 'Mr Redbourn has not yet asked me to marry him. Perhaps he never will. God knows I have hardly been encouraging. And if he does I shall refuse and then that must be an end of it. There may be some unpleasantness, but I cannot see that that can last long.'

Marie sighed. 'I'm sorry your father's plan has not worked out. He was so eager for you to find your rightful place in society and believed that by making Sir Robert your guardian he would achieve just that.'

'I don't think that Papa understood me very well.' Anna spoke sadly, for it had just occurred to her. 'The society he wanted for me was one that he had had for most of his life. But I was only seven when that world vanished. I was never really part of it at all.'

'It wasn't really such good old days either,' said Marie. 'I was lucky to have been taken up by your father. I have met other women who ended up in the gutter.' The Marquis de Sade, who owned the neighbouring château of Lacoste, had regularly demanded the services of local girls who were fortunate indeed if they returned home with only a few bruises.

'If I belong anywhere, it's here,' said Anna. 'I want to live a useful life, not simply be an ornament in the house of a rich man.' She wondered, suddenly, what sort of life Miss Redbourn led in that house in Ludgate Street. Was *she* able to lead a useful life?

The wedding passed off quietly and successfully. Julia dried her tears and transformed into the bride, beautiful, but with a suitable touch of maidenly pallor. Anna, as sole bridesmaid, performed her part with grace. She had not been to an English wedding before and she found it unexpectedly moving, a fact which embarrassed her. God forbid that she was becoming over-romantic, like Julia. The very thought of standing at the altar with Laurence Redbourn was odious. If there were any other candidate hovering at the back of her mind, Anna pushed the thought away.

The wedding breakfast over, Anna took Julia upstairs to help her to change into her going-away costume and in due course the happy couple set off on their seaside honeymoon.

The following day Laurence called, asked to see Sir Robert and his lady and formally asked for Anna's hand in marriage. Anna was summoned down to the library.

Never had she felt more alone as she walked down the stairs and knocked at the library door. She was in the house of her guardian, she owed the very clothes she wore to his generosity, and apart from Tante Marie, there was no living soul who belonged to her or cared about her.

She entered the library with her usual quiet dignity and hoped that nobody noticed that her knees were trembling. Lady Broxhead was sitting by the window, her hands folded piously in her lap. Sir Robert and Mr Redbourn had both risen to their feet as she entered.

'Ah, my dear Anna,' Sir Robert came forward and took her hand. 'Mr Redbourn has done you the great honour of asking for your hand in marriage.'

'Oh?'

Laurence stepped forward. 'Miss de Cardonnel,' he said smoothly. 'Your uncle – if he will forgive me for contradicting him – has got it wrong. Mine would be the honour, the very great honour, if you would consent to be my wife.'

'Very prettily said, upon my word,' said Sir Robert. 'I think I dare answer for my niece's acceptance.'

'I would prefer to speak for myself, sir,' said Anna. She turned to Laurence. 'I thank you, Mr Redbourn, for your estimable offer, but I must refuse. I cannot believe that a marriage between us would serve the happiness of either.' She dropped him a curtsey as she spoke and turned to go.

'Anna!' Lady Broxhead had risen, white with anger. 'One moment, if you please! Sir Robert is your guardian. It is not for you to question his decisions.' She turned to Laurence. 'Mr

Redbourn, I must apologize for my niece. She is all about her head!'

Laurence smiled, a cold smile that didn't reach his eyes. 'Perhaps Miss de Cardonnel has some specific objection to me?' he said silkily. 'I should be glad to know what it is that I may endeavour to remove it.'

'Pooh! What objection could she possibly have?' said Sir Robert. 'It's all missishness.'

'The vicomte would have wanted your obedience, Anna,' warned Lady Broxhead.

Anna drew herself up. There was to be no easy way out. 'My father could scarcely have wanted me to marry a fraudster and an embezzler!'

'How dare you!' cried Lady Broxhead, two spots of colour flying on her cheeks. 'Apologize at once.'

'How do you know this, Miss de Cardonnel?' said Laurence. He was still standing at his ease, but an angry muscle twitched in his neck. 'Surely you have some evidence for so wild an assertion?'

Anna dug her nails into the palms of her hands to stop them from trembling. 'Your brother, Mr Luke Redbourn, told me,' she said.

Laurence paused just a fraction too long. 'I have no brother,' he said. 'I am an only son.'

'Oh,' said Anna politely, 'that is strange, since I visited your brother and sister at the address on your card.' She turned to Sir Robert. 'When my father made you my guardian he did so in the belief that you would look after my interests. If he were here now he would want to know why you did not visit this address yourself?'

Sir Robert sank down heavily on the nearest chair. Laurence strode forward, took Anna's chin in his hand and jerked it up to face him. 'You are too interfering,' he said in a soft undertone that sent shivers down her spine. 'But unless you want to ruin your uncle, you will marry me, understand?'

'Ruin?' whispered Anna.

'Remember what I said; I am not threatening lightly.'

'But why do you *want* to marry me?' asked Anna desperately.

'Love, my dear. What else?' He raised his head and laughed: the frozen figures of Sir Robert and Lady Broxhead were too ridiculous. 'I shall return,' he said, 'so I shall not say goodbye, but rather *au revoir.*'

When the door had closed behind him Anna turned to her uncle, sitting sprawled in the chair, his face ashen, his wig askew. 'How could he ruin you?' she demanded.

Sir Robert moaned. 'I owe him ten thousand pounds, Anna. And I have no hope of ever paying him. If you marry him he has promised to cancel the debt.'

Lady Broxhead had fallen back in her chair. 'You *promised* me,' she cried wildly. 'You promised me that all that was over. There would be no more gambling.'

'Quiet, woman!' shouted Sir Robert, suddenly goaded beyond endurance. 'The house is like a tomb with all your charities and do-gooding and what not. Never a bit of fun to be had with your damned Methodist ways.'

'Do you think I want your disgusting habits here?'

'Am I master in my own house or am I not?' stormed Sir Robert.

'Master!' Lady Broxhead's voice rose to a shriek. 'You're a selfish, stupid oaf, that's what you are ....'

Appalled, Anna quietly left the room, and closed the door behind her.

Helen sat in her rented room in Henrietta Street, Covent Garden, and looked at the small pile of coins in front of her. Five pounds, two shillings and ten pence; it was all she had in the world. Since Laurence had come back into her life she had been unable to save from her usual meagre wages. Although he had said that he would pay her expenses, somehow the money was never forthcoming, or, if it was, it never quite made up what she had had to spend. Her rent was paid, Helen never allowed herself to get behind with that, but there had been that leaving present for Fanny, who had been whisked off to a pretty cottage in Chelsea by her titled lover – lucky girl – and then she had had to buy some new shoes. Her stock was sadly depleted.

She looked round at the room and sighed. It was all right, she supposed, a small boxy room with a patch of damp in one corner and windows that rattled whenever the wind blew, but it was better than others she had lived in. Her landlady wasn't mean with the coals in winter and the mattress was comfortable enough. She had done her best to give it a more homely air by putting up a couple of prints and draping an old shawl over the wooden box that did duty for a bedside table.

But here she was in her late thirties, well, mid-forties, and where was she going to go from here? She turned her chair slightly to look at herself in a mottled mirror that hung on the wall next to the window. She wasn't past it yet, she thought. Her figure was good and her hair still a pretty brown. But she wasn't getting any younger and no matter how many years she took off Mr Kemble was well aware of how old she was. And the big break had never come and, she must face it, now never would.

Suddenly she heard voices down below. Oh God, no! she thought: Laurence. She quickly swept up the money from the table and shoved it hastily into the toe of one of her slippers and thrust them under the bed. She had once seen Laurence take a small netted purse from one of the actresses who'd shared a dressing-room with her and slip it into his own pocket. It had all been done so quickly that Helen had at first thought she must have imagined it. It was only later, when the actress had missed it, that she'd realized that Laurence really had stolen it. Now, she was not taking any chances.

There was a peremptory knock and Laurence entered. His

face was murderous and Helen's hands flew to her throat. Laurence slammed the door behind him.

'You stupid little bitch!'

'Why? What is wrong, Laurence?' Helen faltered.

'Why? Didn't I tell you to keep the cards?'

'The cards?'

'The visiting cards. Didn't I say, don't let the damn butler get them?'

'No,' said Helen. 'You said nothing about the cards.' Surely he'd given them to her to use in the normal way? What was he talking about? 'What ... what else was I to do?'

'Do? You should just have given our names.'

'But Laurence, that wouldn't have done. Ladies would never do that.' Helen still couldn't work out what was the matter. 'What has happened?'

'That damned bitch de Cardonnel took the card and went to see my brother, Luke. God!' Laurence started pacing round the room. 'It never occurred to me she'd be so brassy.'

Helen saw it all. If Miss de Cardonnel had visited his brother, then the game was up. Whatever happened now, the marriage was surely off. Suddenly a wave of thankfulness went through her. She hadn't liked this luring of an innocent girl and now it was all over. She closed her eyes in momentary relief.

Laurence was staring at her. 'By God!' he shouted, 'I believe you did it on purpose. Perhaps you thought to get your hooks into Sir Robert – oh yes, I was watching you.'

'No! No!'

'You betrayed me, you doxy. And you're going to pay for it.' Without warning Laurence's fist shot out and knocked Helen sideways. She fell heavily. She rolled over to protect her face but she couldn't stop the blows as Laurence aimed a series of vicious kicks at her body. Her screams brought the landlady panting up the stairs.

'Miss Clarkson! Are you all right?'

'Thanks to your bungling the wretched girl refused me.'
Laurence gave Helen's inert body a last kick. 'I shall have to
take other measures.' He bent and turned the battered face
towards him. 'Silence, do you hear? If you don't want worse.'
He pushed past the landlady, who had just reached the door,
and left the house.

Half an hour later her landlady had finished her
ministrations. There was a bowl of reddened water on the
table. Helen looked in the mirror at her ruined face. A livid
bruise went from eye to chin. Her lip was split and blood
seeped down from a cut on her cheek. She had three cracked
ribs and her left side was covered with bruises. This was it, she
thought. She couldn't work now. It would be three or four
weeks before the ribs mended and what sort of state would she
be in to rejoin the chorus, even if Mr Kemble kept a place for
her? She had enough money for a month's rent and after that,
what?

If only she'd never told Laurence those shameful secrets
about her past. If only he had stayed in America. If only he
hadn't heard about Miss de Cardonnel's money and
blackmailed and bribed her, Helen, into being his accomplice.
Far better that her secrets came out than this!

Gradually Helen realized that she was feeling angry.
Laurence had said nothing at all to her about the visiting cards,
she was sure. He was frustrated by the failure of his plans and
had come with the deliberate intention of taking it out on her.
Why had she let him blackmail her in the first place? She could
just have said, 'Go ahead' and brazened it out. He might even
not have told if he'd thought she didn't care. Cowardice had
got her nowhere. What she *wanted* to do, she realized, was to
put a spoke in Laurence's wheel. Would that be possible? Was
there any way she could stop him?

Chapter Five

The moment that Anna shut the library door behind her and fled upstairs to her bedroom, she realized that she could no longer stay in Brook Street. Lady Broxhead would never forgive her for being the witness to her humiliation; Sir Robert would see her as the instrument of his ruin. If she stayed it would be tantamount to agreeing to accept Laurence Redbourn's proposal. Suddenly, it felt as though an enormous weight had fallen from her shoulders. She had not understood how oppressive the burden was until she knew, finally, that she must go.

She sat down on the bed and tried to pull herself together, for she was shaking. Oh Papa! she cried silently. Why are you not here? It had been horrible, horrible! She remembered the oily phrases that had tripped off Laurence's tongue with a shudder. And there was a cold ruthlessness underneath it all which frightened her. They could expect no mercy from him: Laurence would exact his pound of flesh. The only small comfort in all this was that her uncle and aunt could now be in no doubt as to Laurence's true nature.

Her first instinct was to leave immediately, but she quelled it. If at all possible there must be a civilized parting from her uncle and aunt. Sir Robert must be thanked for his many kindnesses, and she must at least try to pacify her aunt.

She dried her tears and blew her nose firmly. There was a writing desk in one corner of the room and Anna sat down at it and penned two notes. One was to Marie Bonnieux and in it she said simply that things had come to a head at the Broxheads and she would be coming home on the morrow. The other was to Luke and Hester Redbourn. She explained what had happened with Laurence, and after some hesitation, the hold he had over her uncle. She would therefore be returning home to Somers Town the following morning to live with her Tante Marie. She hoped that in so modest a position she would cease to be of interest to their brother. She wrote encouragingly but, all the same, she was apprehensive. She had not imagined that Laurence would be so determined. Surely, with Tante Marie in Phoenix Street and amongst the French community she'd be safe? But here, in Brook Street, how far dare she trust anybody? Had Laurence already established *moutons* in the house? Sir Robert had never visited them in Phoenix Street, but he must have the address. Would he betray her to Mr Redbourn and perhaps endanger Tante Marie as well?

She opened the bedroom door and paused at the head of the stairs. From her ladyship's room came the sound of muffled sobs and Martha's soothing voice as a sort of accompaniment. Anna tiptoed downstairs. The library door was ajar, but she could hear nothing.

'Are you looking for Sir Robert, Miss Anna?' It was Charles, on duty as footman.

'Yes. No. Is he out?' asked Anna.

'Yes Miss Anna. Gone to his club.' Charles had heard the row – as indeed had all the servants – and rumour was rife downstairs. 'He left orders that nobody is At Home.'

Just as well, thought Anna, with Lady Broxhead still in hysterics upstairs.

'Could you deliver a letter for me, Charles, as soon as I've written the direction?' Anna went into the library. She added a postscript to the Redbourns' letter asking them to deliver the enclosed to Madame Bonnieux, *Pâtissière*, of Phoenix Road, Somers Town, and after folding both letters together, she sealed them up and wrote the Ludgate Street address on the outside. She gave it to Charles and waited until he had left the house.

There, she thought, now I'm safe.

Later Charles, who enjoyed a bit of scandal, whispered about delivering Anna's letter to the scullery maid, a pert brunette whose ways he found very enticing. She, in turn, whispered it to the young man who had recently taken over delivering the Broxheads' vegetables and was showing a gratifying amount of interest in her doings and what went on in the house. The pert scullery maid had never heard of *moutons*. In due course the news reached Laurence.

Anna dined alone. She ordered that her trunk be brought down from the attic and she spent the rest of a miserable evening packing. Thank God Julia was safely married, she thought. The Wellesboroughs would not have liked the scandal and might have terminated the engagement. Julia, fortunately, had inherited some money from a great-aunt after whom she had been named, and had not been dependent on Sir Robert for her dowry. She would write to Julia when she got to Tante Marie's – and doubtless her cousin would be furious at having missed all the drama! Anna smiled fondly for a moment and then turned back to her packing.

The following morning, after a restless and miserable night, Anna nerved herself and went to knock on her aunt's door.

Martha opened it. 'Well, miss?' It was not a promising opening.

'I wish to speak to Lady Broxhead.'

Martha sniffed. 'I'll ask her.' She shut the door.

Anna sighed. It was plain that Lady Broxhead had been

arranging an Authorized Version of events and that Anna was cast in the role of Ungrateful Niece.

The door opened. Martha jerked her head at Anna. 'Her ladyship'll see you.'

Lady Broxhead was sitting up in bed, a wrapper around her shoulders, a Bible beside her and a bottle of smelling salts at her elbow. The inference was obvious; her aunt was armed both spiritually and medically. This was not going to be easy.

'That will be all, Martha.' Martha, after a glare at Anna, went.

'I have come to say goodbye, Aunt Susan,' began Anna. 'But I couldn't leave without thanking you for all your kindness.'

'And where's the gratitude in that?' snapped Lady Broxhead. 'If you hadn't come here, then Sir Robert would never have been drawn into the company of that Mr Redbourn.'

Anna blinked.

'You owe it to us to marry Mr Redbourn.' Two spots of colour glowed angrily on Lady Broxhead's cheeks.

'I'm sorry,' said Anna, quietly. 'I cannot marry Mr Redbourn, but I didn't want to leave without ...'

Lady Broxhead sat up, her night-cap askew. 'Words! Words!' she cried. 'What's the use of saying sorry when Sir Robert will be in King's Bench Prison if you have your way!' Her voice rose.

'I'd better go,' said Anna. 'Goodbye, Aunt Susan.'

'Viper!' shrieked Lady Broxhead. ' "There was given to me a thorn in the flesh, the messenger of Satan to buffet me"!'

Anna left. Martha was standing outside the door, arms akimbo, the picture of disapproval.

'Her ladyship is becoming biblical!' said Anna. 'You'd better go to her.'

There was nothing more to stay for. Sir Robert had gone to White's the previous evening and not returned. She would have to write to him. She went up to her bedroom for the last time to collect her bonnet, gloves and cloak. Her reticule was thrust into her cloak pocket. She looked round the room. Here she had a proper carpet, matching chairs, a four-poster bed with pretty chinz hangings and a marble washstand. But it wasn't, and never had been, home. Tonight, thank God, she'd be back with Tante Marie.

She went back downstairs and arranged with Charles for her trunk to be delivered to Phoenix Street that afternoon. He went to get a cab for her and she waited quietly in the hall. The house was silent. The servants, soon to be disbanded, were downstairs, already the house had an uncared-for look. The flowers on the hall table were wilting slightly, the Sèvres bowl could have done with a dust.

Charles came back in. 'There's a cab waiting for you, Miss Anna.'

Anna thanked him, gave him half-a-crown, which was all she could spare, adjusted her bonnet in the mirror, and left the house. 'Phoenix Street, Somers Town,' she said to the cabby.

He touched his hat briefly and flicked his whip at the horse. Anna sank back against the squabs and closed her eyes. She felt depressed. What would happen to her uncle? Could he really be imprisoned for a gaming debt? What else could she have done? It was hardly her fault if he gambled, but somehow a faint feeling of guilt would persist. She needed Tante Marie to scold her into rationality.

It wasn't until the cab lurched round a corner and came to a halt that Anna realized that they were not in Somers Town. Puzzled, she peered out of the dusty window. They were in a narrow dirty street with a filthy open gutter running down the middle. The houses were in the last stages of dilapidation with broken windows and cracked guttering. Strings of tattered washing crossed the street from side to side.

Where was she?

The door opened.

'Ah!' said a loathsomely familiar voice. 'Our charming visitor.'

Anna opened her mouth to scream. A gloved hand was thrust over her mouth and then a blow on the back of the head spiralled her down into unconsciousness. The last thing Anna remembered was Laurence's triumphant cold blue eyes mocking her.

Word of Helen's misfortunes had got round the theatre and she had received a number of notes, some flowers and ten shillings from Mr Kemble. He had expressed his sympathy but was careful to make no promises for the future, Helen noted. Still, he had sent some money and he hadn't rejected the idea of her return outright. And Peggy had come to see her.

'My, have you got a shiner!' exclaimed Peggy on entering the room. 'Looks like a rainbow, it does.'

Helen tried to smile. 'It could have been worse. I might have lost some teeth.'

'And three ribs broken,' said Peggy gloomily. 'God knows whether you'll ever dance again.'

'If I can't I shall ask Mr Kemble whether he has room in costumes,' said Helen with determined optimism.

'Humph,' said Peggy. 'Your sewing ain't up to much, you know.'

'Don't.' Helen's eyes filled with tears.

'Sorry, pet. I say things I don't mean. I'm sure Mr Kemble will find you something. Oh, that Mr Redbourn. Born to be hanged I say and the sooner the better.'

'I'm worried about what he's going to do next.'

'I shouldn't think he'd come here again,' said Peggy. 'Your landlady wouldn't let him in for a start.'

'No, I mean about Miss de Cardonnel. He talked about "other measures".'

'What can you do?' said Peggy. 'Nothing.'

'I could write to his brother,' Helen suggested.

'What! And you've been impersonating his mother?' cried

Peggy. 'Have some sense, Helen. Do you want to end up in prison?'

'To tell you the truth, Peg, I don't much care. I can't afford to be here, anyway.'

'Well, don't ask me to visit you,' said Peggy. 'I thought you'd have more sense.'

Luke received Anna's letter and duly sent Walter round to deliver the one to Madame Bonnieux. 'I want a full report,' he said. 'The shop. The place. Anything you find interesting. I smell trouble.'

'It don't look too good,' agreed Walter. 'Master Laurence ain't too particular about his methods when his will is crossed.'

'Miss de Cardonnel has the unhappy capacity for getting into trouble.'

'It ain't hardly her fault,' said Walter. Last time he'd met her Anna had tipped him a shilling out of what was obviously a slender purse. She had also thanked him prettily and though at the time he'd just grunted, he was not immune to her charm. Neither was his master, he guessed, from his worried look, for all he was trying to hide it under a show of irritation.

'I have a business to run, you know,' said Luke and went upstairs to show the letter to Hester.

'You'll have to go to Sir Robert now,' she said when she'd read it.

'I know. I'll go tomorrow.'

'What sort of man would be willing to sell his niece into marriage to save his own skin?' Hester was usually so quiet and Luke was startled by her vehemence. Hester's friend, Miss Minerva Leatherbarrow, had been reading her bits of Mary Wollstonecraft's *Vindication of the Rights of Women* and although Hester had been alarmed and shocked by Miss Wollstonecraft's conclusions, she was, nevertheless, converted enough to feel all the unfairness of Anna's position.

Luke spent the following day on a wild goose chase after Sir Robert. He arrived at Brook Street half an hour after Anna had climbed into the cab and was told that Sir Robert was out and Lady Broxhead 'Not at Home'. A small exchange of coin elicited the information that Sir Robert would probably be found at White's. Luke hailed a cab and drove to St James's, only to learn from the hall porter that Sir Robert had just left for the St James's coffee house. Another exchange of coin and the porter helpfully pointed Luke towards number eighty-eight.

By this time Luke was getting irritated. He had had to cancel a meeting to track the man down and the fellow could not be found. Luke had never had much time for gentlemen who frittered their lives away in frivolous pursuits and didn't do an honest day's work.

He eventually ran Sir Robert to earth in the St James's coffee house, sitting slumped in a corner of the upper room, a half-empty bottle of brandy on the floor beside him.

Cup-shot, thought Luke, disgustedly. He doubted whether Sir Robert would be in any fit state to talk.

But he underestimated that gentleman's capacity for drink. If his diction were a trifle slurred and he took some time to focus on the card Luke handed him, he was perfectly aware who his guest was.

'If you've come for the money, I haven't got it,' he announced.

Luke pulled up a chair, sat down and removed his hat. The floor was covered with stains and could have done with a sweep, so after a cursory glance round Luke held his hat on his knee. 'I haven't come about the money.' £10,000 Miss de Cardonnel had written. Was the man mad to gamble away such a sum?

'You haven't?' Sir Robert peered at him. 'You don't look like that damned brother of yours.'

'No,' agreed Luke.

96

'The chit won't marry him anyway, she says, and I'm ruined.'

'He is not a proper husband for her,' said Luke.

'Why not?' said Sir Robert belligerently. 'Good-looking. Earns a pretty packet, he says.'

'He does not,' said Luke. 'He lives by embezzling. I doubt whether he has a penny to fly with.'

'Eh? But he said ....' Sir Robert tried to shake his head clear of the brandy fumes. He wished this persistent young man would just go away and leave him alone.

Luke raised a hand to a hovering waiter. 'Coffee. Strong.'

'At once, sir.'

'Anna's a good girl, really,' said Sir Robert. 'Fond of the chit. She won't let her old uncle go to a debtor's prison.'

So her name's Anna, thought Luke. A simple, elegant name. It suited her. Yes, he liked it. She had courage, too. Not every young woman would be prepared to face Laurence down when he was in a temper. 'Miss de Cardonnel can hardly be expected to marry a rogue to save you from your own folly.' Luke did not mince his words.

'Why not?' Sir Robert sat up. 'Didn't I give her father a hundred pounds a year? Didn't I educate her and take her in when her father died?' He turned suddenly on Luke. 'You sound just like my wife. Always moralizing on about something. I tell you, it drives a man to the dice. She's always on about some damned charity or other. Place like a tomb. She won't have my friends round for a bit of whist. What's a man to do?'

The waiter arrived with the coffee on a tray. He took one look at Sir Robert and saw that that gentleman was in no condition to pour out anything. He placed the tray on a small table next to Luke. Luke did the honours and handed Sir Robert a cup of strong black coffee. Sir Robert took it. He stared at Luke from under bushy eyebrows. 'You married?'

'No.'

'Then you can't know anything about it. Take my advice.

Don't marry a prude, not even for a good dowry.'

'I've no intention of marrying anybody,' said Luke, stiffly.

'It's like that, is it?' Sir Robert became more cheerful. 'Been spurned, eh?'

'I am not here to discuss my affairs.' Luke tried to turn the conversation so as to get some useful information as to Laurence's address or the identity of his 'mother', but to no avail. All that Sir Robert could produce was Luke's own card and make jocular references to Luke's past.

'Pretty woman, though,' he said, 'that Mrs Redbourn. You like them fair, too?'

Luke gave up. He arrived home in no very good temper.

'A whole day wasted,' he said to Hester. 'And the damned fellow was useless when I did find him.'

'You could speak to Lady Broxhead,' suggested Hester.

Luke shook his head. 'Her ladyship is not available.' In fact, until a coin had sweetened him up, the footman had been decidedly off-hand. Luke was not used to being treated with discourtesy and he resented it.

'You did your best,' said Hester. 'It's not your fault if nobody listens.'

'Anyway, Miss de Cardonnel will be safely with this Madame Bonnieux by now, I trust,' said Luke.

He glanced at the carriage clock on the mantelpiece. It was nearly six. There had been a time, before Laurence went to America, when Luke had again spent days on his brother's affairs. Then it was trying to limit the damage done by his embezzling the Carr money. Now, seven years on, Laurence seemed to have the same capacity for making his brother dance to his tune. This time, however, his own business could not be neglected. Luke went downstairs to the office and had a word with his clerks. There were a number of letters awaiting his attention and these he dealt with swiftly.

'The *Artemis* has just come into London Dock, sir.'

'Good. What about that tallow?'

'Twenty barrels in the warehouse, sir.'

'I'll want you to go down in the morning, John. Better be off home now. Put the shutters up, would you?'

'Yes, sir.'

Luke and Hester had their usual quiet supper. Hester ran the house with a maid of all work and Walter. She usually did the cooking which was adequate but unadventurous and this evening consisted of meat pie, spinach and potatoes, followed by bread pudding. Luke ate without noticing what he was putting into his mouth. He took a mouthful of the bread pudding and pushed it away.

Just then there was an agitated knocking at the front door. Luke raised his head and looked across at Hester. 'It seems we have a visitor.'

A few moments later a plump woman, still panting from climbing the stairs, was ushered in. '*Excusez-moi, monsieur, mademoiselle,*' she began, her hands trembling, 'I am Madame Bonnieux and my niece has not arrived home!'

When Anna came to she found herself lying on a straw mattress in a dingy attic room. The back of her head ached, she felt horribly sick and dizzy and her eyes hurt when she tried to open them. What had happened? Where was she? Her bonnet and cloak had been removed and were hanging up on a nail sticking out of the wall. The dizziness was slowly passing but the nausea remained. Cautiously, she opened her eyes and gazed groggily around.

The room was almost empty save for the mattress and a cracked chamber pot. It was also filthy. Plaster hung off the walls, cobwebs so thick hung in the corners that it was impossible to see through them. Beside her, on the floor, was a jug of water. Anna sat up cautiously, tottered to the chamber pot and was violently sick. A drink of water later and she was feeling more herself. Things were coming back to her. She had been kidnapped by Laurence and it was easy to guess why.

But where was she? She went to the window. The panes were broken and patched with newspaper and so dusty that it was difficult to see out. All she could see was a similar attic opposite to hers across the road. She was in a narrow street in some slum. She had been so sunk in her own feelings in the cab that she'd failed to notice where they were going. They'd certainly started out in the right direction. She'd been vaguely aware of the cab rounding Hanover Square and turning into Oxford Street.

There was a creak on the stairs and the sound of the lock being turned. Anna lay down again and groaned.

Laurence came in, flicking the door back with a crash that resounded through her head.

'So you're awake?'

'*Pardon?*' said Anna. '*Je regrette, monsieur, mais je ne suis pas bien du tout. Je suis malade.*'

'Speak English, damn you. Can't understand your cursed French.'

'*Plaît-il?*'

'Listen, bitch.' Laurence sat down on the bed and pulled her up to look at him. 'You're here until you agree to marry me, understand? If you don't, I'll take you anyway.' He thrust one hand between her legs. Anna blenched.

Laurence looked satisfied. 'I see you take my meaning. Well, which is it to be? I'm quite ready.' He stood up and started to undo his trousers.

'I'm going to be sick,' said Anna. 'Immediately.' She reached the pot just in time. When she crept back to the bed she was doubled over.

Damn the bitch! Laurence didn't fancy vomit all over him. He did up his trousers. 'Head hurt eh? You should have been more co-operative, my dear. I'll leave you to sleep it off for now. But I want your answer in the morning.' He left and locked the door behind him.

The moment he'd gone Anna rinsed her mouth and straightened up. Her head still hurt but she was actually feeling better and the second bout of sickness had been as much fear as anything.

The shadows were beginning to lengthen in the room. It must be late afternoon. She went again to the window, undid the catch and with a great deal of effort pushed it open. Outside, was a narrow window ledge and almost immediately above that the roof. She peered out cautiously. To her left was a drainpipe and immediately beyond it the right angle of another house in the adjoining street. The roofscape, so far as she could see, went higgledy-piggledy in all directions.

Anna considered. As a child, aged about five, she had discovered, as generations of de Cardonnels had discovered before her, the delights of the roof of their Provençal château, all turrets and gables. There was a small door from one of the attics that gave out onto the leads and from thence Anna had clambered all over. She had had a good head for heights and the occasional dangers had never worried her.

She was pretty sure that if only she could get out onto this roof she would have a good chance of escape. All the same, it was fourteen years since she'd played on the château roof and to do so now, under the present circumstances, was a very different matter. It was, however, all she had.

It would be safer to wait until dusk. A delicately nurtured female, wearing a cloak and fashionable bonnet, was hardly unnoticeable wandering over the tiles. She went to look at her cloak. It would be cumbersome, but it was at least dark and would provide some camouflage. She would have to take her bonnet. Once back on the ground, no respectable woman would be out without a head covering. She felt in her pocket. It was empty. Laurence had taken her purse.

She stood for some time at the window surveying footholds and wondering whether the drainpipe would be strong enough to hold her weight. Then she shut the window and sat down on the mattress to wait.

Luke listened to Madame Bonnieux' disjointed account in dismay. If Laurence had abducted Miss de Cardonnel, as seemed likely, then there were very real fears for her safety. And they did not even know where Laurence lived. On the one occasion Walter had tried to follow him, after he'd paid a visit at Brook Street, Laurence had given him the slip. Walter didn't think he'd been noticed, but Laurence was plainly taking no chances.

Madame Bonnieux was given brandy and soothed as well as possible.

'It had better be the Bow Street Runners,' said Luke. 'I shall go first thing tomorrow. I suspect he's in the St Giles's Rookery. Where else could be so well hidden and yet so close to the West End?'

Hester patted Marie's hand. 'Try not to worry, ma'am. My brother will do all he can.'

Poor Madame Bonnieux was rocking to and fro. 'She's like a daughter to me,' she sobbed. 'I've looked after her since she was seven. I remember the night she came. Her *bonne* brought her to me after her mother was arrested and the house gutted. Poor little scrap. I can see her now, shivering with cold in a white silk dress, and with huge dark eyes. But she was as good as gold. She had a head on her shoulders for all she was so young. You could see she'd seen too much, but what could you do? It was a time of terror.'

Luke had been pacing up and down and now he, too, came to sit beside Madame Bonnieux. 'You must go home, madame,' he said. 'Your niece might yet come and you need to be there. Walter will take you back. I shall track down my brother, never fear, and Miss de Cardonnel will be restored to you.'

Marie managed a tremulous smile. 'You are very good, monsieur.'

Luke had spoken confidently, but his thoughts were far less sanguine. Laurence had kept himself well hidden. Walter had not been able to discover news of him at his old haunts. Unless there was some unexpected break-through, the chances of finding Miss de Cardonnel, unhurt, were slim indeed.

The sun sank slowly and finally Anna judged it time to go. The street below her had not got less crowded as night drew on. There were still screams from children playing or fighting and women stood on the doorsteps arguing shrilly. But the shadows were lengthening and the faces were becoming less distinct. Anna pushed the window open again. She had worked out how to get onto the roof. The brickwork was badly in need of repair and there were toeholds. If she could just get to the angle only a yard or so away then she thought she would be able to clamber up onto the roof itself. After that she would see. She put on her cloak, secured it and then tied the bonnet on firmly. With one last glance round her, she climbed out, swinging herself backwards over the window ledge so that her toes pointed towards the brickwork.

There was a moment's panic but then she felt the toehold. She edged along the sill as far as she dared and then reached for the drainpipe. It wobbled more than she liked but seemed reasonably secure. It was now or never. She let go on the window sill and reached for the parapet with her spare hand. There was a sickening moment while she groped in vain and then she found it. The bump of her head was throbbing and she could feel sweat pouring into her eyes.

Slowly she edged into the shadow of the angle on the wall, her feet finding minute crevices in the brick. By now both hands were on the parapet. She began to pull herself up, using the drainpipe to climb up with her feet. She had just got one elbow on the parapet when the drainpipe cracked and she lost her balance, her feet kicked wildly, desperate for a purchase. Somehow she found something, an ancient bit of iron sticking out from the wall. Shuddering, she pulled herself up over the parapet and collapsed, her heart pounding.

She allowed herself a minute to recover, but she had to move. The parapet was barely nine inches wide and itself looked dangerously unstable. She climbed cautiously to the top and looked over. Roofs went in every direction. She looked round slowly. The day was waning fast, but she could still make out the bulk of the dome of St Paul's. She turned, scanning the horizon. In the west the sky retained a pinkish glow and to the north Anna could see the windmills on Primrose Hill silhouetted against the sky.

She now knew roughly where she was. This must be St Giles's, an area she had been warned against. Some of it, her father had said, was poor but respectable, but most of it was not. Papa, Anna thought wryly, had been right. However, she now knew the direction she ought to be heading in. Moving cautiously in the shadows of the chimney pots, she set off towards Somers Town and the windmills.

Luke spent a sleepless night wondering what to do and breakfast the following morning showed that Hester, too, had not slept. Neither ate very much. Luke spurned his usual bacon and mushrooms and Hester only picked at her toast.

'Poor girl,' said Hester. 'I can't stop thinking about her. Such a little thing, too. What chance does she have against Laurence?'

'Don't,' said Luke. He was in a mood of impotent rage. He wanted to kill Laurence, but Laurence was not there.

Walter came in with the post and Luke turned it over in a desultory way. Most were business letters, but one plainly wasn't. The writing was small and feminine and there were wild splotches of ink which told of agitation. He broke open the seal.

27 Henrietta Street

Dear Mr Redbourn,
I am the Unfortunate Female who was so Unlucky as to be
caught up in your Brother's dastardly schemes. He has used
me Brutally and I am now recovering on my bed of pain and
seeking Revenge. Alas! I impersonated your Mother. If you
can forgive a Contrite Heart then I may be able to help you.

Yours etc.
H Clarkson

Luke scanned it quickly twice and then handed it to Hester. Now he could act!

'A melodramatic lady,' observed Hester. In fact over the previous twenty-four hours she had felt more and more as though she herself were in a melodrama. It was not an experience she enjoyed.

'Yes, but she may know where Laurence is living,' said Luke. He was already up and shouting for his coat and hat.

'You ... you will be careful, won't you?' Hester was anxious. 'It may be a trap.'

'Possibly,' said Luke. 'But it's all I've got. Here, you had better keep this.' He handed her the letter, gave her a quick peck on the cheek and left the house.

When Luke arrived at 27 Henrietta Street, he was relieved to see that it looked solidly respectable. The front doorstep had obviously been freshly scrubbed, The brass door knocker shone. When he knocked a respectable landlady appeared, a starched day-cap on her head and wearing a neat apron.

Luke raised his hat. 'Good morning, ma'am. I am come to visit a Miss Clarkson. I believe she may be expecting me.' He held out his card. The landlady looked at it doubtfully, then back at him. 'I understand Miss Clarkson has had some unfortunate dealings with a disgraced relative of mine.'

'Relative, is he?' She seemed uncertain.

'Would you prefer me to wait outside while you ask Miss Clarkson?'

That seemed to reassure her. 'No sir, if you will wait in here ....' She ushered him into a respectable room, obviously her lodgers' dining-room.

A few moments later Luke was shown upstairs into a back sitting-room and there Helen joined him.

In spite of liberal applications of arnica, her bruises were still extensive and one eye was still bloodshot and half-closed. A bruise extended right down one cheek. She walked slowly and painfully with a stick. Luke rose and offered her a chair.

'Thank you for your letter, Miss Clarkson,' said Luke when courtesies had been exchanged. 'Pray, please say nothing about the past, I am only too grateful to hear any information you could give me. We had thought my brother to be still in America.'

Helen told her story. If there were occasional melodramatic elements, Luke mentally discarded them. He would have thrown out her tale of the fabulous will if it hadn't already occurred to him that Miss de Cardonnel must have some money somewhere. A dishonest clerk and a substantial legacy certainly explained Laurence's interest, however. It would fit with what he had already surmised. Lastly, shamefacedly, Helen spoke of Laurence's blackmail. 'I have only met Miss de Cardonnel once,' she ended, 'but I could not bear to think of what he might do to her. He spoke of "other measures" which curdled my blood! And so I decided to risk all, and write.'

'We have reason to believe that he has kidnapped her,' said Luke bluntly.

Helen raised both hands as if to ward off a blow. 'He ... he can be violent.'

'So I see,' observed Luke. 'Perhaps you can tell me where he is living?'

'Seven, Charles Street, just off Drury Lane.'

It was Luke's turn to go pale. 'Good God!'

'It's respectable enough,' said Helen. 'If you're not too particular.'

Luke looked around him. This was obviously a reputable lodging house and Miss Clarkson must be a reliable tenant, whatever her unfortunate entanglement with Laurence may have been. 'What about your work, Miss Clarkson? I gather you are employed in the theatre.'

'Yes, the Royal Opera House.' She attempted a smile. 'But it will be a month or so before I can go back – if Mr Kemble will have me.' She looked away. When she had written the letter she had hoped that Mr Redbourn could be persuaded to give her some money to help tide her over. Now he was here, he had treated her so courteously and said not a word about her deception that she felt ashamed to ask.

All attempts at melodrama were gone, Luke noted. 'Miss Clarkson, I am very grateful to you for your information. I was at my wits' end. It is thanks to you that I now know my brother's whereabouts. In return, you must allow me to take some of the worry off you.' Helen opened her mouth. 'No, I insist. Your situation was very difficult and you have suffered at the hands of a member of my family.'

'You are very kind,' whispered Helen.

Luke took his wallet out of his coat pocket and counted out ten guineas. 'I hope that this will make you more comfortable.'

The landlady was hovering in the hall, quite consumed with curiosity. As Luke came downstairs she began energetically whisking a duster. Luke eyed her with amusement. 'Does Mr Laurence Redbourn still come here?' he asked.

'Certainly not! He knows I wouldn't have him in the house, not after what he did to Miss Clarkson. Three ribs broken as well as her poor face. And she's a good hard-working lady, too, sir. Never behind with the rent and always has a pleasant word.'

'If Mr Redbourn ever got to hear of my visit here,' said Luke, 'it would go hard with Miss Clarkson.'

'He shan't hear from me, sir, I assure you.'

'Thank you.' Luke pressed a crown into her palm. 'I knew I could rely on you.' He touched his hat and left the house.

Now there's a proper gentleman, thought the landlady. A whole crown! She would take a trip that very afternoon and have another look at that bonnet in Newton's.

After Laurence had left Anna the previous afternoon he strolled down to the Smyrna coffee house in Pall Mall. It was advertised as a place 'where gentlemen meet to play billiards', but, in fact, one could also play cards and enjoy a drink. Anna's purse had netted him only a few shillings and Laurence was in need of ready cash. His air of fashion attracted the admiring notice of a bored country gentleman who had come up to London (unwillingly) for a niece's wedding. A drink or so later and he had agreed to a friendly game or two of piquet with his new acquaintance. He left twenty guineas poorer.

Laurence spent a portion of it on a pretty little whore he met in the Haymarket and returned to Charles Street about midnight. If he thought at all about his victim in the attic room it was only to smile that she would have had nothing to eat since breakfast and would be rather more amenable in the morning. He toyed with the idea of going in to her at once but discarded it. The whore had taken the edge off his appetite anyway.

Laurence had taken the top floor of the house in Charles Street and Anna had been put into the smaller of the two attic rooms. The other Laurence used as a bedroom and base whenever he had need of it. It was sparsely furnished, but had all that he needed: a reasonable bed, an old cheval glass, a couple of chairs, a table and an oak press where he kept his clothes. Laurence was quite content with his room. It was cheap and convenient. He'd never wasted much time and thought on the comforts of home. What he preferred were public places: the glitter of chandeliers in expensive gaming hells, the rich brocades and gilt in the King Street seraglios.

He did not waken until after eleven and then he opened the door and yelled for the maid to go out and buy him a pint of porter and a meat pie. When he'd eaten, he promised himself, he'd go and see Miss de Cardonnel. She would be in a pitiful state – he smiled – and doubtless would be ready to see reason.

He did not hear Luke come up the stairs. Luke had taken one swift look at the two doors and realized that if Anna were anywhere it would be in the locked room. The turn of the key alerted Laurence who came out of his room just as Luke pushed the door open.

'You!'

Both men rushed in. It was empty. The window was swinging on its hinges. Nothing. Nothing on the cobbles below indicated a fall. A drainpipe was leaning out at a crazy angle.

'How did you find me?' Laurence was white with rage.

'Walter had his ear close to the ground,' said Luke indifferently.

'I've told nobody I'm here.'

Luke shrugged. 'You look much the same and you left something of a reputation.' In fact Luke had had to clear about a hundred pounds' worth of his brother's debts.

'The bitch has gone.' Laurence aimed a savage kick at the water jug, which shattered. 'If you had anything to do with it … I'm warning you, keep out of my affairs.'

'I had nothing to do with it,' said Luke. 'I'd be only too glad to keep out of your affairs if you would keep out of mine.' He left the room as he spoke and pushed open the other door. A swift glance round and he went straight to the oak press. There, in one corner, was a small pile of his calling cards. Luke took them. 'My property, I think.'

Laurence's mouth was rigid with anger. He was several inches taller than Luke and he carried a knife. His hand moved to his belt.

'Don't bother,' said Luke, interpreting his movement. 'Walter knows where I am and it would be a pity to swing before your time. I take it I can now cancel your allowance?'

'That paltry sixty quid!'

'As you wish,' said Luke unmoved. Without a backward glance he turned and left the room.

Chapter Six

Five o'clock that morning and Madame Bonnieux was already up. She had slept badly, alert to every little noise outside. Anna had not come back. But Marie had customers to keep happy and an early batch of brioches and croissants to cook. Several times since the vicomte had died she thought of employing a girl to live in, but an unsatisfactory try had discouraged her and instead she had François, the son of an émigré notary, who came each morning at five to stoke up the ovens and then take the various orders to their destinations.

Marie dressed wearily. Anxiety and fatigue made her clumsy and she kept dropping things. At last she was ready and went slowly downstairs to face another long, miserable day. She had half an ear open for François' knock as she got the dough ready on the baking trays.

A sudden barking from Hercule alerted her and she went slowly upstairs, wiping her hands on her apron.

A slim, slight figure, streaked with dirt, swayed in the doorway. 'Anna!' Heedless of flour and paste, Marie pulled Anna in and embraced her with tears running down her cheeks. 'Oh, Anna! I've been so worried!'

'I'm all right, I'm all right!' Anna kept saying, hugging and crying in her turn.

'And here's François.' Marie looked up as François, jaunty

figure was seen coming down the street. 'Go down, François. I'll be with you in a moment.' She shut the door.

Fifteen minutes later Anna was seated at the kitchen table, a bowl of coffee in front of her and a tartine already half-eaten. She had washed her hands and face, but the rest of her was filthy. Her cloak was ripped in several places and her stockings torn. But she was here.

'The roof!' exclaimed Marie. 'Thank God I didn't know.'

'I was certainly not the first person to have been up there,' said Anna. 'At one point I found a plank across a small gap above a narrow passageway, and at another place, where there was only a narrow ledge to walk along, someone had slung a rope as a sort of hand-rail.'

Marie shuddered. 'But how did you get down?'

'When I reached High Holborn I realized I could go no further. There was a house that had been burnt out. I got down there.' She shuddered, unwilling to go back over it. It had been a perilous descent, for the house was in a dangerous condition, even by St Giles's standards, but the rudimentary scaffolding propping it up had helped. Anna waited on a nearby roof, safely wedged between two chimney pots, until daylight began to appear. She even dozed a little. As soon as she could see she began to climb down. The building had been set on fire at some point and the brickwork was blackened and brittle. A window ledge collapsed just as she put her weight on it and only a lucky grasp of a small tree growing out of a crevice saved her. Once back on firm ground she had gone up Southampton Street to Bloomsbury Square and respectability. It was then about half-past four and getting light. There were few people about and Anna had hurried as fast as she could. She was well aware that she was filthy and her cloak was torn and her bonnet a wreck. Once or twice she'd dodged into side streets to evade a drunk or a nightwatchman, but no further mishaps overtook her.

Marie looked at Anna with a mixture of relief and concern. She was pale from exhaustion and hunger and there was a bump on the back of her head the size of an egg. Her arms were filthy and although she had had a quick wash there were streaks of dirt down the side of her face. Marie got up and took down a big tin tub from its hook on the wall and then went to fill the largest kettle and a couple of saucepans. She pushed the rest of the baguette across the table.

'Eat, *petite*. When the water's hot you can have a bath and I'll have a look at your poor head and then bed. Your trunk came yesterday and François took it up for you. I've made your bed.'

'But ....'

'No buts. You can help this afternoon if you've a mind to. I'll just drop a line to Monsieur Redbourn and say you're safe and then I must get on.'

Luke arrived home to find Hester in a state of high excitement. A note had arrived from Madame Bonnieux saying simply that her niece was back home, safe and well.

'I wonder how she did it?' mused Hester.

Luke told Hester about the empty attic room and the swinging window. It seemed almost impossible to imagine but Miss de Cardonnel must somehow have got up onto the roof. Hester could allow herself to enjoy the drama now she knew that Miss de Cardonnel was safe. 'I'm afraid there's another problem,' said Luke. 'Does Laurence know where Miss de Cardonnel lives? She is far more at risk in Phoenix Street than she ever was at Brook Street. Two women living alone, even with the dog Walter tells me they have. I don't like it?'

'But what can you do?' Hester asked reasonably. 'She is not related to us. We have no right to interfere.'

'I don't want to interfere with Miss de Cardonnel,' said Luke irritably. 'I want to interfere with whatever Laurence has planned for her.' He ran his hands through his hair. He seemed to have passed through so many emotions during the last twenty-four hours that he felt exhausted: anger, fear, anxiety. Not since Caroline had walked out of his life had he felt in such a turmoil. And once again, Laurence was at the centre of it. He sighed. 'I shall have to take a hand.'

'Why? What are you going to do?' Hester was alarmed.

'It's obvious to me that it's all bound up with some will or other – if Miss Clarkson's story is accurate. It would certainly fit what we already know. If only I could find out how?'

'But how can you? You don't even know whose will.'

'I shall start with this emerald.'

'But Miss de Cardonnel said that it was not of enormous value.'

'True, but it was of some value. And it has gone missing in somewhat extraordinary circumstances. I shall go and see Miss de Cardonnel when she has had time to recover.'

'Be careful, Luke. Laurence may be watching you now. If he doesn't know where she lives, isn't it better that it stays that way?'

'Damn him!' shouted Luke. 'Damn him to hell! I tell you, Hester, when I went into that attic room and saw the window open I could have died. That poor child was desperate. She might have been killed! All Laurence was concerned about was himself. "The bitch has escaped", he said.'

'You'll have to use the back,' said Hester practically. The small garden behind the house had a door which led into Holliday Yard and from thence, via a narrow passageway, to Shoemaker Lane. It was perfectly possible to leave the house without being seen by anyone watching, say, from one of the coffee houses opposite, in Ludgate Street.

'Life, since knowing Miss de Cardonnel, is certainly not dull,' said Luke, smiling for the first time that day.

The next morning Anna and Marie Bonnieux were happily

engaged in icing chocolate eclairs. Anna had not slept very well. It had been difficult to lie comfortably and her mind had kept going over the escape, racing round and round like a squirrel in a cage, but she found the icing of eclairs soothing and it seemed to have a calming effect. The shop doorbell rang as it had several times that morning and Marie went through to see to the customer.

'Oh, Monsieur Redbourn!' she exclaimed. For one moment Anna froze. 'How pleased I am to see you! And how kind of you to come! Anna, we have a visitor.'

Anna came through smiling. '*C'est Monsieur Luc,*' she said happily. Suddenly, her world righted itself. They had only met twice, but she felt extraordinarily pleased to see him.

'Miss de Cardonnel.' He bowed and enquired after her injuries. Having satisfied himself that they were not severe he smiled and added, 'I am honoured to be "Monsieur Luc".'

Anna blushed. 'I beg pardon, monsieur. The name Redbourn does not have very happy associations for me.'

'Come into the kitchen, monsieur,' said Madame Bonnieux. 'You will not mind that we are icing eclairs, I hope? But we may be private there.' She bustled about, offering him wine and Anna finished icing an eclair and offered it to him.

'Thank you,' said Luke. 'Delicious. I can now see why Walter is so eager to deliver letters here!' For the first time for days, it seemed, he felt at peace. Luke and Hester had spent many childhood holidays with their Grandmother Redbourn in a little village near Berkhamsted. Suddenly he was back there, in his grandmother's kitchen, a serious small boy, bringing a jar of tadpoles for her to admire and knowing that she would have the kettle whistling on the hob and a cake, rich with currants, on the table. Something of the warmth and comfort of that time was here, too.

Luke heard Anna's story in silence. He then told her of his meeting wih Helen and his subsequent discovery of his brother and the empty attic room with the swinging casement window. 'I feared you'd been killed,' he ended.

'There were one or two nasty moments,' Anna admitted. 'But I am used to heights. As a little girl I used to climb all over the roof of our château in Provence. It had lots of turrets and twisting chimneys, so you see, I had had some experience.'

She was laughing, but Luke's smile faded. Of course, her experiences were very different. This kitchen, though it felt homely to him, probably felt very poor and humble to her.

'Is there anything the matter, monsieur?' asked Marie, looking at him with concern.

'Nothing, I assure you.' Luke pulled himself together. 'I have been trying to put together what I know, Miss de Cardonnel, about the mysterious will Miss Clarkson told me of. So far as I can gather, some unknown benefactor has left you a large sum of money – large enough to tempt my brother – which you, yourself, are not to hear of until you are twenty-one.'

'If I marry before that date does the money then become the property of my husband?'

'Yes, according to English law – unless there has been a legal settlement otherwise.'

'My cousin Julia had her dowry settled on her as part of the marriage settlement,' observed Anna.

'I think we may be certain that my brother had no such settlement in mind. However, there my information comes to an end. The only other thing we know is that your family emerald disappeared in suspicious circumstances. It may be an illogical jump, but it is possible that these two facts are connected.'

Anna looked sceptical. 'I do not think Père Ignace was a rich man.'

'We do not know how many other families he helped escape,' said Marie dryly. 'He could have become very rich indeed, if he had had access to American passports at such a time.'

'May I ask when you will be twenty-one, Miss de Cardonnel?'

'October 4th. But why leave anything to me?'

'We could simply wait until you reached your majority and find out then, but that may be risky,' said Luke.

'What do you suggest?' asked Anna.

'I was hoping, Miss de Cardonnel, that you would accompany me to the jewellers, Rundell and Bridge. We might, at least, ask their opinion on your emerald. They are the best known jewellers in London. If anybody has heard anything of your emerald, it will be them.'

'It would be a start. When would you wish to go? Now?'

'If it would be convenient and if you feel recovered enough from your ordeal.' Anna, after a glance at Madame Bonnieux, agreed. 'You'd better bring any documentation you have concerning the emerald,' said Luke. 'You may have to prove your claim.' When Anna had gone upstairs to get ready, Luke said to Madame Bonnieux, 'I shall bring her home myself.'

'I am worried lest your brother finds her here,' said Marie.

'I, too. I think you should have your locks checked.'

Marie smiled grimly. 'There are none, save on the shop door. Bolts are all we have. And if we got a locksmith in the whole neighbourhood would want to know why. But we do have Hercule.'

'Air Cool?' Luke was puzzled.

'The dog.' She saw Luke's sceptical look and added, 'I know he's too friendly, but he does at least bark.'

Anna came downstairs, carrying a small clutch of papers. She was still a little pale Luke noticed as he offered her his arm. He was relieved that he had decided to keep the cab waiting. Miss de Cardonnel was in no state to walk. He handed her in and climbed in after her. In a short time they were bowling back towards the City, for Rundell and Bridge was on Ludgate Hill.

'I should have asked your aunt to come as chaperone,' said Luke, in a worried tone.

'I have never been able to understand why girls may not be in charge of their own reputations,' observed Anna. 'The constant chaperonage was one of the most irksome things about living in Brook Street. Anybody would think females were imbeciles!'

'It is for your protection,' said Luke mildly.

'Ha! Fine protection!' So far as she could see, all that chaperonage had done for her was put her in the position where she was forced to listen to Laurence's advances.

'I might have dishonourable intentions.'

'I thought we had settled – the first time we met – that you had no intentions at all!'

Luke laughed. A faint tinge of colour touched his cheek, but all he said was, 'Why is your dog called Air Cool?'

Anna laughed in her turn. 'His name isn't Air Cool. It's Hercule – Hercules. We are hoping that he will be as strong and fierce as his namesake.'

'You'll have to teach him not to rush up and lick strangers,' said Luke, still smiling.

Rundell and Bridge was an imposing establishment, as befitted the foremost jewellers in the capital, with an impressive doorman who came forward to open the cab door and assist Anna to alight. Inside there were a number of immaculate black-coated assistants. One of these came forward as Luke ushered Anna into the shop.

'I called in earlier. The name's Redbourn,' said Luke. 'I believe Mr Bridge is expecting me.'

'I shall go and enquire, sir.' Within a few minutes they were shown into Mr Bridge's office and Anna was introduced.

'I have been looking over our records, Mr Redbourn, since I spoke to you this morning, and I find that we had a visit from the Vicomte de Cardonnel about this very matter in '94. Unfortunately, we were unable to help him then.'

'You have heard something since?' Anna looked up eagerly.

Mr Bridge bowed. 'About three years ago we were asked for a valuation to do with a will.' He paused. 'Would you be able to describe this emerald to me, Miss de Cardonnel?'

Anna did so. 'I was only seven when I last saw it,' she finished. 'My memory may have been playing me tricks.'

'No, no, you have described it very accurately. It is indeed a beautiful piece. In normal circumstances I would not consider breaking a professional confidence, but in this case, having seen your receipt and the letter from Child's Bank, we are dealing with a piece of jewellery that was undoubtedly, if not stolen precisely, then certainly misappropriated. The lawyer who approached us was a Mr Hargreaves of Gray's Inn. The name of the client, if I remember correctly, was a Mr Henry Ignatius.'

Anna and Luke exchanged glances 'I must thank you for your trouble,' said Luke, rising. 'You have been most helpful.'

When they were once more in the cab Luke said, 'Would you like to go home now Miss de Cardonnel, or shall we pay a visit to this Mr Hargreaves? I cannot help but think that your Père Ignace and this Mr Ignatius must be the same person.'

'I think so too. A visit by all means.'

Things were much less easy at the lawyers. They were kept waiting for half an hour in a dingy room and Mr Hargreaves, when he eventually saw them, was suspicious and uncooperative. He examined Anna's letters carefully, taking a magnifying glass to the signature of Père Ignace which was on the receipt for the emerald. He examined the Letters Patent of Nobility for the vicomte and then he looked up.

'How do I know that you are Mademoiselle de Cardonnel?' he said at last.

'But why would I want to lie?' Anna was affronted. She might be small, thought Luke, looking at her, but at that moment she looked every inch the aristocrat.

'Many reasons.'

'I don't know whether you have heard of Abbé Carron de la Carrière?' said Anna, after a moment's thought. 'He has set up many charities to help the émigrés and is very highly thought of in the English community as well, I know.' Mr Hargreaves merely bowed, but made no comment. Anna continued, 'The abbé knew both my father and myself. In fact, I was educated at his academy for young ladies. I am sure he would vouch for me.'

'Humph. I shall need an affidavit from this abbé before I can even consider going any further in the matter. And I shall have to consult with Miss le Vivier.'

Who was Miss le Vivier, wondered Anna. This was a new name. Aloud she said, 'You shall have your affidavit. Good day to you.' She rose as she spoke and swept out, leaving Luke to follow.

'Insufferable!' Anna was still fuming as they climbed back into the cab. 'He was hardly polite.'

'He was protecting his client's interests.'

'Rather late in the day,' snapped Anna, 'since one of his clerks has already spilled the beans to your brother.'

'If we could find Miss le Vivier we might be able to do without this suspicious Mr Hargreaves.'

'I shall pay a visit after church to Madame de Gontaut,' said Anna after a moment's thought. 'She always seems to know everybody.'

Life in the Broxhead household was far from happy. Lady Broxhead was maintaining an attitude of saintly forgiveness which was exhausting to her husband. Somehow the word had got round that the Broxheads were no longer good credit risks and the bills had flooded in. There was a really staggering amount due for wax candles. Cook reported that the provisions merchant, who had the honour of supplying the family with tea, sugar and other comestibles, was running out of patience;

amounts had been left outstanding for several years. And, of course, on top of it all were the vowels for £10,000 held by Laurence Redbourn.

Lady Broxhead sold some fine diamond ear-drops, which had belonged to her grandmother, and paid the most outstanding bills. The receipts were placed, ostentatiously, on her husband's desk.

'Oh, my lady, your beautiful ear-rings,' cried Martha. 'Oh, that wicked French hussy.'

'The Lord giveth and the Lord taketh away,' said Lady Broxhead, piously.

Even White's was not so welcoming these days, Sir Robert found. Word had somehow got about that Broxhead was in trouble. Most of the members were sympathetic, but all the same, a gaming debt was a debt of honour.

'D'ye know,' whispered Mr Torkington to Lord Zennor over the brandy, 'I hear Lady B. sold her diamonds and paid the tradesmen: Damme, why pay a load of tradesmen? I never pay mine.'

Lord Zennor shook his head. 'I hear she's an Evangelical,' he muttered. 'One of those damned abolitionists, I daresay.' Lord Zennor spoke feelingly, for the bill for the Abolition of the Slave Trade had gone through earlier that year and the noble lord feared for the consequences to his Jamaican sugar plantations.

'Unsound,' agreed Mr Torkington. 'Not Broxhead's fault, of course. Must be fair.'

'He should control his own wife,' argued Lord Zennor. 'Still, the poor fellow looks pretty down in the mouth these days.'

They finished their brandy. 'How about a game of piquet?' suggested Mr Torkington. 'A friendly. Ten shilling points, say.' They moved across towards one of the green baize-topped tables.

Worse was to come. Sir Robert had retreated to the St James's coffee house and was drowning his sorrows when a familiar figure came into the room. It was Laurence. He looked every inch the gentleman. His cravat was impeccably starched, his coat fitted him to a nicety and his boots shone. He nodded to various acquaintances and exchanged a few words before sitting down opposite Sir Robert.

Sir Robert groaned.

'As bad as that, eh?' Laurence laughed. 'Come, man, you know the rules as well as I do.'

'I shall need time.' Sir Robert hated himself for saying it and hated Laurence for having put him, as he saw it, in this position.

'I don't have much time,' said Laurence. 'Either your niece marries me by the end of July, or you pay up. You have about three weeks.'

'She's gone! She went home and we haven't heard from her since.'

If the bitch were dead, then all hope of that fortune was gone. 'Where does she live? Dammit, you're her guardian.'

Sir Robert shook his head. 'Can't remember where she lives. Never visited the place. Somewhere in Somers Town.'

'Somers Town,' said Laurence thoughtfully. He saw that there was nothing more to be got out of Sir Robert. 'End of July,' he repeated and left him.

That evening Sir Robert hailed a cab and made his way to Ludgate Street. Luke saw him in the little room where he'd first met Anna. Sir Robert was decidedly shakier than when they'd last met, though whether this was drink or ill health, Luke did not know. He rang the bell and said a few words to Walter. Somehow, Sir Robert wasn't quite sure how, but in a few moments he was sitting by the fire with a coffee jug and a plate of beef sandwiches beside him.

'Thank'ee, Redbourn. Civil of you.' His wife never spoke to him now if she could help it, and if he wanted anything to eat he had to ask for it himself.

Luke sat down opposite. 'I take it you've been having problems with my brother again?'

'Collared me in the coffee house and demanded the money. Either I pay up or my niece marries him before the end of July.'

Laurence must be getting desperate, thought Luke.

'Always thought she was fond of me,' went on Sir Robert. 'She's my ward, she's supposed to marry where I tell her.'

'Did you know that he had her kidnapped?' Luke asked abruptly.

'Kidnapped?' Sir Robert sat up. His look brightened. 'She'll have to marry him now. Otherwise she'll have no reputation.'

Luke controlled himself with an effort. 'It may interest you to know that he also beat up the actress who has been impersonating my mother.'

'What! That pretty Mrs Redbourn?' Sir Robert was genuinely concerned.

'Her name is Helen Clarkson,' said Luke, watching his guest carefully. 'She lives at twenty-seven Henrietta Street. She was lucky to escape with three broken ribs and extensive bruising.' Sir Robert seemed incapable of understanding the threat to Miss de Cardonnel. Perhaps his understanding would return if he saw Miss Clarkson.

'I should have come here first,' said Sir Robert, after some moments' silence. 'I wanted to believe him, that was the trouble. M'wife's been on at me about getting m'niece off our hands. Met Redbourn. Seemed ideal. Should have checked.'

'It would have saved us all a lot of trouble,' said Luke with restraint.

'I told him she lived in Somers Town,' said Sir Robert contritely. 'Should have thought.'

Luke shrugged. 'He would have tracked her down eventually. There are only certain areas where French refugees live. A few enquiries are probably all that is necessary.'

Sir Robert finished his beef sandwich and put down his cup.

'Never marry a woman with a mission, dear boy,' he said. 'They make your life a misery. I daresay we shall shut up the town house now and leave London. Either that or the King's Bench Prison.'

'We have until the end of the month,' said Luke. 'I doubt whether my brother will do anything precipitate, though he may threaten.'

'You think so?' Sir Robert brightened up. 'Can't bear the country,' he confided. 'It's too damn full of sheep. Prefer the town. Always have.' He stood up. 'Where d'you say this Miss Clarkson lives?'

Miss le Vivier lived in Queen's Gardens, just off Brompton Row in Knightsbridge, Anna discovered. It was not an address favoured by the refugees and the Duchesse de Gontaut expressed her surprise to Anna that Mademoiselle le Vivier should have chosen it.

'She was rather a strange woman, as I recall,' said Madame de Gontaut. 'She was reluctant to mix and kept herself to herself. I believe she came over with an uncle who was in Holy Orders. But I never really knew her.'

Anna conveyed this information to Luke by letter and it was agreed that Luke should visit this Miss le Vivier in his capacity as family friend and see what was to be learned. Anna herself would visit Abbé Carron and ask for his help.

'You will be careful, won't you?' said Hester.

'Of course. But I hardly think that visiting a middle-aged lady in Knightsbridge constitutes danger.'

'All the same,' said Hester, 'things have been too quiet these last few days.'

'Getting to like the life of adventure, are you?' said Luke, amused. He was in something of a hurry. He had briefed his clerks on the day's business, signed a number of business letters and tried to set up a meeting with various fellow insurers. Such was his haste that he forgot to exit by the back door, and it was only when Hester heard the front door slam that she realized.

Laurence, sitting in the coffee shop nearly opposite, saw Luke leave and hail a cab. He got up, threw a shilling on the table, and left hastily.

Hester decided that she was being fanciful and reached out to pick up the paper. Turning idly to the Court and Social page an item caught her gaze which made her forget everything else. Under Deaths she read:

On July 3rd, of an apoplexy, William Simpson, alderman of the City of London. He leaves a widow and two daughters.

Oh my God, she thought, Caroline a widow. Now we are in the soup. After the break-up of her engagement with Luke, Caroline had hoped that Laurence would marry her. When he refused point blank she dissolved into a torrent of tears and for a while seemed in danger of going into a decline. Nothing in her short, indulged life had prepared her for such an eventuality. She had then written a number of pathetic ill-spelt letters to Luke, begging for his forgiveness. Luke had not replied.

Later, she had written to Hester; Hester had been kind but firm. It was not for her to interfere in her brother's concerns, she wrote. In fact, she had been overwhelmingly relieved. Even though she felt upset at the sight of Luke's misery, she could not wish the betrothal resumed. She had never thought Caroline to be at all worthy of her brother.

Six months later Caroline had married William Simpson, a man nearly thirty years older than herself, rich and doting enough to spoil her to her heart's content. Hester's only feeling was one of profound relief.

Now Mr Simpson was dead and Caroline was a widow.

Hester seriously hoped that she would not return into Luke's life. Her betrayal had affected him deeply and, as no other woman had taken her place, it was to be inferred that he still had a soft spot for her.

She pushed the cat off her lap and went to write Caroline a stiff letter of condolence.

While Anna had been questioning Madame de Gontaut, Luke had been making enquiries among his business associates and, as the cab made its slow way down towards Knightsbridge, he went over what he had learned. According to his information Henry Ignatius had arrived in this country in the wake of the French Revolution on an American passport. He had not gone to London, but instead headed north and made a fortune by investing firstly in canals and then in various iron-smelting processes. He had been well respected for his business acumen.

'Rarely came to London, though,' his informant had told him. 'He was based in the north. Somewhere near Ironbridge, I believe.'

All this sounded most unlike some émigré cleric and Luke had begun to doubt whether it could possibly be the same man, when his informant added, 'Rumour had it that he was a disaffected clergyman, abbé or some such. Unlikely, if you ask me. But there was a certain austerity about him ... perhaps that helped to fuel the rumours. He always fasted on a Friday, for example.'

'Odd,' said Luke non-committally.

He had no idea how he was going to tackle Miss le Vivier. He could say that he wished to pay his respects to the niece of an old business friend, perhaps. Might he have discussed insurance possibilities with Mr Ignatius? He doubted whether Miss le Vivier would know whether he had or not.

Queen's Gardens proved to be a row of modest houses all

with well-scrubbed front steps and polished brass. A very tidy
little maid opened the door to him and took up his card.

A few moments late he was shown into a little parlour
decorated in apple green. A tiny woman rose to greet him. Miss
le Vivier was built in miniature. She was probably about fifty,
he guessed, with grey hair kept neatly under a cap and a rather
old-fashioned gown in a crisp blue and white print. Clear blue
eyes looked him over shrewdly.

'Mr Redbourn?' Her English was impeccable.

All at once Luke realized that this woman was far too
intelligent to be taken in by flummery. It would have to be the
truth – or at least a part of it. Swiftly he revised his story.

'I am here in my capacity as family friend to a Miss de
Cardonnel,' he began. 'Though I warn you that I may be on a
wild goose chase and, if so, can only apologize for taking up
your time.'

'Please sit down, Mr Redbourn,' said Miss le Vivier. 'You will
chase wild geese more comfortably from a chair, I am sure.'

Luke smiled.

'I was wondering, ma'am, whether your uncle, Mr Ignatius,
could possibly once have been known as Père Ignace?'

'And if he were?' Miss le Vivier was composed.

'Then he was instrumental in getting passports for Miss de
Cardonnel and her family to escape in '93.'

'Ah,' said Miss le Vivier.

Luke saw that she was not going to help him further.

'Miss de Cardonnel was only a child at the time and her
father, alas, is now dead. If your uncle and Père Ignace were
the same person, then she is anxious to express her thanks for
his help and courage during those difficult times.'

'And that is all? Miss de Cardonnel is, perhaps, in financial
difficulties?'

'No, ma'am.' Luke spoke coldly. It was intolerable that she
thought that Miss de Cardonnel might be after money –

especially when this Mr Ignatius had not returned the cabochon emerald to its rightful owner. 'She is in need of nothing. She lives with a Madame Bonnieux in Somers Town and they run a successful pâtisserie.'

'Miss de Cardonnel is not yet twenty-one. Am I correct?'

'She will be of age in October.'

'My uncle was a secretive man,' said Miss le Vivier. She had apparently decided in Luke's favour. 'He told me very little and I rarely saw him. However, I can confirm that he was indeed Père Ignace, but like so many others, his experiences in Paris destroyed his faith.'

'A tragic time indeed.' Luke, too, could be uncommunicative, and if his tone held a trace of scepticism, Miss le Vivier did not allow it to discompose her.

'However, Miss de Cardonnel's name is not unknown to me. He once spoke of an obligation; of what kind, I do not know. He left her a small legacy to be given to her when she is twenty-one.' Miss le Vivier's gaze was open and candid. It was plain that Mr Hargreaves had said nothing to her of any emerald.

'That was very good of him.' Luke was somewhat at a loss. He would have to consult with Miss de Cardonnel before he said anything more, he decided. It must be her decision whether or not to take it further. 'I am pleased to have discovered the identity of my young friend's benefactor,' he said as he rose to go. 'Perhaps you will permit me to bring Miss de Cardonnel herself to visit you?'

'I should be delighted.' She rang the bell. 'I am pleased to have met you. Mary, please show Mr Redbourn out.'

Luke bowed and left. The cab was waiting and he climbed in. 'Ludgate Street.'

The cabby touched his cap.

Luke drove back towards the City lost in thought. He liked Miss le Vivier, he decided. That touch of reserve was not unpleasant and he felt that she was a woman to be trusted. She was naturally cautious, but when she had decided to be more open, she was clear and to the point. He thought Miss de Cardonnel would like her. He found himself hoping that she would allow him to escort her to Knightsbridge one day. However, there were still some unanswered questions. His City informant had spoken of Mr Ignatius as being a very warm man indeed who had made a considerable fortune. Miss le Vivier lived in modest circumstances. So what had he done with the rest of the money?

The cab had been bowling up Sloane Street and now turned into Knightsbridge. It was just slowing up for the Hyde Park turnpike when a shot rang out. The horse shied and started plunging wildly and Luke threw himself onto the floor. Two bullets tore through the cab window, shattering the glass.

There were confused shouts, more shots and then silence. The cabby had somehow managed to steady the horse. Luke picked himself up. One hand had been gashed by flying glass and was bleeding profusely. The door was wrenched open.

'You all right?' Luke, dazed, looked up. The man, obviously a military gentleman, turned to shout to his companions. 'Fellow hurt in here.'

A small troop of Life Guards, resplendent in their scarlet jackets, galloped up.

'Take him to hospital,' said one. The cab had come to a standstill almost opposite St George's Hospital.

'You want to kill him? I can do better than that.' The man turned to Luke, who was groping for a handkerchief to stem the bleeding. 'Colonel Blackburn, Life Guards. Just returning to barracks and heard you were in trouble. Here, let's see.' He helped Luke out of the carriage, removed his coat and checked him over. 'A few cuts and bruises. Apart from the hand, nothing serious.'

'Perhaps, the hospital,' Luke suggested.

'Nonsense, man. Here.' He took out a flask of brandy, tipped half of it down Luke's throat and swabbed the wound with the rest before wrapping it carefully in a clean handkerchief. 'Does the cabby know where you are going?'

Luke, feeling somewhat dizzy, managed to nod.

'Good. Here, Thorn, you go with him. See he's all right. Jones, take Thorn's horse. Shocking thing, footpads. In broad daylight, too.' He sketched a salute, vaulted into the saddle and left.

'Not footpads,' muttered Luke.

'Enemies, then?' said Thorn interested. 'Next time don't choose a piebald horse. Makes it too easy to spot. And take the second cab that comes along, rather than the first.'

'I've led a very humdrum life,' said Luke with a short laugh. 'I never thought to look at either the cab or the horse.'

'One doesn't,' agreed Thorn. 'But you learn fast in the army. It's not a mistake you make twice.'

'I don't feel very heroic,' said Luke. All he'd done was to throw himself down on the floor.

'Heroic! Who wants heroics? The last man I knew who was heroic got his head blown off by a cannon ball.'

'I didn't give a very good account of myself.'

'Nonsense, you ducked, which is what any sensible man would do and you're alive to tell the tale.' He paused and eyed Luke tolerantly. 'You want a fine story to tell the ladies, is that it?'

Chapter Seven

Helen was sitting in the landlady's parlour that was specially reserved for her female lodgers. It was not a big room and was somewhat overcrowded with little tables and knick-knacks, for the landlady liked her 'bits and pieces' as she called them, and her numerous nephews and nieces often brought her pretty china and other curios. One of the housemaids had come up to Helen's room that morning and helped her to wash her hair – a painful business – and Helen was now content to recline on the sofa with her feet up and doze.

She had been unwilling to go to the expense of a doctor, but Peggy, who had seen all sorts of injuries in the theatre, assured her that she was healing well. Her bruising made it difficult to sleep other than fitfully, but there was no evidence that Laurence's kicks had done any serious damage. Her split lip was healing and one eye, which had been quite closed up, was beginning to resume its normal shape.

There was a knock at the door and the landlady came in, quite breathless with excitement.

'A gentleman to see you, miss,' she said. 'A real nob by the sound of it.' She handed Helen a card.

Helen looked at it and turned pale. Sir Robert Broxhead! Whatever should she do?

'You don't have to see him, miss, if you feel poorly.' The

landlady had regaled all her friends with stories of how she had given Laurence 'a piece of her mind', though in fact this had been expressed merely by a scowl at Laurence's back as he had left the house. She now imagined herself saying to Sir Robert – with a toss of the head – 'Miss Clarkson is indisposed and she'll thank you not to come a-bothering of her.'

Helen pulled her shawl up round her shoulders as if for protection. Had he come to have her arrested for false impersonation? Could he do that?

'Is anybody with him?' she asked.

'Oh no, miss.'

'Show him up then, if you please.' There was no point in postponing things. He knew her name and where she lived. She was in no position to run away in any case.

Sir Robert came in, puffing slightly from his exertions up the stairs. He stood for a moment and looked down at her. Helen played with her shawl fringe. She had glanced at him once, under her lashes, as he came in, and was relieved to see that he did not seem to be angry.

'The brute,' he said. 'He's no gentleman.' He suddenly realized the full extent to which he'd been duped. Doubtless Redbourn had come to that very gaming hell with the intent of seeking him out. Redbourn had known of his weakness and deliberately set out to exploit it.

'I'm afraid I'm no lady,' said Helen, trying to smile. She had not expected such concern. 'I am truly sorry, Sir Robert.'

'Why did you do it?' Sir Robert sat down heavily on a small chair which creaked ominously.

'He ... he knew things about me....'

'Blackmail, eh? Well, who am I to blame you for that? He did the same to me.'

Tears of relief shone in Helen's eyes. She didn't deserve that he was so kind to her. She pulled herself up to a sitting position. 'I should have told him to go to hell,' she said.

Sir Robert blinked. 'So should I, m'dear. Damn fools, both of us.' He reached out and patted her hand. There was a short companionable silence.

'How did you find me out?'

Sir Robert told her.

Helen's mind worked rapidly. Mr Luke Redbourn was no fool. He must have given Sir Robert her name and address deliberately. And Sir Robert had come to see her. Suddenly her future looked a little brighter.

'I am sorry not to be at my best,' she said. 'If I may persuade you to come again in a few weeks' time, I hope I shall be more myself.'

Sir Robert sighed heavily. 'If I could get this damned debt off my back I should be delighted to get to know you better, m'dear. But, m'hands are tied.' He stayed long enough to exchange views on Laurence to their mutual satisfaction and then took out his pocket watch and looked at it. 'Time I was off.' He stood up, kissed her hand with old-fashioned gallantry, and left. Helen heard him stumping heavily down the narrow staircase.

Half an hour later a large basket of fruit arrived with Sir Robert's compliments.

It was still too early to get up, but daylight was already banishing the night shadows from Anna's bedroom. Anna, for reasons she did not understand, was feeling sadly flat. She had what she thought she had wanted. She was back with dear Tante Marie, she had work to do and she slept in her old bedroom with all her familiar things around her. It was the room she had thought about most when she was at Brook Street. Anna lay and looked at the ceiling. There was a simple egg and dart cornice and a pretty ceiling rose which Anna had always liked, but today these things failed to please. There, sitting on one corner of her chest of drawers, as she had done ever since Anna arrived in England, was the rag doll Tante Marie had made for her in place of Princesse Clothilde. The doll had brown wool hair, the almond shape of her eyes had been carefully feather-stitched and her irises were small tortoiseshell buttons. Her dress was made out of the white silk that Anna had been wearing when she had arrived, terrified, with her *bonne* on the evening of her mother's arrest. It was the only thing remaining from the time before.

Usually, when she contemplated the rag doll, Anna felt better, but this time it didn't work. Suddenly, for no reason that she could see, just when she thought she would feel secure again, she felt adrift. What was there for her in the future? Where was she going? Helping Tante Marie in the shop, certainly. And then what? Was that all?

Now Anna was back permanently in Somers Town, she began to be invited to the various soirées held by the French refugees. The guests were mainly those of her father's generation who were still in London. The short-lived Peace of Amiens had induced a number of émigrés to swallow their pride and return to France, even if the price was to acknowledge Napoleon Bonaparte as First Consul. The Vicomte de Cardonnel had been among those who decided not to return. What was the point? His château had been looted and burnt; everything he owned had been confiscated. What would he be going back to? In France he had no means of support and he would have to grovel to that usurper from Corsica in the hopes of getting back some of his property. At least in England he had his dear Marie and a thriving business.

Those who remained in England tended to be the die-hard royalists. So far as their means allowed they attempted to reproduce the soirées of pre-Revolutionary Paris. There was good conversation; serious talk about philosophy or the arts – not the English preoccupation with horses or the weather. There were impromptu concerts or recitals – and all in the elegance of the French language. The guests might bring a candle or some wood for the fire and leave a discreet shilling or two towards the expense in a little vase on the mantelpiece, but apart from that, it was as near as they could manage to the salons of Paris they missed so much.

Anna had been to one such salon only the previous Saturday.

'Ah, *mademoiselle*,' a young comte had sighed. 'Shall we ever go back home?'

'You don't think of England as home now?' asked Anna. The comte could not have been more than a year or so older than Anna herself; what would he remember of France?

'Never!' He shuddered eloquently. 'The food! The abominable weather!'

'There are things to admire, too, *monsieur*.'

'I cannot think of any.'

'The English are more egalitarian. The classes are less rigidly divided. With intelligence and application a man may rise.'

'And you like that! *Tiens!* We have a Jacobin in our midst.' He turned to Madame de Saisseval. 'Mademoiselle de Cardonnel here has no respect for breeding.'

'Birth isn't everything,' said Anna stoutly. She thought suddenly of Luke Redbourn, a City businessman. In Paris he would be unacknowledged by the circle into which she had been born. And who was the loser? Surely a healthy society needed the intelligence of all its citizens?

'*Mademoiselle* was only a child when she came here,' said Madame de Saisseval, tactfully. It was well known that the Vicomte de Cardonnel had been living with his mistress who had actually been a *pâtissière* on his estate! And the child had been allowed to absorb who knew what notions from such a woman. 'You must not deny your birth, *ma chère*,' she said to Anna.

'I am not denying who I am, *madame*,' replied Anna. 'But I must live in the present, where I find myself.'

'Ah,' said Madame de Saisseval, 'it is true, perhaps, that we live in the past.'

'And now this Bonaparte, this self-made emperor,' cried the comte. 'Who knows when we shall get home now? I, for one, can never acknowledge him.'

Anna edged away. As far as she could see there was not much to choose between the autocracy of King Louis and that of the Emperor Napoleon. She was just wondering how long she would have to stay when a stocky young man came over and stood before her. He looked vaguely familiar but Anna could not place him. He was certainly not from one of the émigré families she knew.

'I see you do not recognize me?'

'I must confess, *monsieur*, that I do not.'

'Why should you, indeed. It must be thirteen, fourteen years since we last met.'

Anna gasped. 'Good heavens! Are you ... you cannot be my cousin Bertrand?'

The young man bowed. 'And now, since your esteemed father's death, Vicomte de Cardonnel.'

'But ... your father, your brothers?'

'My father was executed in '94 and both of my brothers are now dead.'

'I beg your pardon, *monsieur*,' Anna collected her thoughts together. 'I remember now, my father did tell me about your father. But both your brothers! That is very sad. May I ask how it came about?'

'They were with the Duke of Brunswick's army. Auguste was killed last year fighting the French and Marcel died of wounds after Eylau. I came to England with the La Ferronays.'

But after the family news had been exchanged there was nothing much to say. Bertrand was a stolid, unimaginative young man, very aware of his own importance as the new Vicomte de Cardonnel and uninterested in the trivialities of

Anna's own life. She was pleased that he had survived, pleased that the line would not die out with her father, but that was all.

They parted with mutual expressions of regard and conventional hopes of meeting again. Bertrand had his eye on a position with the Duc de Berri. He said nothing to Anna, but his family owned a small estate in Switzerland and the new vicomte was financially better off than many of his compatriots. It would have been well within his means to have offered his young cousin a small allowance. Bertrand chose to say nothing: the appearance of a possibly indigent relative could only be a drawback to his hopes of advancement. Anna was relieved by his lack of interest. She had already received various expressions of concern that she should be living with her father's mistress: 'I'm so afraid, dear *mademoiselle*, that it will damage your chances,' Madame de Gontaut had said. Anna did not want the new head of the family making things difficult.

She had felt out of place, too, with the Broxheads. The meaninglessness of their daily round irked her; the lack of interest in things of the mind; the stifling limitations imposed on ladies. There seemed to be no end of things she couldn't do. She might not go out by herself. There were certain places she must never go under any circumstances; down St James's Street, for example, or shopping in Bond Street in the afternoon. Anna had no particular desire to be a lady patroness of the local workhouse like her aunt, but although Lady Broxhead's involvement with her various charities might smack of a high-handed interference in others' lives, at least she was trying to fill the vacuum of her days with something useful.

Well-brought-up young English ladies, Anna was told, had no opinions. They smiled prettily and had good manners. They danced and they rode, but little else. Lady Broxhead had once chidden Julia for stating her views rather too forcefully.

'We are Whigs, dear,' she said firmly. 'That is all you need to know.'

'Why?' muttered Julia.

'Are ladies allowed no opinions at all?' Anna asked. How odd these English were.

'Certainly, she may have opinions, but she must never express them – and they will naturally coincide with the views of her husband, or father, if she has no husband.'

Later, Julia had said to Anna, 'I doubt whether Papa has ever had a political opinion in his life!'

'Women in France have gone to the scaffold for their political opinions,' Anna replied.

'Then perhaps it's safer not to have any!' retorted her cousin.

Anna stirred. The daylight had become stronger now. Already she could hear Tante Marie moving around in her room. François would be here soon and the day would begin. She must get up and make breakfast. There was no use moping about things. Life, Papa always said, was what you made it: you simply had to do your best with the materials that came to hand. What she must do, which she had put off, was go and see Abbé Carron about the affidavit proving her identity for Mr Hargreaves, then at least steps might be taken about finding the cabochon emerald.

Luke was feeling more shaken by the attack than he liked to admit to Hester. Thorn had chaffed him on wanting to impress some unknown fair, but it was not that: it was the awful realization that his own brother, in all probability, wanted to put a period to his existence. Luke had known for a long time that Laurence resented him, but to be the focus of such hatred was another matter, and Luke found it hard to come to terms with.

'I'm all right!' he said testily when Hester exclaimed at the sight of him. 'A few cuts and bruises, that's all.'

'Walter! Run for the doctor!'

'Stop fussing,' shouted Luke. 'For God's sake, there's nothing wrong. If you want to do something useful, you can organize a bath for me.'

Luke rarely spoke other than kindly to Hester and she was almost more shocked by his outburst than by the blood all over his clothes. When he had left the room she said to Walter, 'Find out what happened. I want the truth, Walter, not such bits of it as my brother thinks suitable.'

'Don't you worry, Miss Hester. I'll get it out of him.'

Later, over supper, Luke apologized for his show of temper. He was looking better, even to Hester's anxious eyes. The cut on his hand was bandaged and after the blood from the numerous bits of flying glass had been wiped away the scratches were seen to be less alarming than Hester had feared. His right hand was obviously hurting him and he allowed Hester to cut up his food into manageable portions.

'You were not yourself,' said Hester. 'Do you really think it was footpads?' (She had had a word with Walter.)

'They occasionally operate around Hyde Park.'

'That does not answer my question,' said Hester, severely.

'All right, I don't know.' Luke put down his fork. 'If there's a choice between footpads and my brother trying to have me murdered, I'd rather it were footpads.'

Hester blenched. 'Surely he wouldn't murder you?'

'There was a gun, Hester.' Luke spoke abruptly. He found it difficult to accept the possibility that his brother might have wanted him killed.

Hester winced. Even less than Luke could she face the implication of the gun. Hester had not enjoyed a happy relationship with her mother, and her father had always been a somewhat distant figure. Her brothers, therefore, meant all the more to her. Though she dearly loved Luke, it was Laurence, the baby of the family, who had been her darling. 'Do you think Laurence might attack Miss de Cardonnel?' she whispered at last.

'I doubt he'd do that. She, after all, is the one he wishes to marry.'

Hester forced herself to say the unsayable. 'He might kidnap that aunt of hers, or one of the Broxheads.'

'He would be unwise to kidnap the Broxheads – Society tends to look after its own. Besides, if all else fails, he wants that ten thousand from Sir Robert. He would be foolish to risk that by having the law brought against him. Madame Bonnieux, however, is another matter. Her disappearance would be unlikely to interest the authorities.'

'But what can we do?'

'I'll send Walter over to Somers Town tomorrow with Jeremy Jackson. See what needs doing in the way of security.' Jackson was the odd-job man who occasionally did work about the house.

'Thank goodness Father isn't still alive,' said Hester, sighing. 'He had such hopes of Laurence.'

'He must hate me,' said Luke sadly. He remembered when Laurence was born and how he, Luke, aged seven, had proudly raced to school the following day to tell them of his new baby brother.

There was a silence while both of them tried to master their emotion. Then Hester suddenly remembered. Caroline! She put her hand to her cheek. 'Oh! I'm sorry to bring this up now. Other things drove it quite out of my head. You ought to see this.' She rose and went over to the table by the window and picked up the folded copy of the morning's paper. She handed it to him, pointing to the item about Alderman Simpson.

Luke read it in silence. Hester, looking at him, had no clue as to how he felt.

'You must write, of course,' he said at last.

'I have already done so. Sent both our condolences.'

'Good.'

There was a pause. Hester searched frantically for something to say. 'I daresay she will be a wealthy widow,' she managed.

'Probably,' agreed Luke. 'Caroline will like that.'

It was the first time he'd used her name since the break up of his engagement and Hester couldn't decide whether it betokened interest or indifference.

Anna had agreed with Luke that she would go and see Abbé Carron and ask if he would swear an affidavit for Mr Hargreaves. She did so on the Sunday after church. The abbé was interested to hear that there was news, albeit unconfirmed, of the cabochon emerald, but was very distressed to learn of the possible complicity of Père Ignace.

'Alas, my dear Anna,' he sighed. 'We are all frail. Père Ignace, too. But we cannot know how he was tempted.'

Anna said nothing.

At last the abbé roused himself. 'Of course, my dear. I shall do what I can for you. Arrange a time with my secretary and we'll sort it out.'

The abbé was swift and efficient and in no time, it seemed, Anna had gone with him to the lawyer with whom the abbé usually dealt and sworn the affidavit. Anna knew that Luke intended to visit Miss le Vivier and she thought that she would wait until he had done so and give him the affidavit when he reported back about the visit, as he had promised to do. When Walter, with Jeremy Jackson in tow, arrived in Phoenix Road with news of the attack on Luke, Anna and Madame Bonnieux were horrified. Anna turned quite white.

'He is not hurt, I hope?' she said anxiously. She was feeling most peculiar, as if a gaping hole had suddenly appeared inside her.

'A few cuts, miss. He'll be as right as rain, don't you worry.'

Anna sat down suddenly.

'He wants you to have your shutters and locks checked, Mrs Bonny,' said Walter. 'Madame Bonnieux' was too much for an

141

Englishman to swallow. Mrs Bonny sounded more English; it suited her too, thought Walter, who rather admired Marie's plumpness and bright eyes. 'A precaution, he says. And you're not to argue.'

Marie laughed. 'We are grateful to Monsieur Redbourn for his concern.'

Jeremy Jackson took a pencil from behind his ear and asked Marie to show him round. 'Top to bottom, Mr Redbourn says.' He had a carpet bag with him which contained, among other things, a ruler and a grubby notebook.

An hour later Jackson had finished. 'You'll be wanting proper shutters back and front,' he announced with gloomy satisfaction. 'Iron bolts – them you have is wooden. Shutters to the shop repaired. New locks on the front and back doors – the ones you have now wouldn't keep out a mouse. And broken glass on the top of the garden wall.' As his list lengthened he became more and more animated.

'Anyone would think we housed the Crown Jewels,' said Anna.

'But can we afford all this?' worried Madame Bonnieux.

'Not to worry, Mrs Bonny,' said Walter. 'It's the master as is paying. And no argufying about that neither.'

'Will you have some coffee before you go?' asked Marie. 'I have some brioches.'

'If that's them little cakes, they're just grand,' said Walter, sitting down with alacrity. Jackson hesitated. He wasn't sure whether sitting in the kitchen with a couple of ladies was right.

'Please sit, Monsieur Jackson,' said Madame Bonnieux, getting down the coffee beans and measuring them into the coffee grinder.

They were Frenchies, Jackson thought to himself. Didn't they believe everyone was equal and chopped the heads off their king and queen? He sat.

When Walter and Jackson were ready to go, Anna shyly

handed Walter a note. 'For Mr Redbourn. We both hope he is better soon.' She also enclosed the affidavit signed by Abbé Carron to prove her identity. Now that Luke had been hurt it seemed more and more imperative that the whole mystery be solved as soon as possible.

Jeremy Jackson returned that afternoon with a horse and cart in which were various bolts and locks, a bag of cement, some pieces of wood and several pails filled with broken glass.

'What will the neighbours think?' asked Marie.

'You sound like Lady Broxhead!' said Anna.

'But what will they think? It'll be all over the place by tomorrow.'

Anna thought. 'Sir Robert ordered it,' she said finally.

'But why would he want to do that?'

'That's what we are wondering,' said Anna promptly. 'One of the eccentricities of the English, perhaps?'

Marie laughed.

Laurence paced up and down his dingy room in Charles Street and swore. Never in his life had he been thwarted as he was now and he couldn't stand it. Curse this country where everybody had always been against him. His father had always preferred Luke, old Carr had begrudged him a few paltry hundreds, and that prissy little Caroline had squealed when they'd been caught. If she'd kept quiet they might have brazened it out and he could have enjoyed more of her charms at a later date. But the stupid wench had actually thought that he would marry her!

Then that French hussy had turned him down. She'd escaped too – doubtless bribed the slut who acted as the landlady's slavey. He should have raped her while he had the chance. She'd have been more compliant then. And those damn fools he had hired had failed to do more than break a window of the cab and that precious brother of his had got clean away.

Morality was a concept Laurence had never bothered to

understand: if a man wasn't out for himself then he was a fool. The world was a tough place, and if you weren't on top then you were likely to get crushed underfoot. He was never concerned about the hurt and distress he caused others.

Just now he felt sorry for himself. Luke had a good living, he thought resentfully. He must be worth a thousand a year, at least. There were rich opportunities for fraud and embezzlement in the commodities market if only Luke had the wit to see them. If Luke had met with an unfortunate accident now, no one would have been more upset than his brother. He would have gone to Hester and wept on her shoulder. She would have allowed him to stay – Laurence felt he could rely on Hester's soft heart – and in no time at all he would have milked the business for all it was worth. Laurence's fingers itched to get back into that cash box. But the damned fools had let Luke escape with only a few cuts.

Now Laurence had to start all over again. He must get hold of Miss de Cardonnel and this time he would mean business. Thanks to Sir Robert he now knew more or less where she lived. Somers Town was hardly a distinguished area and there would probably be few servants to raise the alarm. It must be easier.

At that moment the slavey knocked on the door. She carried yesterday's paper and a bottle of brandy.

Laurence uncorked the brandy and took a swig. 'Get out.'

'Please, sir, that's three and sixpence.'

'Chalk it up.'

'Please sir.' The girl was trembling. 'Missus says there's two weeks' rent owing and when's she going to be paid?'

Laurence picked up an old empty bottle and threw it at her. It hit her on the elbow. She gave a cry of pain and fled. Laurence laughed and opened the paper.

A moment or so later he was staring down intently at an item which interested him very much. So old Simpson had stuck his spoon in the wall, had he? Cut up rich, doubtless. Caroline was still only – what? – twenty-four or so, and a hot little thing, if his memory served. The trouble with rich widows, though, was that their husband's wills often tied things up damned awkwardly. All the same....

Laurence took another swig of brandy and turned the problem over in his mind.

The wind gently ruffled the curtains in the open window of the pretty drawing-room in Cheapside, overlooking the church of St Mary le Bow, where Caroline Simpson sat and opened her letters with a slim ivory paper-knife. They were all condolences on the loss of her husband and several, gratifyingly, were from fellow aldermen who would not be averse, Caroline suspected, to pursuing a closer acquaintance with her once her year of mourning was over. She turned her head slightly to admire herself in the glass. A slender figure with pale-gold hair, admirably set off by her black silk dress, looked back at her. Caroline refused to wear crape, whose matt surface was considered more suitable for the first stages of mourning. Her husband would not have liked it, she told her friends, raising a wisp of lace-edged handkerchief to her eyes. She knew that the black silk, which was cut in the very latest fashion, set off her fair prettiness admirably.

She grieved for her dear William, naturally. An indulgent older husband had just suited her – though there had been times when she missed the fun and excitement of a passionate young man. The handsome clerk at Christmas, for instance, who ... Caroline hastily pushed the memory away. Nothing had really happened after all. Anyway, at Christmas a few stolen kisses were permissible, surely?

Absently, she slit open another letter and scanned the signature: *Hester Redbourn.* Caroline sat up. *My brother joins with me in sending his condolences.* Caroline's pretty lower lip quivered for a moment. Luke might have written himself! Had he still not forgiven her? She had been young and foolish and Laurence had been so persuasive. Luke ought to have forgiven her.

He was doing very well now. Her husband had spoken of him with respect as someone who was worth watching. 'Got a good business head on his shoulders, young Redbourn,' he'd said. 'Should go far.'

Somehow the steadiness of Luke's character, which at seventeen had seemed prosy and dull, now had its attractions. Steady men, who were doing well, could support pretty wives and indulge them.

Alderman Simpson had left £4,000 each in trust for their two daughters and Caroline, apart from her own dowry of £3,000 which had been settled on her, had a jointure of £500 a year. She was a young, attractive widow with a handsome competence. When her year of mourning was over she would look about her a bit.

Of course, she couldn't do much until then, but it would not do any harm to pay a visit to dear Hester.

Things in Phoenix Street now settled into a busy, purposeful routine. François, who had come in the mornings to help stoke up the ovens and do any heavy lifting, was now employed full time. Anna and Madame Bonnieux had felt it necessary to tell François something of what had been going on to quash his amazement at the bolts and locks. 'Mademoiselle de Cardonnel has been pursued by the good-for-nothing brother of Monsieur Redbourn,' he was told.

François promised to keep his ears and eyes open. Their news didn't surprise him; several times he'd been set on by a local gang of English lads, who'd found it good sport to attack 'a frog'. François was small and seemed an easy target, but he was wiry, too, and had surprising strength. Once he'd banged a few heads on the cobblestones and knocked out a tooth or two, the gang had left him alone and gone in search of easier prey.

'Don't you worry, *madame*,' he said to Marie. 'I'll spread the word. Mademoiselle Anna will be safe here.'

Whether it was François' vigilance or that Laurence had lost interest, they didn't know, but things were quiet. Anna tried to feel settled and happy. They had had a brief note from Hester, thanking them for their kind letter to her brother: *He begs to offer his apologies for not replying himself,* she wrote, *but he cannot yet use his right hand.* Anna told herself that she didn't mind – she was content only to know that Luke was all right.

Somehow it didn't stop her worrying about him.

'I wonder how Monsieur Luc is?' she said one evening a day or so later, when she and Madame Bonnieux were having their evening meal. 'We have heard nothing since Miss Redbourn's note.' She tried to sound casual, but to her annoyance she found herself blushing.

'I'm sure we'd have heard if he were seriously ill,' said Marie. 'I daresay he has work to catch up with.' She was only half listening. Her new strawberry palmiers had sold briskly and she was wondering whether to do an extra batch tomorrow if François could get the strawberries.

'Of course,' said Anna. 'This business must have taken up much of his time.' She tried to feel satisfied.

Anna had not been sleeping well. She woke easily and once awake found it difficult to get back to sleep. And there were noises, scratches in the roof that Tante Marie said were mice, the occasional bark of a dog and the dawn chorus. That night Anna lay and stared up at the ceiling. There were scratches now. Mice again. They really ought to get a cat.

The scratching stopped. Anna shut her eyes. Then there was a creak. Her eyes flew open. Houses always creaked, she told herself. Another creak and then a slight thud. Heart thumping,

Anna sat up. There was a trapdoor on the landing between her room and Tante Marie's, which led to the loft. Could it be … surely not? Jeremy Jackson had secured the trapdoor that led from the loft out onto the roof, but not this one. She took the tinder-box from her bedside table, lit the candle with trembling fingers, and tiptoed to the door.

The trapdoor was being stealthily pulled up.

Anna screamed.

Instantly, there was pandemonium. Marie shot up and Hercule, who was sleeping in the kitchen, woke up and started barking. Anna pulled on her dressing-gown and ran downstairs. The front doorbell clanged whenever a customer pushed open the door, but it could be rung by anybody who pulled at the little chain that hung down from the coiled spring and Anna pulled it now.

Suddenly, there were lanterns outside and voices, French voices, asking if they were all right. Anna drew back the bolts and opened the door.

'There's somebody in our attic!' she panted.

By the time a ladder had been got and a burly neighbour climbed up to look, whoever it was had gone.

'But we had the trapdoor out onto the roof secured,' said Marie. She was only half awake and at first wondered if it were all Anna's imagination. She, herself, had heard nothing.

'He pulled the slates off,' said her neighbour. 'There's a hole. You can see starlight.'

François, alerted by the noise in the street, now came running up.

'There's nothing we can do tonight,' said Marie, when a thorough inspection had been made. 'I doubt whether he'll come back.'

'I shall stay, *madame*,' said François. His eyes were alight with excitement. 'I have brought my father's sword! I can sleep on the landing floor.'

The neighbours eventually left. Anna locked and bolted the front door behind them and the house settled down to sleep if it could. Marie found some cushions for François to lie on and Anna got back into bed. I shall have to write and tell Monsieur Luc in the morning, she thought. She fell asleep surprisingly quickly.

'Oh no!' cried Hester. 'They were not hurt, I trust?' She was buttering Luke's toast as the use of his right hand still pained him.

Luke looked up from reading out Anna's letter. 'It says not. Though I imagine they must have been frightened.' Anna's letter had been perfectly coherent, but the occasional blot and somewhat wild signature spoke of her agitation.

'Yes, indeed. Poor things. What shall you do, Luke?'

'I can think of one thing,' said Luke slowly. 'Though I'm not sure whether Miss de Cardonnel would agree.'

'I should think she'd agree with anything that would secure her safety.' Hester, looking at him, saw that he had flushed slightly.

Luke gave a short laugh. 'I hope you're right. Ring the bell please, Hester, and ask Walter to fetch Jeremy Jackson. I want to go over later this morning, say, eleven, if that suits Jackson.' He left the room looking, to Hester's amazement, quite animated.

The pâtisserie in Phoenix Street was more than usually busy. Everyone had heard of the attempted entry and customers were crowded into the shop. Anna was behind the counter. Business was obviously going briskly.

'Oh, Monsieur Luc!'

'Miss de Cardonnel.' He raised his hat. 'I've brought Jeremy Jackson with me to inspect the damage.'

'How very kind,' said Anna. She went to the door and shouted. *'Tante Marie! C'est Monsieur Luc.'* She turned to Luke. 'We have been worried about you,' she said, shyly. 'How is your hand, now?'

Luke held it out. It was still bandaged but he flexed his fingers and said, 'Much better, thank you. My sister assures me it is healing as it ought.'

Marie came in, wiping her hands on her apron. 'We are pleased to see that you are recovering so well, monsieur. How good of you to come so promptly. Anna, why don't you take them up?'

Anna stripped off her apron and they went upstairs. The ladder had been propped up in a corner by the staircase. Jeremy Jackson climbed into the loft. Anna and Luke were left standing on the landing.

'I'm sorry there's more for you to worry about,' said Anna. 'I suppose it could be housebreakers.'

'Unlikely.'

Anna sighed.

Jackson's head now appeared. 'He's pulled the tiles off to get in, but I can't see any other damage.'

'Can you deal with it?'

'Yes, sir. And I could put a bolt on the inside of the trapdoor onto the landing.'

'Well, do so,' said Luke.

Jackson disappeared.

'Miss de Cardonnel,' said Luke. 'I should like a few words with you in private, if I may. Is there anywhere we could go?'

'The garden?' offered Anna. 'You will see that we are rather crowded today. The excitement last night caused quite a stir. Tante Marie says that it's all good for business and got up early to bake an extra batch of cakes!' She led the way downstairs.

The Redbourns' garden was a similar size to the one here, but never were two gardens so different. Luke's mother had had the outside paved and used it only for hanging out the washing, for she was not a gardener. Hester liked a garden and had improved the place with a variety of tubs; pansies in winter and cheerful clove pinks in summer. Sometimes she sat out there to shell peas or hull strawberries.

This garden, however, was quite different. Outside the house there were the usual offices, but beyond an arched doorway was the garden proper. It managed to be entirely French, formally laid out like a miniature garden by Le Nôtre. There was a gravel circle in the centre, kept in place by neat little box hedges. Outside there were geometrical parterres, each with its different green herb. Some were dark and some pale. There were some with feathery grasses whose name Luke did not know. Nearest the kitchen were clumps of herbs that Luke recognized; a rosemary bush, shaped into a neat ball, some thyme, chives, parsley, sage and tall angelica. There were several mints and, in a small terracotta pot, some basil. The general effect was green and peaceful. There was very little colour apart from the scarlet pom-poms of the bergamot. At the far end of the garden was a stone urn filled with ivy and beside it a wooden bench.

Luke looked around. 'This is charming,' he said. 'My sister would like this. Tell me, can you eat everything here?'

Anna laughed. 'Almost. Tante Marie is a great believer in herbs.'

They sat down on the bench.

'I have two things to discuss with you,' Luke began. 'The first is about this affidavit. I could send it to Mr Hargreaves and put in a formal request that, if he knows of its whereabouts, the cabochon emerald be returned to its rightful owner. I must confess, however, that I am somewhat reluctant to pursue that course of action.' Luke then told Anna of his meeting with Miss le Vivier. 'It is obvious to me that she had no idea of any wrongdoing on her uncle's part and I think it would distress her considerably. At any rate I was unwilling to take any further steps without consulting you.'

'I don't want Mr Hargreaves thinking of me as an impostor,'

said Anna with a lift of the chin. 'Could he be sent the affidavit and a letter stating that you have met Miss le Vivier? As she mentioned that I am a beneficiary of her uncle's will, I am willing to postpone the problem of the emerald until I am twenty-one. He will need the affidavit then, anyway.'

Luke considered. 'That would be an excellent compromise. Would you like me to write to him on your behalf?'

'Thank you. That would be kind. If you are certain that is what you want. After all, monsieur, you have suffered consequences too. You must consider your own safety, as well.'

'I am satisfied,' said Luke, shortly. He turned to study the garden. His gaze seemed fixed by the bergamot and its scarlet flowers swaying in the breeze. 'I have been wondering whether there might be some way we could stop Laurence's activities once and for all,' he said, still looking intently at the bergamot.

Anna got the sudden impression that he was ill-at-ease; something had embarrassed him. But what? 'Short of murdering him I cannot see what else is to be done.' Anna spoke lightly.

'You could marry me.'

'*What!*' It came out as a squeak.

'I can see that the idea does not appeal to you.' Luke removed his gaze from the bergamot and turned to look at her. His tone was light but his eyes held a disturbing expression she had never seen before.

Anna's heart began to thud. 'Could you explain, please?'

'It's very simple. It seems to be more and more difficult to protect you adequately. I don't wish to alarm you unnecessarily, but there is a possibility that those you care about, Madame Bonnieux, for example, could be used as a hostage.'

'True.' Anna's voice had steadied.

'If you married me then you obviously cannot marry my brother. We would have a proper settlement to ensure that any money you have or will have remains yours absolutely. And, after your birthday, when presumably, this whole mysterious business will come to light, we can get an annulment.'

'An annulment?' Anna stared blindly out at a garden she could no longer see.

'Yes.' Luke looked down at the gravel and seemed intent on turning over a small pebble with his foot. 'I would not wish to hold you against your will. Once you are of age you may do as you wish.'

'You are thinking of a *mariage blanc*?' Her voice did not seem to be her own.

'The marriage would not be consummated,' said Luke stiffly. 'I believe that in such circumstances an annulment is a mere formality.'

Anna's thoughts were in confusion. 'I ... I should like to think about this, please.' She realized, to her amazement, that she was both upset and angry. Why?

'Of course. You will wish to discuss it with your aunt.'

Anna rose and led the way back to the house without a word.

Chapter Eight

So far as was practicable, Hester ignored her lameness. She was perfectly well able to walk with a stick, she would say testily to any well-meaning interference. Every morning she and her maid went to Covent Garden to choose her fruit and vegetables to be sure of getting the best. She personally inspected the fish and meat she bought and her grocer had long since learnt not to send Miss Redbourn inferior goods.

However, she did get tired and sometimes longed to have things a little easier. As well as the shopping there was the cooking and cleaning and all the work involved in running a house. The maid, a slightly vacuous young woman named Emmy, did the heavy work and every fortnight Mrs Meakins came to help with the washing. Walter helped too. Neither Hester nor Luke could imagine life without him. He was Luke's confidant, valet and a sort of supernumerary clerk when the occasion required. He acted as a butler and footman upstairs, delivering messages and introducing visitors, and he could always be relied upon to help Emmy lift a heavy table or escort Hester, if she had to go out. Even so, running the house was a strain.

Of course, Luke would allow her more help if she asked, but it had become a point of honour not to. She was well aware that most of Luke's capital was tied up in his business and she did not want to add to the expense. Hester knew that her friend, Miss Leatherbarrow, thought she was intent on martyring herself, but then Minerva had the poorest opinion of men and didn't understand that Hester wanted to contribute something, too. She could not go out to work; but she could see that the house ran efficiently on as small a budget as was reasonable.

Hester's one concession was that she tried to allow herself a couple of hours in the afternoons to sit, with her feet on a small footstool, the cat on her lap, and read in peace and quiet.

Luke had gone out that morning to Phoenix Street with Jeremy Jackson and had not yet returned. He'd probably gone straight on to some business in the City and would doubtless take his luncheon in some chop house. She had the house to herself. The clerks were in the office downstairs and Emmy could be heard clattering about with broom and dustpan, but neither disturbed her. Hester took Ben onto her lap and closed her eyes.

She was just beginning to doze off, when there was a knock at the door and Walter entered with a card on a tray. Hester's eyes shot open. She sat up abruptly, dislodging Ben, and tried to straighten her cap and collect herself before taking the card. She took one look at it and sighed.

'Show Mrs Simpson up, Walter. And ask Emmy to bring up tea and the honey cake.'

'Yes, Miss Hester.' Walter left and Ben jumped back onto Hester's lap. Mechanically, she began to stroke him.

'Dearest Hester!' Caroline peeped round the door. 'Oh! I'm disturbing you. Shall I go away?' She came in, kissed Hester affectionately, took off her cloak, gloves and bonnet and sat down.

'Why, it's just like old times,' cried Caroline. 'You sitting there with Ben on your lap and the dear old room – just as it was.' She looked across at Luke's chair and sighed. The room hadn't changed. When she was seventeen it had all seemed impossibly old-fashioned, now she found it reassuring. Hester was older and thinner, perhaps, but really very much the same. And Luke? Caroline didn't dare bring the subject up just yet, but she knew that he had never married.

Hester looked at her guest. Caroline, she saw with dismay, was much improved. Her figure had filled out and she looked both fragile and ethereal in her black silk. 'Is this just a courtesy call, Caroline?' she asked with a touch of scepticism.

'Oh, you naughty thing!' cried Caroline. 'You have found me out in an instant. I declare you are so sharp it frightens me. I would not have you think me coming for the world.' Hester, she remembered, had never been too keen on her engagement to Luke.

'I have not seen you for seven years,' said Hester. 'It would be impertinent of me to guess why you are here.'

Caroline pouted. 'I am here because of your kind letter, naturally. I am sure you cannot blame me for that.'

'No, indeed. And I was sorry to hear of Mr Simpson's death. Was it unexpected?'

'Oh yes!' Caroline mopped at her eyes. 'My poor husband. He was so dotingly fond of me – and of my two little girls – I do not know how I shall go on without him.'

Hester was anxious to get away from any discussion of what, exactly, Caroline might have in mind. 'It's a sad thing for daughters to lose a father.'

'I don't think they understand what has happened,' said Caroline. 'Poor Mr Simpson was such a busy man. He scarcely saw them, except occasionally if he were in at tea-time. That's the problem with an older husband. He didn't really care for childish prattle.'

'They will feel the loss more as they grow up, I daresay,' said Hester.

Emmy now came in with the tea and some moments were occupied with the tea tray. But such tactics could not long delay things. Hester hated any unpleasantness and however was she to discourage Caroline without the young widow dissolving into a flood of tears – which Hester was well aware she could do?

'I was such a silly girl, myself ...' began Caroline.

But she was interrupted. Walter knocked on the door and announced, 'Miss Leatherbarrow!'

'Minerva!' cried Hester, overcome with relief.

Miss Minerva Leatherbarrow, she who had attempted to introduce Hester to the thoughts of Miss Wollstonecraft, was a tall thin woman with large teeth and a long face. She scorned feminine airs and trickeries, as she termed them, and now strode into the room wearing an ill-fitting gown in an indeterminate shade of grey. She took one look at Caroline and gave a snort of laughter. 'Well, Caroline! And what are you doing here? Husband-hunting again?'

Caroline bit her lip. She had been a pupil in the school run by Miss Leatherbarrow's parents and still held Minerva in some awe. 'I am come to visit Hester,' she said defensively. She could cope with dear, compliant Hester, she thought, but Minerva made her mind go all woolly.

'So I see. But isn't it a bit soon to come chasing after gentlemen?' No more than Hester, did Minerva believe that Caroline had come with the sole purpose of spending an afternoon with a middle-aged spinster.

Caroline flushed. 'And why should I want to chase after gentlemen, when I'm only just widowed? You are unkind, Minerva.'

Minerva looked sceptical. Caroline said waspishly, 'You always thought the worst of me! It was you who accused me of getting Nelly Tytherly to do my hemming for me!'

'And so you did.'

Caroline gave an angry sob and rose to her feet. 'I shan't stay. I can see when I'm not wanted.' She began to put on her cloak and bonnet, tying the ribbons with jerky fingers. 'Goodbye, Hester. I hope that when I come again we shan't be interrupted by this – this beanpole!' She picked up her gloves and left the room. The door closed behind her with a snap.

Hester sank back against the cushions and mopped her brow. She could never cope with Caroline's emotions. 'You were uncivil, Minerva,' she said reproachfully.

'Yes,' said Minerva, with satisfaction. 'And if you let her get her claws into your brother again, you're a fool, Hester. Now, how about some of that honey cake?'

The following day Luke received a stiff little letter from Anna. She thanked him for his proposal, which she had now discussed with Madame Bonnieux. She was inclined to accept it, she told him, but there were a couple of points which she must discuss with him first. Could she possibly come and talk about it with him in privacy?

What she did not say was that she had found herself snapping at Tante Marie, who was being calm and practical, and ended up in floods of tears. She had then spent a sleepless night and was still no nearer any coherent thoughts on the subject. Marriage with Mr Redbourn was a rational solution, she knew, and one that would help guard them both from further malice on Laurence's part. But there was another part of her that found it upsetting, almost insulting, that she couldn't account for.

An hour later Walter was round with an answer. *Dear Miss de Cardonnel*, she read in Luke's handwriting. *If you would like to return with Walter we may talk privately in my office. Yours etc. L. Redbourn.*

Anna read it twice. That was all it said.

When Walter ushered Anna into Luke's office and offered to take her pelisse and bonnet, Luke was sitting at his desk, absently going through some business correspondence. He had been through it several times since Anna's letter arrived, and he was well aware that it was making no sense at all. He rose as Anna came in and offered her a chair at the round table in the centre of the room.

Walter left the room and Luke sat down opposite her.

'I have two points,' said Anna, stiffly. She was feeling awkward and embarrassed and trying desperately not to show it.

'Yes?' Luke drew a piece of paper towards him and dipped his pen in a small glass inkpot that stood on the table.

'Tante Marie pointed out that your brother could just as well marry me as a widow – particularly if he thought I might be going to be a wealthy one. I don't wish to place you in more danger. So you will please make a will which does not benefit me at all.'

'That is not necessary,' said Luke. 'All I have to do is state that if you marry Laurence, the money goes to charity.'

Anna gaped at him. 'But … I could not possibly benefit from this marriage under any circumstances.' Had she understood him aright?

'Have no fear, Miss de Cardonnel. I have no intention of dying before October. What is your other point?'

Anna hesitated. What she had to say was skirting a very difficult area. 'It is about Tante Marie,' she began. 'You must know that … that she is not really my aunt.'

'I gathered that,' said Luke unperturbed. 'Are you trying to say that she was your father's mistress?'

'Yes.' Anna raised her chin as she had done at the impertinence of Mr Hargreaves, daring Luke to disapprove. 'In my view that fact concerned nobody but my father and Madame Bonnieux. There have been a number of people who have been shocked at my living with her. I have always ignored them. Tante Marie is one of the best people I know and she has been like a mother to me.' She stopped and thought a moment.

'More in fact. I rarely saw my mother. It was not the custom then.'

'I understand all this,' said Luke gently.

Anna's eyes filled with tears. 'I cannot give up seeing her.'

'Of course you must see her,' said Luke.

Anna began to relax. Perhaps it would be all right. This awful feeling of there being something important that she had missed would go. Mr Redbourn was an honourable man. There was no reason for her to be upset.

'I have come up with a problem, too,' Luke continued. 'I am worried about getting consent to the marriage. You are a minor and it is hardly to be supposed that your uncle would voluntarily agree to it.'

'Must it be my uncle?'

'Isn't he your guardian?'

'Yes, he is,' acknowledged Anna. And then suddenly a thought struck her. A rather boring, stocky young man bowing in front of her.... 'Bertrand!' she exclaimed. 'I met my cousin Bertrand de Cardonnel last week at Madame de Saisseval's. He is now Vicomte de Cardonnel.' She laughed. 'Other émigré friends have told me that he has a snug little estate somewhere in Switzerland. But he has kept this fact very quiet from me! I suppose he fears lest I start making demands on him. I think he would be willing to give the necessary permission. In fact, I'm sure he'd be delighted to know that I was safely married.'

'The question is whether an English court of law would agree that the head of the family has rights above an appointed guardian?'

'It is arguable, though, isn't it?' said Anna.

'Oh yes. I believe a case could be made. I just don't want your name dragged through the courts.'

'Who would bring the case?'

'Sir Robert Broxhead.'

'Could he afford to do so?' asked Anna. 'And would it be

161

worth his while?'

'He stands to lose ten thousand pounds to my brother otherwise,' Luke reminded her. 'On the other hand, by the time it got to court you would almost certainly be twenty-one. I think we should risk it and ask your cousin to give the necessary permission. What do you think?'

'And afterwards,' said Anna, hedging, 'are … are you thinking of my living here with you and your sister?'

'Of course. How else may I protect you?'

'I thought perhaps....' Anna was scarlet. 'Well, if it is a *mariage blanc* then I can't see it matters where I live.'

'Don't be a fool, Miss de Cardonnel. We have got to convince Laurence that the marriage is real.'

'I suppose so.'

Luke looked across at the shut little face. 'My dear Miss de Cardonnel,' he said gently, 'I wouldn't distress you for the world. Why don't you look on this as a visit? Hester and I will do our best to make you welcome. You will miss your aunt, I know, but she can come and visit us and I hope that you would make a friend of my sister.'

Anna took a deep breath. 'You are right,' she said with resolution. 'I must be rational. I accept your offer, Monsieur Luc, and if I am to stay in your house then I would like to be a part of it, not just a guest. I can cook, you know.'

'My dear – Hester does the cooking.' Anna looked at him. Luke laughed. 'I daresay she could do with your help. Cooking is not one of her favourite occupations. And I know what you French think of our English cooking!'

'Then – everything is settled?' Anna asked shyly.

'Certainly it is settled. Let us go upstairs and tell my sister.'

He rose as he spoke and held out his hand to her. She took it and allowed him to lead her to the door. Just before he opened it he paused and raised her hand to his lips. As they went upstairs

Anna could still feel the warmth on her hand where his lips had been.

Bertrand de Cardonnel gave his most willing consent to his cousin's marriage to Mr Luke Redbourn. As Anna had suspected he was pleased to be rid of any obligation in so unexceptionable a way. He did not even ask too many questions about the actual ceremony. If a proper Catholic wedding was not legal in this benighted country and his cousin content to be married in some Protestant church, so be it. Anna had expressed some alarmingly democratic views, Madame de Saisseval had told him: doubtless she was half-heathen anyway. He would give her away and his duty would be done.

Anna and Luke were married by special licence in St Bride's Church on Monday, 27 July, 1807. There were only four guests: Hester, Walter, Marie Bonnieux and Bertrand de Cardonnel. Anna wore the cream lutestring dress she had worn at Julia's wedding and a new cream satin bonnet trimmed with rosemary and moss roses. Luke had discarded his usual sober businessman's clothes for a dark green coat with straw-embroidered waistcoat, buff pantaloons and black pumps.

'A handsome man, your husband,' Bertrand whispered.

'Yes,' replied Anna. The sudden discovery of his good looks was somewhat disconcerting.

Introductions were made and the usual compliments exchanged. It was cool and dark inside the church after the sunlight outside and Anna shivered. Luke, seeing it, took her hand and tucked it into his arm.

'There,' he said, smiling down at her. 'I hope you're not suffering from cold feet as well?'

Anna looked up at him with wide dark eyes. She scarcely knew this stylish stranger with his elaborately tied cravat and carefully cut hair. 'It's just that I've never been married before,' she said idiotically.

'Neither have I,' responded Luke. 'Do you think we might manage to support each other through the ordeal?'

Anna smiled shakily, but she felt better. This was the Monsieur Luc she knew.

Bertrand watched the ceremony critically. He had never been in a Protestant church before and he knew very little English. He had had a vague preconception of alien rites, some travesty of religion. He was astonished that it seemed to be very similar to the ceremony he knew. He was further surprised to find that he approved of Luke. A well-set-up man, he thought. Good-looking and obviously prosperous – why he was almost a gentleman! His cousin had done well for herself.

The service drew to a close. Luke bent to kiss his bride and Anna flushed prettily, just as she ought, Bertrand noted. However, enough was enough. Bertrand declined to attend the wedding breakfast – a previous engagement – but he presented Anna with a pretty pair of garnet ear-rings that had belonged to his mother.

Anna thanked him. 'I am truly grateful, *monsieur*. Everything that belonged to my own mother was lost. I shall treasure these.'

The vicomte gave Anna a chaste kiss on the cheek, bowed slightly to Hester, totally ignored Walter and Marie, shook Luke's hand cordially and left. With his departure the atmosphere lightened.

'We have organized a small wedding breakfast,' said Hester. 'At least, I hope Emmy has not failed us. You will come, Madame Bonnieux, I hope?'

The dining-room was filled with the scent of roses and pinks. There was a huge bowl of flowers on the table and another on the mantelpiece. Emmy was there in a new print dress, grinning from ear to ear. The wedding breakfast was simple: hot rolls and butter, ham, tongue and eggs. Hester and Emmy had made a small fruit cake (with marzipan and a white icing) in honour of the occasion.

Anna suddenly felt better. It was not just the prospect of food – for she had been quite unable to eat anything that morning – but the fact that Hester and Luke had obviously gone to some trouble to make her feel welcome.

Madame Bonnieux was relieved, too. She had not expressed her doubts to Anna, but, whatever the provisions of the marriage settlement (and Mr Redbourn had been scrupulously just) marriage did put a woman completely in the power of her husband. As she watched Luke pour out the drinks and hand Anna her glass she became aware of something else. Mr Redbourn, though he was trying to hide the fact by light banter, found his bride very attractive. Anna, she knew, was determined to regard the marriage as entirely one of convenience. Marie was pretty sure that other feelings had simply not entered her head: in some ways she was curiously immature.

There might be problems ahead.

'How dare you, sir! I shall have the law on you for this! It's illegal, I tell you.' Sir Robert's face was crimson with rage. He was in the Redbourns' small parlour and, as he spoke, he banged on the floor with his cane. Hester and Anna, who were in the drawing-room on the other side of the landing, exchanged worried looks.

'My wife's cousin, the Vicomte de Cardonnel, gave his consent,' replied Luke. 'He is now the head of the family.'

'And I am her guardian!'

'You may take it to a court of law if you wish, Sir Robert.' Luke looked at the florid face in front of him with a certain pity. 'But I wouldn't recommend it.'

'I'll have you in prison for this!'

'I doubt it. There is also the little matter of your debt to my brother. I don't think any court of law would think much of a guardian who was willing to sell his niece.'

Sir Robert seemed to collapse. 'What am I to do?' he whispered. 'A gaming debt is a debt of honour.'

'Tell me, Sir Robert, if it were not for my brother would you have any objection to my marrying your niece?'

'Objection, why should I?'

'You might prefer somebody more of your own background, perhaps?'

Sir Robert shook his head. 'She has no dowry. Taking little thing but ... no money. If you're fond of each other, you're welcome to marry with my good will. But, Redbourn, I'm in a damned mess.'

'The IOU, how did you word it?' Luke asked next.

'Usual thing. Wrote it on the back of one of his cards, I remember. I owe Mr L. Redbourn the sum of ten thousand pounds. Date. Signature.'

'You're sure it was one of his cards? Like this?' Luke took out a card from his waistcoat pocket.

'The same. But what is that to the purpose?'

Luke laughed, scribbled something on the back of the card and handed it to Sir Robert.

Hester showed Anna round the house and helped her to settle in. The second floor was much bigger than she had expected, for at some point in the past a wall had been knocked through to number eight.

'There is a bookseller next door, which I daresay you have noticed,' said Hester. 'My father bought the top two floors from him. He didn't need it and at the time my father had a growing family.' She led the way upstairs. There were four bedrooms and a closet.

'My brother is in here.' She indicated the front room over the bookseller's. 'Behind is a spare room. Next to that is my room and you're in the other front room.'

'But ...' exclaimed Anna, 'surely, you should have the front room? You mustn't leave it because of me!'

'No, my dear. The back room has always been mine.'

Anna's room was panelled like the others. There was an old-fashioned oak chest of drawers and a large cupboard which took up most of one wall. Along the top was carved *Lemuel Redbourn, born August ye fifteenth 1716. Married Mary Bayley, June ye twelfth 1737.*

'It was my grandfather's,' said Hester. 'Too big and clumsy for modern taste, I fear.'

'I like it,' said Anna. The smaller panels were heavily carved with bunches of grapes. The two central panels were of Adam and Eve. Eve had long wavy hair, round high breasts and a strategically placed bit of ivy. She was holding out the apple. Adam, on the other panel, had one hand outstretched towards the apple while the other shielded his modesty. The serpent's body coiled round the tree behind Eve, seemed to disappear into the cupboard and the head reemerged somewhere above Adam's shoulder and looked enquiringly at him. It had a forked tongue and appeared, to Anna, to be smiling. Anna was charmed by it.

The bed was an equally old-fashioned four-poster with bulbous posts and what looked like a large pineapple on each corner. The bed hangings were heavy and embroidered with an elaborate trellis of flowers and birds. It looked utterly English. Revolution, surely, had never touched it. Anna said as much.

'We had our Revolution a hundred and fifty years ago,' said Hester, smiling. 'My family fought for Parliament. We have an old pike somewhere to prove it.' She paused and looked round. Emmy had put some flowers on the dressing-table and Walter had brought up Anna's trunk. 'I shall leave you now, Anna. I hope I may call you Anna, now that we are sisters. You will want to settle in.'

Apart from the visit by an irate Sir Robert, there were no untoward occurrences. Nobody, however, believed that

Laurence would give up that easily. Luke forbade Anna and Hester to go out without Walter to escort them. 'I know it's a nuisance,' he said. 'But we must be careful.'

'But you need Walter,' protested Hester.

'I can do without Walter if I have to. And I'd rather know that you were safe.'

Hester and Anna, accompanied by Walter, went to Covent Garden every morning and did the shopping. Anna bought whatever herbs she could find and began to grow them in various tubs. She persuaded Hester to let her take over the cooking. The result was that the food instantly improved. There was now a pot-au-feu permanently on the hob and fresh pâtés in the larder. Hester was initially horrified to find Anna putting wine into the beef stew and pressing garlic into a lamb bone, but Luke only laughed.

'You must learn not to be so insular, Hester,' he said, one evening after dinner.

'But ... wine!'

'It's only cooking wine,' Anna expostulated.

'And it's delicious,' said Luke. 'Don't you like my wife's cooking, Hester?' He smiled at Anna, who flushed.

'Yes, indeed. All that wine, though. And the cream. It seems so sinful.'

'I cannot understand why you English despise food so,' said Anna. 'Good food is a gift of God. It seems ungracious, to me, not to make the best use of it.'

Later, when Hester had left the room, Luke said, 'I hope you don't think that Hester is criticizing the way you run the kitchen? I'm grateful that you've taken it over. All that standing about was not good for her.'

'Hester and I understand each other, I hope,' said Anna. 'This is her home after all, Monsieur Luc, and I try not to usurp her position.'

'Yet in some ways you're a stickler for convention, Anna.

"Monsieur Luc" sounds very formal to me.'

'Would it be proper for me to call you by your Christian name?' Anna felt a sort of pleased confusion.

'In private, certainly. We are married, after all.'

'Luke is a good name, I think,' said Anna shyly. 'Your brother's name would never have done for me. In France it is a girl's name!'

'I didn't realize until the wedding that you were Anna Charlotte.'

'My ancestors were Scottish. I was named after Anna Cardonnell who came to France in 1517 after the battle of Flodden. Charlotte is for Prince Charles Edward Stuart. My grandfather was with him in '45.'

'A Jacobite, to boot.' Luke was amused.

'You are talking to somebody who sat on his knee as a baby!' Anna shot him a mischievous look.

'I don't believe it!'

'It's true. I was born in Rome and christened by Cardinal Henry Stuart in his palace at Frascati. So you must be respectful.'

'But Bonnie Prince Charlie. I thought he ended his days drunk and gouty?'

'He did,' said Anna. 'I don't think I sat on his knee for very long! My father told me I bounced too much, so I had to be removed.'

Luke laughed. 'But what were your parents doing in Italy?'

'My father was often employed on diplomatic missions. He was very good at languages and spoke fluent Italian. My parents were there for a year or so.'

'But why did you not go to Italy when you left France? Surely the Cardinal would have been in a better position to have helped you than poor Broxhead?'

'England was closer. And besides, Papa had a little money here.'

'I, at any rate, cannot regret his decision,' said Luke with a smile.

Anna looked at him warily. Should he be saying such things? Should she be pleased to hear them?

Caroline Simpson, sitting at her breakfast table, took one horrified look at *The Morning Post* Court and Social columns. Luke married! Hester had said nothing of this to her. There must be some mistake. But there it was: *On July 29th at St Bride's Church, London, Luke Redbourn, Esquire, to Mademoiselle de Cardonnel. The bride was given in marriage by the Vicomte de Cardonnel.*

To say that Caroline was put out would be an understatement. She was furious. That Hester should keep it from her – no doubt with the sole intention of enjoying her discomfiture.

Caroline had always set her heart on things she was told she couldn't have. It had been part of Laurence's attraction that he was forbidden fruit. It was all Luke's fault for being so staid, the seventeen-year-old Caroline had decided. If he'd made sheep's eyes at other women, she would have fought tooth and nail to keep him. But where was the fun in being engaged to a man who would never give you a moment's unease?

She reached out, rang the bell, and said pettishly when her butler appeared, 'This coffee is cold, Ribble.'

'I'm sorry, madam.'

'I want some fresh. And tell Mary that the eggs were overcooked.'

Downstairs Ribble said, 'She's in one of her pets.'

'It'll be that announcement in the paper,' said Mary. 'Mr Redbourn's been and got married.'

'Serve her right,' said Ribble. 'You'd better watch it, Mary. Her upstairs will find something wrong with her luncheon, you mark my words.'

The widow's annoyance reverberated round her household

for several days. The two little girls, up in the nursery, were hushed and put on their best behaviour. Poor Mary, down in the kitchen, had her meals sent back and Mrs Simpson's lady's maid nearly gave in her notice. Fortunately, a few days later Caroline's temper found a more satisfactory outlet. For one of her morning visitors was Laurence Redbourn.

Caroline had not seen him since that last humiliating meeting when she'd expected him to marry her. Laurence had been very persuasive on the sofa and Caroline had allowed a number of deliciously alarming intimacies. The shock, therefore, was severe when he said, 'Marry you! Don't be foolish, Caroline. If I married every girl I played with I'd need a harem.' He'd laughed at her tear-struck face. Caroline demonstrably preferred himself and he'd paid Luke back for being the elder and his father's favourite.

Laurence had forgotten most of this when he came to pay his call. Caroline was a rich widow, that was all that concerned him. And, if she hadn't gone off, she could be quite a tempting proposition. A widow knew what was what. Once he'd got her into bed he didn't doubt she'd pay handsomely for him to keep quiet about it.

Caroline, however, had neither forgiven nor forgotten. She remembered very well the resentment Laurence always felt towards his brother. Doubtless he would not be too pleased about the marriage. Caroline had developed considerable needling skills towards those who displeased her. She intended to use them now.

'Mr Redbourn!' she exclaimed as he entered. 'How delightful of you to call.'

'Mrs Simpson!' Laurence bowed elegantly over her hand. 'My deepest condolences.' He cast a quick look around. Everything of the best. He mentally priced the furniture and the pictures. There was a pretty penny here.

'I was just thinking of your family,' said Caroline, indicating that he should be seated. 'The announcement, you know.'

'What announcement?'

'Oh! Did you not see it?' Caroline reached out one graceful arm and picked up the paper. 'Here, in *The Morning Post*.' She handed it to him.

Laurence read it. His face darkened. For a moment he looked so murderous that Caroline reached reassuringly for the bell.

'Married!'

'Yes. Isn't it delightful? French aristocracy, too! Your brother must be moving up in the world.' She looked at him innocently.

Laurence got up and began pacing up and down. Luke had actually married her! It was Luke who would get his hands on all that money! He'd pay him out for this. This time there would be no mistake. He spun round and caught a satisfied smirk on Caroline's face. 'You little bitch ...' he began.

Caroline rang the bell sharply. Ribble appeared. 'Show Mr Redbourn out,' she said, coldly. 'He will not be welcome here again.'

She waited until she heard the front door close behind him and then she rang the bell again. 'Do you know, Ribble,' she said, when her butler entered, 'I feel quite peckish. Tell Mary that I'd like some of her delicious veal and ham pie for luncheon.'

That afternoon Caroline wrote to Luke to congratulate him on his marriage. She begged, very prettily, that she might be introduced to his wife, who she was sure must be charming. So far it was a conventional, if somewhat effusive, letter. It was the postscript that was designed to alarm Luke and overcome any inclination to refuse her request. *Your brother called this morning. He was astonished and not best pleased by the news. His behaviour was despicable and I have forbidden him the house.*

This, Caroline calculated, would serve to make sure that she was indeed invited. She had heard rumours of Laurence being at odds with his family before, for her husband once said, 'I hear Redbourn has packed that rascally brother of his off to America. Just in time, if you ask me.' He had refused to enlarge on the topic saying it was not fit for her ears. Caroline was not worried about her ears and promptly cross-questioned her maid who could be relied on to know these things.

'Embezzlement, madam,' her maid had hissed.

Caroline couldn't help thinking that Luke would want to know more about her meeting with his brother and, naturally, as an old friend, she would tell him. The lure of forbidden fruit still beckoned.

She was duly invited to tea on Sunday afternoon.

Hester heard of the invitation with dismay. What was she to say to Anna? Should she tell her that Caroline had once been engaged to Luke? Surely it was up to Luke to tell her? When she had tried to broach the subject with him he had curtly dismissed her fears and she had not liked to persist. She vacillated for so long that in the end it was too late.

Anna disliked Caroline on sight. The widow, looking deliciously ethereal in a clinging black silk dress and with pretty jet drops in her ears, came in hands outstretched.

'Hester! My dear!' She kissed her affectionately. 'Luke!' Luke bowed. 'And this must be your wife. Charming, my dear Luke, charming!' She surveyed Anna through a raised lorgnette and let it drop with just a hint of dismissal.

Anna curtseyed rigidly. Who was this woman who called her husband by his Christian name and who dared to patronize her?

They sat down and Hester, flustered and apprehensive, rang the bell for tea. Caroline chattered on. 'Everything is just as it was!' she exclaimed. 'Ben, perhaps, is a trifle more portly. But you, Luke, I declare you're as handsome as ever you were.' She caught sight of Anna's face and trilled, 'You must forgive me, my dear Mrs Redbourn. I have known Luke and Hester for ever! Indeed, at one time....' She gave Luke an arch look and turned in pretty confusion to toy with her bracelet.

There was an awkward pause.

'Mrs Redbourn made the cakes,' said Hester, brightly. 'She is a famous cook.'

'Really?' Caroline's eyebrows arched delicately. 'How quaint.'

Normally, Anna would have been amused by such obvious malice and manipulation, but today she was powerless against it. Every playful look Caroline gave Luke, every reference to shared intimacy in the past, went through her like a knife. Jealousy had claimed her. And with it anger and despair. At last Anna recognized the cause of all her sense of dislocation and unease over the last few weeks.

She was in love with her own husband.

This Mrs Simpson was clearly indicating that she had once been very close to Luke – perhaps she had even hoped to marry him now that she was a widow? And Luke? After his marriage to her was annulled would he then wed this predatory woman? Anna was now acutely aware that she did not want a *mariage blanc* at all.

'I gather Laurence did not meet with your approval,' said Luke. He was furious with Caroline for her needling of Anna, furious with himself for not realizing that she would be up to her old tricks and, even more, for not telling Anna about his past engagement. He could see from her set little face that she had put the worst construction on his relationship with Caroline and he blamed himself.

'Laurence was quite abusive,' said Caroline with a pitiful sigh. 'I cannot imagine why he came to see me if it were only to insult me.' She peeped at Luke, expecting a compliment.

It was Hester who said, 'Laurence would be after your money, Caroline. Make no mistake about that.'

'And could it not be for my charms?' asked Caroline coquettishly, glancing up at Luke.

'Laurence is out for himself, first and foremost,' replied Luke. 'You, of all people, should know that, Mrs Simpson.'

Caroline saw that she had gone too far. She offered a small olive branch. 'He was very put out by your marriage. Quite violent in fact. I felt it only proper to warn you.'

'You are very good,' said Luke tonelessly.

Anna listened. She became aware of hidden shoals of meaning. Something was going on here. The Redbourns, whom she had been so sure of as trustworthy, now seemed dangerously deceptive.

Whenever Julia had been in love, whether with the footman or Signor Puglietti, it had always seemed to entail rather more agony and tears than pleasure. Anna had never been very sympathetic to her cousin. This afternoon, during the couple of hours that Caroline Simpson took tea with them, Anna felt she had passed through an emotion spectrum. There was pleasure and tenderness, certainly, in knowing how she felt about Luke, but there was also jealousy, rage and despair.

She mentally offered Julia an apology.

Chapter Nine

Laurence dressed with unusual care. His shoes were polished, his cravat impeccably tied in the Oriental mode and his linen was fresh and starched. Today he was going to collect £10,000 from Sir Robert and tonight he promised himself a night on the Town. He had taken the precaution of writing to Sir Robert and (with only a hint of coercion) suggested that it was time he was paid.

There was no excuse. A man's gaming debts must be honoured and Laurence had every intention of seeing that Sir Robert's cronies in White's were fully informed if he attempted to renege on his obligations. Sir Robert had several times confided that White's was a home from home for him, a place of escape. Sir Robert was too well bred to say 'from Lady Broxhead' but Laurence understood him well enough.

If no draft for £10,000 were forthcoming, then Sir Robert would shortly be finding himself ostracized in all the St James's clubs and coffee houses – Laurence intended to be very thorough about that. But he did not think such a step would be necessary; Laurence prided himself on knowing to a nicety the amount of pressure needed to produce results.

He picked up his cane and weighed it carefully in his hands. It looked an elegant trifle, an ebony shaft with a silver-mounted top, but the butt was weighted with lead and any ruffian in

Charles Street who thought he was some fop who had missed his way and an easy target would very soon find that he was mistaken. However, Laurence was not accosted. Word had got round; he was known to be quick on his feet and he carried a knife, which he had no hesitation in using.

He made his way down to Drury Lane and hailed a cab.

In Brook Street Sir Robert was waiting in the library. He, too, had been busy over the last few days and his mood was unusually sober. He had ordered his wife to remain upstairs during Redbourn's visit and such was his tone of voice that Lady Broxhead, having opened her mouth to expostulate, shut it again.

Laurence arrived, punctually, at eleven o'clock. Normally, only one footman, or even a maid, was at hand to open the door. Today, there were two footmen, both splendid specimens over six foot with powerful muscles. They bowed impassively as he entered, one relieved him of his hat and cane while the other conducted him into the library.

Laurence's eyes narrowed. This show of strength was not quite what he had been expecting and he was faintly disconcerted. Sir Robert rose to his feet and shook his hand cordially. 'Ah, Redbourn. Come in, come in.' He bustled about offering him a chair.

Laurence sat down. What was going on?

'Now, Redbourn. What can I do for you?'

'You know very well what you can do,' snapped his guest. 'Your niece has married my brother and, in default of our agreement, you owe me ten thousand pounds.' He pulled out the IOU and held it out to Sir Robert.

Sir Robert glanced at it. 'But my dear fellow, I have paid it! Naturally, I would never default on a debt of honour. I have the receipt somewhere.' He rummaged around on his desk.

'Ah, here it is! Thought it couldn't be far.' He handed it to Laurence and sat back, the picture of geniality.

Laurence took one look at the signature. 'Is this some kind of joke?' His voice was like ice. Sir Robert felt a prickle of unease. Thank God he had taken his nephew-in-law's advice and his two stalwart footmen and the bell were within easy reach.

'No, it's not a joke,' he answered with tolerable steadiness. 'The gentleman to whom I owed the money was the one whose name is on the card. As you know it is an offence to use somebody else's name to get money by fraudulent means. I could have you arrested.'

'I *am* Mr L. Redbourn,' snarled Laurence.

'But you are not the Mr L. Redbourn who lives at Seven Ludgate Street,' responded Sir Robert pleasantly. 'It is that Mr Redbourn whose name is on the IOU you are holding and it is he who gave me the receipt.'

'You never paid him a penny.' Laurence was now white with rage. A muscle twitched dangerously in his forehead.

'That is none of your business.'

'Isn't it? We'll see.' Laurence jumped up and was angrily pacing the room. £10,000 was slipping from his grasp. 'You very much mistake the matter if you think I'll let you get away with this. I fancy your friends at White's won't be so complaisant. Nor those who were with us in King Street where I won the money.'

'Try it and see,' was all Sir Robert replied. On Luke's advice he had overcome his reluctance to talk about his affairs and asked the opinions of Lord Zennor and Mr Torkington, when he met them in White's. Both were of the opinion that Redbourn's deception was disgraceful. The receipt Broxhead held was proof enough that he had honourably discharged his debt.

'Damn tuft-hunter, that Redbourn fellow,' remarked Lord Zennor. 'I know the type.'

'Like a leech,' added Torkington. 'You did right to come to us, Broxhead. He'd have been demanding membership next!'

'We'll put the word round.' Lord Zennor gave him a friendly clap on the shoulder. 'Come and have a drink.'

Sir Robert watched Laurence warily. He had stopped his pacing and was standing with his back to his host. Suddenly, he spun round and there was a knife in his hand.

'I ... don't ... like ... cheats!' With one bound he went for Sir Robert. There was a crash of a fallen chair. Sir Robert staggered back and shouted, 'Charles! George!' The two footmen rushed in.

Laurence had managed to slash Sir Robert's arm and now bounded onto the desk and raised his arm to strike again. His face was murderous. For one moment Charles and George were immobile with shock. Then Charles seized the poker and George went for Laurence's legs. Laurence leapt off the desk just as the poker crashed down. It caught him a glancing blow, not enough to fell him but, in the split second's hesitation, George seized Laurence's right arm and, after a short struggle, the knife dropped. Both men fell to the floor, wrestling furiously. Charles kicked the knife under the desk and went to help George.

'Put him in the cellar,' said Sir Robert, thickly, when eventually Laurence was overpowered. Blood was seeping from his arm and he sank heavily onto a chair.

Laurence suddenly sagged and as the footmen's grip loosened, recovered himself, twisted free and leapt for the door. He grabbed his hat and cane and in one savage movement smashed at the hall mirror with the lead-weighted butt. Another second and the front door slammed behind him. All that could be heard was the sound of tinkling glass.

'Vicious!' panted Charles. 'You all right, George?'

'Get Lady Broxhead,' whispered Sir Robert.

Anna found that being in love was a full-time occupation and one that she was powerless to control. All her pride in her Gallic good sense and the superiority of reason was suddenly shown to be quite inadequate to explain this new emotion. Everything about Luke enchanted her. It was as if he had imprinted himself on her very soul.

Anna remembered with astonishment how she'd listened politely to Julia's raptures on the footman's splendid physique or Signor Puglietti's expressive black eyes, whilst privately thinking that her cousin was being very silly.

The sudden realization that she herself had fallen in love and could have been quite as rhapsodic about a man's charms if there had been anybody to listen, was a shattering revelation. She had had no idea it was possible to feel so deeply or to be so shaken by the emotion. It was, she thought, like learning a whole new language. Luke's warm brown eyes, the crinkles round them when he smiled, the strength of his shoulders, all filled her with an alarming mixture of pleasure and excitement.

She now looked back with incredulity on that day when she had gone with him to Rundell and Bridge. She had been quite unconcerned about being alone with him and quite uncon-scious of his proximity. How could she have been so insensible? Now, she was acutely aware of his very presence in the room. She had to stop herself from making opportunities to touch him and when he smiled at her she felt her whole body respond.

But. There was a big but. He had offered her a marriage of convenience, one which was expressly to secure her safety and which had a definite end after her twenty-first birthday. He had not asked her for love. If she weren't married to him she could at least have set herself to please and hope that her feelings would be reciprocated. Any advances he made would be because he wanted to.

Now she could do nothing. The end had already been set. In October, after her birthday, he would seek an annulment. Then she would be bereft indeed. In the present circumstances to hope for a greater intimacy, knowing that it would be snatched away from her, was like a form of torture. Anna sighed. How could she have been so stupid as to agree to this marriage?

The night after Caroline's visit Anna tossed and turned, sleeping only fitfully. When she woke up she found that it had been raining in the night and the morning was overcast and grey. Normally Anna enjoyed this period of the day. She liked to sit up in bed and admire the Adam and Eve panels on the wardrobe. Today however Eve looked less confident than she usually did. Adam seemed more than half-inclined to repudiate the apple and the serpent was looking seriously worried.

She forced herself to think about Caroline's visit and, in doing so, some measure of common sense returned. Whilst it was true that Mrs Simpson was probably out to entrap Luke, it could not be said that he had responded to her advances. Of course, thought Anna, unable to stop torturing herself, it could be that he was constrained by the presence of his wife and sister, but a saner part of her didn't think so. All the same, there had once been some sort of understanding between Luke and Mrs Simpson, she was sure. She wondered whether she dare approach Hester on the subject.

She was still agonizing over this the following morning when she was sitting outside on a kitchen chair, shelling peas. A rush basket for the pods was on a small footstool and a saucepan for the peas was on the ground. There was a pile of peas in her apron.

A shadow fell over her.

'I won't be long, Emmy.'

'It's not Emmy.'

'L ... Luke!' Anna clutched at her apron.

'I'm sorry I startled you.' Luke removed the rush basket and sat down. 'I wanted to talk to you.'

'Oh?' Anna's fingers stripped the pods with sudden energy.

'Yes, about Mrs Simpson. I am sorry you were subjected to her impertinence.'

'I was obviously *de trop*,' said Anna, as neutrally as she could.

'No, dear Anna,' said Luke, reaching out and taking her hand. Peas scattered. 'It was Mrs Simpson who was unwanted, never you.'

Rubbing his thumb gently over the back of her hand, Luke then told her of his youthful engagement to Caroline and its ending. 'My father and Hester were never happy about my betrothal,' he finished. 'At the time I thought they were prejudiced against her. I was eight years older than Caroline and imagined, like a greenhorn, that she would change when we were married. Responsibility would settle her, I thought.' He gave a rueful laugh. 'But, of course, Father and Hester were right. We were really quite unsuited.'

'She's very pretty,' observed Anna, trying to ignore what Luke holding her hand was doing to her pulse rate.

'If you like those sort of looks,' said Luke. 'My taste now runs to something very different.' He looked at her as he spoke.

Anna pulled her hand away in confusion. Did he mean ...? Could he be saying that ...? All of a sudden she couldn't cope with it all. Her emotions had been turned topsy-turvy by the revelations following Caroline's visit. She didn't dare trust what she hoped he was saying. It might so easily be the product of her own wishes.

Luke sighed. 'I just wanted you to know.' He stood up. 'I shan't be in to luncheon. I have to go down to the warehouse.'

Anna, miserably aware of her cowardice, bent her head over the peas.

The house in Ludgate Street did not learn of the attack on Sir Robert until the following day when Luke received a letter from him written in a shaky hand. Out of consideration for his niece, he wrote, he was in two minds whether or not to press charges. He would be glad to discuss it with them. He ended with a formal invitation to dinner. Lady Broxhead joined him in extending their good wishes.

It seemed that there was to be a reconciliation.

Anna made a face. 'The last time I saw Aunt Susan she said I was a viper's brood, or perhaps it was the Devil's spawn. Anyway, something of the sort.'

'Perhaps I should reassure her that your price is above rubies,' said Luke.

'Oh, I don't think she'd care for that at all! That would give her a very poor opinion of your understanding.'

Luke laughed.

'I'd better help you with the new underskirt to your rose-pink dress, Anna,' said Hester practically. 'When is this dinner, Luke?'

Luke scanned the letter. 'Wednesday, August 19.'

'I shall be out, too,' said Hester. 'Minerva has invited me to go with her to Mr de Clifford's Recitations.' She saw Luke and Anna looking blank and added, ' "Remarks and Specimens shewing and inculcating the propriety of the just delivery of written language" – at least so it says in *The Times* here!'

'Shall you understand it, Hester?' asked Luke smiling.

'Probably not.' Hester was unperturbed. 'But Minerva does enjoy having somebody with whom to discuss things, so I shall have to do my best.'

Anna picked up the paper. 'Fortunately, it will be "diversified or relaxed by some excellent vocal music"!' she said mischievously. 'I hope you don't fall quite asleep!'

The three of them had discussed the question of pressing charges against Laurence without coming to any firm conclusion. Hester had been very tearful and begged for one more chance. There was good in Laurence somewhere, she knew. She remembered, fondly, how he had sent her the fine beaver wrap from America. Surely, somehow, it was possible to reach his heart and lead him away from his evil ways?

Luke was less sanguine. Laurence had already been offered

several fresh starts and had taken none of them. This time he hadn't stopped at fraud; he now included violence. Sooner or later somebody would be seriously hurt, if not killed – and he did not want a relative of his to end on the scaffold.

Anna tried to keep out of it. Laurence was not her brother. Personally, she thought he was quite obnoxious; but she perfectly understood how difficult a decision it must be for the Redbourns. All she was prepared to say, when pressed by Luke was, 'I will support whatever you decide. The only thing I ask is that you do not concern yourselves about my name being mentioned in court. I cannot say I like it, but, if you decide that justice must take its course for the sake of others who might be harmed, then I shall, of course, do my duty as a citizen.'

The Broxhead invitation was duly accepted and on Wednesday evening Anna and Luke set out for Brook Street. Privately, Anna thought Luke looked very distinguished in his dark-green evening coat, buff knee breeches and the correct evening pumps. Anna wore the newly trimmed pink silk. It was the first time since leaving Brook Street that Anna had seen either her uncle or her aunt and she was feeling nervous. She was also acutely aware of the proximity of her husband. She knew he was not as handsome as his brother, but she was left in no doubt as to which she found the more attractive: his nearness was having an alarming effect on her pulse.

'I still don't know what to say to Sir Robert,' said Luke, when they were in the cab. 'Poor Hester is so distressed.'

'Ultimately it must be Sir Robert's decision.' Anna was grateful for the neutral topic.

'It could be a hanging matter, though,' worried Luke. 'Or at least transportation. The Redbourn name would be disgraced.'

Anna's private view was that as Laurence had kidnapped her and tried to have her husband shot, it could only serve him right if he found himself in Botany Bay. Remembering her own mother who had died in prison for no crime at all, Anna had very little sympathy to waste on Laurence.

'During the Terror the de Cardonnel name was proscribed and our property confiscated,' observed Anna. 'Did that really make us all villains?'

'You think Sir Robert should go ahead, don't you?' Luke turned to look at her. Anna's face was in shadow.

Anna sighed. 'Luke,' she said gently, 'I understand how difficult it all is. I have said that I will support whatever you decide. All I wanted to say was that one disgraced member of the family does not sully the whole name. You and Hester will be respected and valued wherever you are known, I am sure.'

'Thank you. But it is your name too, Anna, while you are married to me.'

'Yes,' said Anna soberly. 'I know that. I cannot see that I have anything to be ashamed of in being Mrs Luke Redbourn.'

'You mean that?' Luke tried to scan her face.

'Yes. Oh, we've arrived.' Anna's voice held a mixture of relief and disappointment. Perhaps it was just as well, she thought. The darkness of the cab had engendered a dangerous mood of giving confidences: she wasn't sure how safe it was to do so.

As Luke paid off the cab Charles flung open the front door. Graciousness was obviously to be the order of the day. Both Sir Robert and Lady Broxhead were in the hall to greet them. Lady Broxhead surged forward with determined affability.

'My dear Mrs Redbourn.' She offered a cheek to Anna. 'Mr Redbourn.' She extended two fingers.

Sir Robert was more natural. His right arm was in a sling, but otherwise he looked fit and well. 'Anna, you baggage.' He kissed her on both cheeks and held her away from him. 'Marriage agrees with you, eh?' He nudged Luke in the ribs. 'I see you know what's what, eh, Redbourn, you dog!'

Luke smiled faintly. 'How are you, Sir Robert? I'm pleased to see that you are no worse.' He indicated the arm.

'Pooh! Just a scratch. Nothing serious.' He lowered his voice.

'You were right to warn me, dear boy. As it turned out I was fortunate to have m'footmen within call.' He glanced up to where the hall mirror used to hang. It had been beyond repair and had now been removed. A large, rather dreary picture of Sir Robert's grandfather with a somewhat dispirited dog by his side hung in its place.

'And now,' said Lady Broxhead majestically, leading the way up the stairs to the drawing-room, 'we have a surprise for you, Mrs Redbourn.' She opened the door.

'Julia!' cried Anna joyfully. 'And Mr Wellesborough too! How wonderful to see you.' She embraced her cousin affectionately and introduced Luke.

Julia, she saw with a touch of envy, was looking blooming. She seemed quite reconciled to Mr Wellesborough. He was her 'dear Wellesborough' on every occasion. She couldn't talk fast enough: their honeymoon, their new house: it was all perfect.

Julia, after an arch look at her husband, put up her fan and whispered to Anna, 'Marriage was much more fun than I expected! Mama never mentioned that to me!' She giggled. Julia, thought Anna, had plainly inherited Sir Robert's robust enjoyment of life rather than her mother's more prudish disposition.

Some minutes were spent in exchanging courtesies and then the butler entered to announce that dinner was served. 'As we are just a family party, I do not propose to stand on ceremony,' said Lady Broxhead, as they moved through to the dining-room. 'Mr Wellesborough, will you please sit here on my right? Mr Redbourn?' She indicated the other side. Julia caught Luke's eye and grinned.

Anna, at the other end, was looking furious.

'Now don't take on so,' said Sir Robert, patting her hand. 'You know what your Aunt Susan is like. She just wants to put your husband through his paces.'

'My husband is not a horse!' objected Anna.

'He's a sensible chap. He'll have her measure. You'll see.'

This time Sir Robert had done his homework. He had informed his wife that Luke Redbourn was a well respected up-and-coming businessman, easily worth a thousand a year and very likely more. Anna had done well for herself. Lady Broxhead, naturally, gave the first ten minutes to Mr Wellesborough before turning her attention to Luke. Quite correctly, he was talking to Julia on his left, but kept an eye open for Lady Broxhead to claim his attention. When she did, he gave Julia an apologetic smile and turned towards his hostess.

Lady Broxhead could not fault his company manners. Somewhat to her chagrin he behaved as she would have expected a gentleman to behave. His manners were unaffected and he talked like a sensible man. One must move with the times, after all. Perhaps she could persuade Mr Redbourn to support one of her charities? Maybe even sit on the board? A wealthy businessman was by no means to be despised.

Later, over port, the gentlemen discussed the vexed question of Laurence. Sir Robert had obviously explained matters to Mr Wellesborough, who was surprisingly supportive. An uncle of his had gone to the bad – he'd been caught free-trading – and excuses were made for him. The uncle had promptly gone on to wrecking. Mr Wellesborough didn't see that forgiving crime did a particle of good. He coughed, 'Understandable, though, that you want your name kept out of it, Redbourn.'

Luke shrugged. 'I'm inclined to agree with you. When my brother was first caught embezzling, his then employer agreed not to prosecute out of respect for my father. I'm not saying he was wrong – the shock of it certainly hastened my father's death in any case – but I'm convinced that our leniency meant that my brother felt he could return to England after I had packed him off to America. After all, if we had forgiven him once, why not again?'

'Several people have already been hurt, too,' said Sir Robert.

'You, Redbourn, my niece and myself.' And pretty Helen Clarkson, he thought.

'I would have said enough is enough,' said Mr Wellesborough. 'Though, of course, it's none of my business.'

'It could be a hanging matter,' said Sir Robert soberly. His arm was hurting him, but all the same, he was not sure he wanted a man's death on his conscience.

'Why don't you go ahead, sir, and Redbourn here can write to warn his brother. If the fellow has any sense he'll slip out of the country,' said Mr Wellesborough. Presumably, he thought, neither Redbourn nor his father-in-law would care too much, so long as Laurence Redbourn were out of the way.

'It seems a pity to foist him on the Americans again,' said Luke. He had had business dealings with some Americans and liked their fresh openness.

'It's arranged, then?' said Sir Robert, after some more discussion. 'Very well. Shall we join the ladies?'

Peggy watched Helen critically. They were up in Helen's room and Helen was practicing *pliés*, one hand on the back of a chair. She was as graceful as ever she was, thought Peggy, but somehow she had lost her former suppleness. Perhaps it would return eventually.

'What do you think, Peg?' Peggy always ventured on the side of caution, she knew. Helen needed an honest assessment of her chances of getting back into the chorus. She was well aware that she was not as fit as she should be, but money was beginning to run short again. She had been as careful as she could with the windfall from Luke, but she was still going to have to find some paid work within the next two weeks.

'You look older,' said Peggy at last.

Helen glanced at her reflection in the mirror. The bruising on her face had faded away and her split lip was now healed, but she had taken a battering and no longer had the resilience of youth. 'I have improved, though, haven't I?' she asked hopefully.

Peggy sat down on the bed. 'It's wonderful how well you've done, Helen, and you've been ever so good about exercising. But whether Mr Kemble will....'

'He must,' said Helen desperately. 'I don't know what ...'

There was a knock at the door and the landlady entered. 'It's Sir Robert Broxhead again, Miss Clarkson!' she whispered in a state of high excitement. 'I've put him in the small parlour.'

Helen exchanged a swift glance with Peggy. 'Thank you. Pray tell him I shall be down directly.'

The moment the door closed, Peggy said, 'That's your best chance, Helen. You'd never have to do no more *pliés* again.' She went to the cupboard and flung it open. 'Here, put this on. You can't leave nothing to chance.' She took out a low-cut dress in cerulean blue. 'You always looked good in this. Quick. Can't keep a gentleman waiting!'

'You will stay till I come back?' Helen hastily began to strip off her old dress.

'Wouldn't miss it for the world.'

Sir Robert was standing by the fireplace gazing abstractedly at a pair of china dogs on the mantelpiece when Helen entered. He looked up and Helen was gratified to see his jaw drop. As a widow in her blacks she had looked respectable and demure. Last time they had met she had had a black eye and was reclining on a sofa, bundled up in a shawl. Now, in a clinging dress tantalizingly cut to reveal her full breasts she looked, to Sir Robert's appreciative eye, most delectable.

'Miss Clarkson.' He bowed over her hand. 'Delighted to see you looking so much better.' Egad, and a luscious armful for any man!

'Thank you, Sir Robert – and also for the delicious fruit you sent me. I didn't write in case it might be awkward for you.' Tactful too, approved Sir Robert. Helen continued, 'I'm certainly feeling fitter. I have been upstairs doing my exercises.' She sketched him a graceful curtsey and tried to ignore the twinge in her back.

'Going back to work, eh?'

Helen sighed. 'I have no choice, Sir Robert – if Mr Kemble will have me. But what about you? I see you have hurt your arm.'

Sir Robert gave her a brief summary of his own experiences and Helen, recognizing her cue, provided a chorus of suitable exclamations on his bravery and her horror.

'He might have killed you!'

'Pooh! Just called my footmen. Two big strong fellows, y'know.'

'You are making light of it, I am sure,' said Helen admiringly. 'You must have been very brave to face him when he had a knife. I'm sorry he got away.' Helen did not like the idea of Laurence still being loose in London. 'But you're out of debt, that must be the main thing.'

'I've given up gambling,' announced Sir Robert. 'Not even for chicken-stakes. Too risky.'

'That's hard,' said Helen sympathetically. Practically all the clubs, coffee houses and taverns revolved around gambling in some form or other. 'You will miss it, I know.'

'That's kind of you, m'dear,' said Sir Robert gratefully. His wife had simply sniffed and said 'About time too'. 'But there's no help for it. I've known for some time that I don't really have the head for it. I don't mind admitting that the last few weeks in Redbourn's clutches have been damnable.'

'Anybody who gets caught up in one of Laurence's plots goes through hell,' agreed Helen with feeling.

Sir Robert had been standing up, propped against the mantelpiece. He now moved and sat down beside Helen on the sofa. He took hold of her chin and turned her to face him. 'I have a different diversion in mind,' he told her. 'I'm not a

191

young chap any more, Helen, but, if you're interested, we might do a deal?'

Helen smiled. 'What are your terms, Sir Robert?'

'No point in beating about the bush,' said Sir Robert bluntly. 'I never could make pretty speeches. You come to bed with me and I look after you. That's about the sum of it. What d'you say, eh?'

Luke wrote to Laurence and, although there was no reply, there were no more attacks. Walter reported that he had left his rooms in Charles Street. The Redbourns devoutly hoped that Laurence had had the sense to leave the country. The end of August came and went and they were into September. It was now about a month until Anna's birthday. The days had become perceptibly shorter and there was a faint chill in the evening air.

A new element entered Anna's life in Ludgate Street. One lunchtime Luke came up with a letter in his hand.

'Anna, could you translate this for me, please?'

Anna scanned it. 'Yes, of course. I didn't realize you did business with France. I thought there was a blockade on?'

'There is,' Luke grinned. 'Fortunately, it's not very efficient. This letter's from Luxembourg. Many of them resent the French occupation of their country and are happy to circumvent the blockade if they can get away with it.'

'I'll do you a proper copy,' said Anna. 'Though there are a number of technical terms here I'm not sure about.'

'Thank you.'

'I shall enjoy doing it,' said Anna sincerely. If she were a man, she thought, she would probably have tried to make a living doing this. She knew she wrote an elegant sentence and she was fluent in both languages. It was good to be able to exercise her brain.

In due course Anna was asked to translate Luke's reply into

French. 'I've always liked languages,' Anna told him, when she handed him the translation. 'Aunt Susan was very put out when Julia and I started singing lessons with Signor Puglietti and I insisted on learning Italian! I wish I still had lessons. I hated having to stop.'

'Really, Anna?' Luke looked thoughtful. 'How good were you? Your Italian, I mean.'

'Quite good enough to translate business letters into English.'

'And vice versa?'

'Probably, though I'd have to take up lessons again, I think.' She paused and looked at him hopefully. 'Oh, Luke! Would it be possible? I won't tease you, but if it would be of any use to you in business, please let me.'

'Of course you may have your Italian lessons, Anna. I had no idea that was how you felt. Do you have Signor Puglietti's address?'

'Thank you!' Anna went towards him, hesitated, then touched his arm briefly.

'I see it doesn't merit a kiss,' Luke observed, half-playfully, half-ironically. 'Never mind. Give me Signor Puglietti's address and I'll see what I can do.' He left the room.

Anna looked at the closed door with hopeless longing. Why was she such a coward? She knew the answer, though. She was afraid of being rejected and all the awkwardness that would ensue.

'Translating business letters,' said Hester doubtfully that evening after dinner, when she heard of Anna's new activity. 'Should a lady be doing such things? Not that I wish to dictate to you, dear Anna.'

Anna put up her chin. 'I am sure your friend Miss Leatherbarrow would approve of my work,' she observed. 'Why may a woman not translate business letters, if her talents lie in that direction?'

'She's got you there, Hester,' said Luke amused. 'So you agree with our Athene of Islington, do you, Anna?'

'I like exercising my brain,' said Anna shortly. 'That was something Aunt Susan could never understand. To be able to warble an Italian song prettily was acceptable. To want to learn Italian seriously was not.' She stopped and stared rather sadly in front of her. 'Papa would have understood me, though. He spoke five languages. I suppose I have inherited the facility from him.'

'I am very grateful for your help,' said Luke. 'It's certainly good for business if Redbourn and Sons can correspond in French. If we can do so in Italian, that's even better.'

'But Luke! You cannot employ Anna as a clerk!' cried Hester, scandalized.

'I think he's wonderful,' said Anna slightly breathlessly. She looked at Luke and managed a shy smile.

Anna had met Minerva Leatherbarrow briefly once and been rather taken with her, finding her refreshingly lacking in social hypocrisy. Her occasional gaucheness she ignored and she was reluctantly impressed by her staunch support for women's rights. Minerva's parents were plainly somewhat alarmed by their forceful daughter, but there was no doubt that her strong personality had contributed to the success of their little school for young ladies. Minerva was plainly a 'character'. Recalcitrant daughters quailed under Miss Leatherbarrow's eagle eye. They learned their lessons and did as they were told. She was a bit of a blue-stocking, of course, worried many an anxious Mama, but they consoled themselves with the thought that any unladylike knowledge would soon brush off Laura or Jane as soon as they came out for the season.

Even empty-headed girls like Caroline had done surprisingly well at the Leatherbarrows' school. Caroline had never had two thoughts to rub together, but her writing was neat and her spelling perfectly adequate and her father was well content to pay thirty pounds a year for that. He was sure that she would soon forget any nonsense about Political Economy.

Anna went with Hester to visit the Leatherbarrows in their cottage in Islington. Apart from going to Ramsgate with Julia shortly after her father's death, Anna had rarely been out of London and she much enjoyed the open fields and hills and the view back down over the City. The Leatherbarrows' cottage stood in a couple of acres of orchard and, when they arrived, a number of girls were running around playing tag, their white dresses and coloured sashes fluttering in the breeze.

'Were you at school here too, Hester?' asked Anna.

'Yes, I stayed here during the week and went home at weekends. I loved it here.' Hester looked round affectionately at the gnarled apple trees. 'They were very good to me after my accident.'

'Poor Hester.'

'It was my own fault,' said Hester with determined cheerfulness. 'I used to enjoy sliding down the banisters at home – something I was strictly forbidden to do. I fell. You must have seen the new bit of banister on the first landing. I was fortunate not to be killed.'

'I have seen it, yes.' How awful, thought Anna, to have to live with a constant reminder of your youthful high spirits and its tragic aftermath.

'Poor mother,' said Hester sadly. 'She found a lame daughter very difficult to cope with. Not marriageable any more, you see.'

'I don't see that.' Anna tried not to sound indignant. What she had heard of Mrs Redbourn had not led her to feel much sympathy for her. Critical of Hester where she should have offered support; indulgent towards Laurence where she should have given a firm guidance, Mrs Redbourn frankly sounded like a foolish woman. Luke hardly ever mentioned his mother, except once to say that he knew he was not as good-looking as his brother, for his mother had often told him so.

'I never much fancied marriage anyway,' said Hester smiling. 'You will think it odd, I daresay. I've often thought I should like to help Minerva here, with this school.'

Minerva now came down the orchard path to greet them. 'Here you are. Splendid! Mother's just put on the kettle.' She kissed Hester and wrung Anna's hand. She then turned heel and strode back up the path to the house.

Miss Leatherbarrow, Anna noted, ran things as she wished. Old Mrs Leatherbarrow, having done the honours at tea, after a curt nod from her daughter, left the three women to themselves. They sat in a small room which Minerva had evidently appropriated for her own use. There were a number of books, some of which, Tom Paine's *The Rights of Man*, for example, and an English translation of Voltaire's *Lettres Philosophiques*, indicated where Miss Leatherbarrow's sympathies lay.

There were no ornaments – Minerva thinking them fripperies – but there were some robust satirical prints on the wall, Hogarths mainly. Hester averted her gaze, but Anna would have liked a closer look. It seemed an unlikely friendship, Anna thought, but perhaps it was the attraction of opposites. Minerva was bold where Hester was timid, and possibly Hester's affectionate nature was one of the few allowed through Miss Leatherbarrow's somewhat prickly exterior.

'So, Mrs Redbourn, I hear you met the inconsolable widow.' Plainly Miss Leatherbarrow did not believe in beating about the bush.

'I have met the widow,' said Anna dryly.

'Ha!' Minerva gave a bark of laughter. 'A proper little madam, isn't she? I dare swear she didn't take to you.'

'Minerva!' Hester was moved to expostulate. 'Mind what you say! You make it sound almost insulting. Take no notice, Anna, she always goes on like this.'

Anna laughed. 'But Hester, we have discussed this. We agreed that Mrs Simpson was being deliberately malicious. It is plain that Miss Leatherbarrow is of the same mind.'

'Luke was foolishly besotted once,' stated Minerva, thinking poorly of male taste. 'I've never seen a man so moonstruck. He seemed to lose all common sense.'

Anna felt her stomach knot. I do not want to hear this, she thought: that Luke had once been wildly, passionately in love with Caroline Simpson.

'He's over it now,' said Hester. 'After she went home he said that he was glad to have seen her once more, but would be quite happy never to see her again.'

'So I should hope,' sniffed Minerva. 'If a man can't pull himself together after seven years then he deserves everything he gets. However, as he's married our friend here, presumably he's come to his senses.'

'He's very fond of Anna, certainly,' said Hester.

Fond! thought Anna. Yes, possibly. Unfortunately, that was no longer enough for her. Not nearly enough.

Anna and Hester did not leave Islington until six o'clock. Minerva had commandeered the parson's gig to take them home and the clerk, a thin, dry little man, who looked somewhat nervous at being asked to drive two ladies, duly arrived at the cottage gate. Anna and Hester, after thanking Minerva, climbed in.

Gigs were only built for two people but, as both ladies and the driver were thin, they managed well enough. The evening was pleasantly cool and Anna enjoyed the view, with the great dome of St Paul's and all the City spires rising above the roofscape. The last time she'd noticed it, she remembered, was from the roof above Laurence's attic room.

'It's pleasant to get out of London.'

'Yes, I know. I used to feel it every Monday when I came to school, even in winter. The air is so crisp and clean.'

'And so peaceful,' added Anna. They were passing a flock of sheep on the green. 'All this so close to the City.'

'What's for dinner?' asked Hester. 'All this country air has made me hungry.'

'Gigot à la Bretonne, if Emmy has remembered to put it on. I left her with firm instructions. I even wrote them down, but you know what her reading's like.'

The gig turned into Ludgate Street and drew up. The ladies descended and thanked the clerk, who touched his hat to them and turned the horse round.

'The shutters aren't up yet,' said Hester puzzled.

'The front door isn't locked,' said Anna. They looked at each other alarmed. Anna pushed the door open. 'Walter! Emmy!' There was no answer. Hester went through to the kitchen.

Anna opened the door to the office and gasped. The room had been ransacked. Luke's desk had had all its drawers pulled out. The chairs were broken, the clerks' stools overturned. Worst of all the strong-box, which always sat in one corner of the room, had been hacked open. Splinters of wood were everywhere. Anna was just about to call Hester when she heard a groan.

Luke, trussed up, blindfolded, and with a piece of rag twisted cruelly tight over his mouth, was lying motionless behind the desk. Anna's heart seemed to stop in sheer horror. Luke groaned again.

She looked swiftly round. There, on the floor, were the office scissors. Grabbing them, she knelt down by Luke and cut gently at the blindfold. He seemed only half-conscious, for his eyes, after fluttering open for a moment, shut again. Anna cut the gag.

Working feverishly Anna then cut the ropes. Laurence, for

who else could it have been, had done a thorough job. The ropes had bitten into Luke's ankles and wrists, leaving great weals. Eventually the last rope fell away.

There was a bowl of flowers on the table. Anna threw the flowers on the floor and brought the bowl to Luke. She dipped the rag into the water and gently cleaned his face. Luke's eyes flickered open.

'Anna?'

'Hush, it's all right.' Tears of relief were pouring down Anna's face. 'Oh, Luke, I thought you were dead!' She dropped the rag, put both arms gently round him and held him close. At that moment she didn't care if Luke knew how she felt. All she wanted to do was to hold him and to know that he was alive.

Luke rested his head wearily on her shoulder. His hands came up to stroke her hair. There was silence.

'Anna!' There was an exclamation from the doorway as Hester took in the damage.

Anna raised her head. 'There has been a break-in,' she said unnecessarily. 'Luke has been hurt, though not, I think, badly. Where are Emmy and Walter?'

'Poor Emmy was locked in the coal-hole,' said Hester. 'She's having hysterics in the kitchen. I don't know where Walter is.'

'Walter's out on business,' said Luke faintly. 'Anna, sweetheart, get me some brandy.'

'I'll get it.' Hester left the room.

Luke slowly sat up, still holding on to Anna. He looked round the room, taking in all the damage, the broken chairs, the scattered papers. 'The strong-box,' he said at last.

'I know,' said Anna. 'But you're safe. That's all that matters.'

'No,' said Luke more forcefully, struggling to rise. 'There were important business documents in there. If I don't get them back I'm ruined!'

Chapter Ten

Anna and Hester did what they could for Luke's bruises and cuts. Fortunately, these were not serious. Luke remembered nothing of what had happened. One moment he was working at his desk, the next he had been overpowered, blindfolded, a gag stuffed in his mouth and his hands and feet bound. 'I heard nothing!' he kept saying, as if by repeating it he might remember more. 'God knows how he got in.'

'The door was unlocked when we returned,' said Hester. 'Oh, Luke, are you sure it was Laurence?' Hester didn't think she could bear it. She had somehow managed to blot out the full significance of Laurence's attacks when they were outside the home. After all, she had never met Sir Robert, and had not seen Anna after her flight over the rooftops. The Knightsbridge attack on Luke could have been footpads.

Neither Anna nor Luke replied.

Hester burst into tears. 'Oh, what went wrong?' she wailed. 'Laurence had everything!'

'Hester,' said Anna gently, 'why don't you see to Emmy? She's still very shaken. I believe a sleeping draught and bed would be the best thing for her.' Hester left the room. Anna turned to Luke. 'There's not much to eat – poor Emmy was bundled off to the coal-hole before she could prepare dinner, but I can heat up some potage if you could manage that.'

Gradually, some semblance of normality returned. Hester went to bed. Luke and Anna managed to drink a few spoonfuls of soup though neither of them felt hungry.

'Now, please,' said Anna firmly. 'Explain the position to me. What is it that Laurence has taken?'

Luke sighed. 'The strong-box contained about a hundred and fifty pounds in cash. That's gone, naturally. But far more serious are the bonds and credit notes.'

'What, exactly, are they?'

'They are either payments due to me – like IOUs, if you like, or else money in the form of bonds. Insurance bonds, for example.'

'Are they very valuable?'

Luke rubbed his head wearily. 'Oh yes. You might say my professional integrity rests on them. For instance, I have a bond from a gentleman who doesn't want it to be known that he is trading in Shanghai.'

'Why not?'

'Because his brother has an opium concession there and my client is, in fact, trading against his brother's interests.'

'It all sounds very complicated.'

'It is complicated. You'd be surprised how many personal secrets are wrapped up in business.'

'But could Laurence use these bonds and credit notes?'

Luke considered. 'It would be difficult to get money from them directly. In theory he could get money from the credit notes, but he must know that I would alert the banks. His best bet would be to blackmail me – that would save him the trouble of working out who owed what. Or, if he were prepared to do his homework, he could blackmail my opium trader, say, and threaten to tell his brother. Either way, Laurence stands to gain.'

Anna's eyes widened. 'What can you do?'

'Find Laurence before he does any damage,' said Luke flippantly.

That, of course, was easier said than done. It had only been by chance, in the form of Helen Clarkson's letter, that had let Luke know Laurence's address before. Walter had reported that Laurence had moved. Luke could not expect such luck a second time.

'Bow Street?' queried Anna.

'Hopeless incompetents. However, I shall inform them, of course. It may be that they are more efficient where large sums of money are involved.'

'Shall you tell your clients?'

Luke grimaced. 'Not if I can help it. Once I do that I really am ruined. The word'll get round.'

'Does Laurence know that? I mean, is he out to ruin you, do you think? Or does he just want money?'

'It would pay him to have me solvent. He could then milk me for money whenever he liked. And I must be grateful he didn't kill me. I suppose he must have some faint family feeling after all.'

'So it is in his interest to keep his mouth shut with regard to your clients?' persisted Anna.

'For the moment, yes.' Luke looked slightly more hopeful. Then he said soberly, 'You'll be well out of this mess after your birthday, Anna.'

'Thank you,' said Anna, hurt. Was that all Luke thought of her? Somebody who ran away at the first hint of a problem, who would desert her friends? She bit her lip to hold back the tears and tried to swallow the lump in her throat.

Luke spent the next day closeted with Walter and the two clerks trying to assess the damage. Several officials from Bow Street came round and made notes. Luke had been right: some of the names on the bonds were important and the officers of the law were quite as anxious to get their hands on Laurence as Luke could wish.

Banks were discreetly alerted. Word was put round various

brothels and gambling houses that Laurence Redbourn was wanted for questioning by Bow Street and a reward was offered.

Forty-eight hours later, the blackmail letter came. Laurence was willing to return the bond and credit notes in return for £20,000. Luke was to signal his acceptance through an advertisement in *The Times*.

'£20,000!' gasped Hester.

'I doubt whether I can raise such a sum,' said Luke. He was still pale from the attack and there were rings under his eyes from sleepless nights.

'Could you negotiate?' asked Anna. She, too, was tense and drawn.

'I shall have to try.'

The following morning Anna received a letter from Madame Bonnieux. Could she please visit? Tante Marie did not explain further and Anna was worried. Was she all right? She had not yet had time to tell Marie about the attack. Had Laurence, God forbid, involved her as well in his nasty games? Anna did not want to worry Luke or Hester further, so she simply said that she felt she must visit her aunt and, if it were not inconvenient, she would go that morning.

'Of course,' said Luke absently. 'Walter will get you a cab.'

Anna arrived to a frenzied storm of barking from Hercule, who leapt up and tried to lick her face the moment she stepped through the door. Marie, who had been in the kitchen, bustled through, arms outstretched.

'Anna, *petite*, how good of you to come so promptly!'

Anna hugged her gratefully and then took off her cloak and bonnet and hung them up. She looked round. Everything was the same. Imperceptibly she began to relax. Here she was loved and welcomed. Hester and Luke had been very kind, but she couldn't forget that conversation with Luke in Tante Marie's garden: he had made it very clear that it was only a temporary marriage.

'But you don't look well!' exclaimed Marie, when they were sitting down in the kitchen over the inevitable cup of coffee.

Anna explained about the break-in. Marie was as horrified as Anna could wish.

'Poor Monsieur Redbourn!' she exclaimed. 'Such a good man, too. It's always those who suffer while the wicked flourish.'

'Like the green bay tree,' added Anna.

'Green bay tree?' Marie looked out of the kitchen window in a puzzled way to where her own bay tree sat in its pot. It was certainly flourishing.

Anna laughed. 'The English have a habit of quoting from the Bible, at least, I think it's the Bible. It was one of Aunt Susan's favourites.'

As they exchanged news Marie looked at Anna. She had not seen much of her since the wedding and she was worried at the change she saw in her. Of course, it could be worry over Laurence, but Marie had an idea that it went deeper than that. Anna had insisted that Luke and Hester were kindness itself, but something was wrong. Anna's usually candid gaze held shadows that had not been there before.

'A packet arrived for you, Anna. That is why I wrote. It came yesterday by special messenger. A foreign gentleman.' She rose as she spoke and went to a small box where she kept odds and ends and took out a small packet, wrapped in brown paper and sealed with sealing wax. It was addressed to *La Donna Anna de Cardonnel*.

'The cabochon emerald?' said Anna. 'It seems too small. Pass me the knife, please, Tante Marie.' Deftly she cut the string and broke open the seal.

Inside was a letter and a small leather box. The letter was in Italian. Anna put it to one side and opened the box. Inside were ten small buttons, of the sort that had once belonged to a waistcoat of the previous century.

'Buttons!' said Marie incredulously.

'But aren't they pretty!' exclaimed Anna. She picked one up and examined it closely. They were in a deep blue and gold cloisonné in the shape of a flower and with a tiny seed pearl in the centre.

'But who are they from?'

Anna picked up the discarded letter. 'Good Heavens!' She read it again. 'How extraordinary. This is from Monsignor Angelo Cesarini, Bishop of Milevi, and executor of the will of his late Majesty, his Eminence Henry Stuart, Cardinal York.'

'I never knew he had died,' put in Marie. 'Mind you, he must have been an old man. Well, go on.'

'His Eminence was saddened to hear of the death of his old friend, the Vicomte de Cardonnel. He regretted that his age and infirmity did not allow him to reply personally to your kind letter. He instructed me, however, to send you some small memento when the time came in appreciation of your esteemed father's friendship and as an affectionate remembrance from one who received you into our Holy Church.' Anna looked up frowning. 'At least I think that's what it says. It's rather long-winded.'

'How very kind of the cardinal to remember you, Anna,' said Marie.

'I can't imagine why he should,' said Anna frankly. 'I don't remember him at all! But he was fond of Papa, I know. Papa was one of the few people who never pestered him for money. It seems odd to send me buttons, but they are certainly very pretty.'

'They would make a lovely necklace,' said Marie, turning over the buttons gently. 'You could even turn one into a cravat pin for Monsieur Redbourn.'

'Yes,' said Anna woodenly.

So that's it, thought Marie. She was just about to frame a careful sentence, when Anna looked up.

'Oh Tante Marie!' she cried. 'I'm so in love with him and he doesn't care for me at all!'

Laurence's second letter said, gleefully, that as Luke's wife would shortly be inheriting a fortune, he was willing to wait until after October 4 for his £20,000. Luke had better settle then, for the price would go up each succeeding week. He was not prepared to negotiate.

Laurence enjoyed writing the letter. At last he had Luke on his knees and he intended to milk him for every penny. His brother was lucky he didn't sting him for more, he thought. It was only his kindness for his sister that kept him from demanding double the sum. Laurence was not quite sure how much Anna would inherit, but le Vivier had assured him that £20,000 would be the least she could expect.

As Walter had discovered, Laurence had moved from Charles Street. He had, reluctantly, paid his landlady what he owed her, fearing that otherwise she might be only too willing to co-operate with any law officers on his track. By and large, Laurence knew, the inhabitants of the St Giles's Rookery kept their mouths shut when confronted by the law – or any others who came nosying about – but he would run no foolish risks.

His new lodgings were in Red Lion Street; a couple of backrooms overlooking the Blue Boar Yard. It was in a slightly more respectable area and his rooms on the second floor had an escape route in the shape of a pulley and chain attached to a cast-iron bracket sticking out of the wall just outside his window. This was to haul hay and straw up to the upper floors for storage, for the Blue Boar stabled forty horses, but Laurence had seen its other possibilities immediately. The Yard also had two useful exits, onto High Holborn and Eagle Street and Laurence reckoned that it was as safe as anywhere: he was well aware that this time he was playing a dangerous game.

If he lay low and avoided his previous haunts in St James's he should be safe enough. The last time he had been to the Smyrna Coffee House in Pall Mall it was made clear that he was no longer welcome. The waiter served him but he was cut by two former acquaintances with whom he had formerly enjoyed some pleasantly profitable rounds of piquet. Sir Robert – curse him – had obviously talked.

Fortunately, there were drinking places and plenty of brothels near to hand in Covent Garden. He did not notice that a man, sitting in the corner of the Unicorn Inn, was sizing him up.

This time, thought Laurence, his plans would work. He held the bonds and the credit notes. It was he who held the whip hand. He was just about to order another pint when there was a tap on his shoulder. Laurence spun round, one hand reaching for his knife.

'Whoa! That's no way to greet an old friend!' A shuffling, wizened little man wearing a red-spotted neckerchief, was looking at him.

'Le Vivier!' Laurence cursed under his breath. 'Where the devil have you sprung from?'

The man shrugged. 'Off the boat. Things got difficult in New York.'

'Things could get difficult over here,' said Laurence significantly.

'You wouldn't split on an old mate, Redbourn. Didn't I tell you about that fortune? Though from the look of you you ain't got it yet!' He gave a snigger, but hastily turned it into a cough when he saw Laurence's face. 'Sorry, no offence meant.'

'The bitch wouldn't play,' said Laurence sullenly. Le Vivier couldn't know anything about his plans and Laurence certainly wasn't going to tell him. 'My brother stole a march on me and married her himself.'

'Whew!' said le Vivier admiringly. He himself wouldn't care to get on the wrong side of the man in front of him. 'Cut his throat yet?'

Laurence gave a reluctant laugh. He surveyed the little man in front of him. Why the devil had he said anything? He didn't want le Vivier muscling in. He reached into his pocket and flicked him a guinea. 'Keep out of my way, le Vivier. I'm warning you. Or you could get hurt.'

'I don't want no trouble and I ain't seen you.'

'Good. Just keep it that way.' He watched as le Vivier shuffled his way over the sawdust-strewn floor and left. Laurence turned back to the bar. 'Another pint, Molly,' he said.

Le Vivier left the Unicorn and went towards Covent Garden which was full of stalls, semi-permanent wooden structures selling everything from eel pie and mash to vegetables. He stationed himself behind a coffee stall and waited. He was not finished with Redbourn, not by a long chalk. But first of all he needed to know where the bastard lived.

Miss le Vivier sat upright in the chair facing her lawyer in his rooms in Gray's Inn. She had dressed carefully for the occasion, for she had a difficult task in front of her. She knew that she was a little dab of a thing and whenever she had previously met Mr Hargreaves he had treated her with a sort of impatient condescension which Miss le Vivier found infuriating. She wore a grey pelisse with imposing steel buttons and a grey Capote bonnet embellished with a number of tall ostrich feathers, which she hoped would give her the dignity of height. 'I am extremely worried about the whole thing,' she informed him crisply.

Mr Hargreaves bowed impassively across the desk. 'I cannot reveal anything about your late uncle's affairs, Miss le Vivier. You must see that.' Plainly, the ostrich feathers had not impressed him with any notions of their owner's intelligence.

'It appears you already have!' snapped his visitor. 'You employed my cousin, Raymond le Vivier, if you remember.'

'He was dismissed.' Mr Hargreaves was tight-lipped. About two years ago he had come back unexpectedly into the office to find le Vivier poking his nose into business which did not concern him. The uncomfortable truth was that Mr Hargreaves had carelessly left a cupboard unlocked.

'And I know why,' stated Miss le Vivier. 'Raymond is as leaky as a sieve. Always was. He found out something he shouldn't have done about my uncle's will and sold the information.'

'Nonsense. Female hysteria.' Mr Hargreaves disliked being in the wrong, and still more being told of it by this diminutive female.

'Is it indeed! Raymond came to see me yesterday. He has been in America where he met a man named Laurence Redbourn, a good-for-nothing who had been got out of the way by his family after some embezzling. Now they're both back. My cousin is rather the worse for wear, but he tells me there's a reward out for this Laurence Redbourn. Unfortunately, as he jumped bail, he cannot go to Bow Street himself.'

'And what has this to do with me?' Mr Hargreaves glared at his visitor. He was remembering Luke Redbourn's and Miss de Cardonnel's visit and their story of the cabochon emerald.

'Merely that le Vivier told Redbourn that Miss de Cardonnel would inherit a fortune when she is twenty-one, in a few weeks' time. Redbourn returned to London in order to secure it by marrying the girl. Doubtless he then meant to get his hands on the money and desert her.'

Mr Hargreaves swallowed. 'Very well. I will confirm for you that Mr Ignatius left Miss de Cardonnel the bulk of his fortune. However, Miss de Cardonnel is now married to a Mr Luke Redbourn. There was a notice in *The Times*. My information is that he is a well-respected businessman. I have no reason to suppose that he is guilty of any wrong-doing.' He smiled grimly. 'Unless it was of getting a criminal young relative out of the country.'

'Are they related?'

'I imagine so. It can hardly be a coincidence that two Redbourns are both interested in the same young lady. But I will check on it, if you wish.'

'Thank you.' So that nice Mr Luke had married Miss de Cardonnel. At last they seemed to be getting somewhere, thought Miss le Vivier. Why was it that men always seemed to think that women had no brains? She had had to fight to get the smallest co-operation. If she'd been credited with some commonsense the problem could have been discussed in half the time. As it was, she felt exhausted and was longing for a cup of coffee.

Her uncle, Henry Ignatius, had always been one to hold his cards close to his chest, she reflected. He had left her £250 a year and the house, and she was very happy with that. But she was aware that he was, in fact, worth much more. She had not allowed her mind to dwell on it. He had provided for herself and the rest was not her business.

Miss le Vivier took a deep breath. 'I want you to do something for me, Mr Hargreaves. I am still concerned for Miss de Cardonnel's safety. My cousin seemed convinced that Laurence Redbourn had something planned. He knows where Mr Redbourn is living, but he can't go to Bow Street because of your charges against him. Of course, I could go myself....'

'Very well. If you wish it I shall withdraw my charges against your cousin.'

'Thank you.' Miss le Vivier said nothing more. They both knew that if she told Bow Street that the information about the will had originally gone astray because of Mr Hargreaves' carelessness then his reputation would be badly affected. But, having gained her point, she had no wish to humiliate him.

Mr Hargreaves, however, had different ideas. 'You should also know that Mr Ignatius founded his wealth on a very fine emerald belonging to the de Cardonnels, which had been given as security for money he'd paid out to get them out of France. He kept the emerald.'

'What do you mean? If the money wasn't forthcoming then he was entitled to do so!' Miss le Vivier flared up in defence of her uncle's integrity.

'Ah, but the vicomte had the money waiting. He made a number of well-publicized enquiries for Père Ignace, but in vain. Père Ignace was not to be found. No, Mr Ignatius decided to keep the emerald.'

'This cannot be true!'

'I'm afraid it is. Mr Luke Redbourn and Miss de Cardonnel came to see me about it. Their evidence was unimpeachable. There is absolutely no doubt that this emerald morally and legally belongs to Mrs Luke Redbourn.' Mr Hargreaves sat back and contemplated his visitor with some satisfaction. She was looking horrified and distressed. Serve her right, he thought, for thinking she could blackmail him, for that was what she'd done over her cousin. It would do her good to know that her sainted uncle was little better than a crook himself.

Miss le Vivier took a deep breath. 'If my uncle has not given it back to Miss de Cardonnel on her twenty-first birthday, I shall cease to have a mass said for him on the anniversary of his death!' she announced, two spots of pink flying on her cheeks.

Mr Hargreaves did not bother to suppress a smile.

Laurence had never been very good at inaction and the fact that he'd agreed to wait until after Anna's twenty-first birthday galled him. But there was no help for it. £20,000 was by far the biggest sum he'd been after in his shady career. He spent much of the time thinking what he would do with it, and indulged in some pleasant daydreams about strings of brothels and gambling dens. Some really high-class brothels, say, with the madam giving him a twenty per cent cut? Why, in no time he'd be rolling in the stuff. Laurence always preferred easy money.

The thought that le Vivier might try anything never crossed his mind: he had long ago written him off as a harmless little tick. He'd pulled a knife on le Vivier once in New York and the chap had practically blubbered! No, le Vivier would keep out of his way, if he valued his skin.

His mind turned to gambling dens. Now what was needed there was a hostess who was up to all the rigs. Somebody who was attractive but clever enough to run the place without falling into the trap of either gambling herself or drinking too much.

Helen Clarkson! Now she'd make a good hostess. She might just jump at it, too. Laurence doubted whether she would have been able to get a job at the theatre after he'd roughed her up. Yes, Helen would be grateful to see him. And if she needed a little persuading ... well, he knew one or two things about her....

Where the devil did she live? Ah yes, Henrietta Street. He'd go this very minute.

The landlady at 27 Henrietta Street was politely uncooperative. 'Miss Clarkson does not reside here hany more,' she informed him in arctic tones.

That did not surprise Laurence. She was probably shivering in some cheap attic. She couldn't have had much in the way of savings when he'd last seen her.

'Her address then, woman,' he said impatiently.

'She didn't leave hany haddress.'

'But she must have done....'

The door shut in his face. Laurence kicked it but it remained unyielding. A drink or two later in the Unicorn and he felt better. He still had some of Luke's money from the strong-box. Maybe a night with a whore would be as good a way of passing the time as any? He stopped at one of the Covent Garden stalls and bought himself a pie and then made his way homeward. It was still a bit early to visit a brothel, things only livened up there in the evenings. He'd go home, get some money, have a drink and then, in an hour or so, set out.

As he crossed over High Holborn he did not notice a burly individual in a shop doorway. Behind him was a weasly little man wearing a red-spotted neckerchief.

'That's him, guv. Tall cove with the blue coat.'

'All right. Now you make yourself scarce.'

'But the reward?'

'We ain't got him yet, 'ave we? Don't you worry. We've been after this'un for some weeks. We ain't likely to let 'im go.'

The landlady let Laurence in. If she looked at him strangely, Laurence did not notice. He was still put out about not being able to get hold of Helen and her landlady's rudeness rankled. Nor did he notice that the moment he had gone up the stairs and the front door had shut behind him, a man came and stood there, blocking the exit.

Out the back, in the Blue Boar Yard, a man had just finished removing the chain from the bracket and pulley. Nobody was saying anything but, although the yard was quiet, a number of stableboys and ostlers were standing at the windows. News had got round surprisingly fast that an arrest might be made and nobody wanted to miss the fun.

It wasn't until Laurence opened the door to his rooms that he realized that they were already occupied. Two law officers, one with handcuffs swinging from his belt and both with cudgels, were waiting.

'What the …?' He swung round. Another officer was on the landing behind him.

'I arrest you, Laurence Redbourn, for theft, blackmail and attempted murder!'

Laurence slammed the door onto the landing and shot the

bolt. He whipped out his knife. 'I'll kill anyone who comes a step nearer.' Neither of them had guns. If he could just get to the back window he could make it. The two officers exchanged glances. Laurence backed slowly towards the window, one hand behind his back to fumble with the catch. The officers moved slowly forward but kept out of range of the knife, Laurence noted.

Cowards and fools. He'd never had much respect for the forces of the law. The casement window flew open. Laurence turned and leapt for the chain.

Down in the yard someone flung an old horse blanket over the spreadeagled body on the cobblestones. A man came forward with some straw to soak up the blood.

It was several hours later that Luke, escorted by two officers, entered the room. Laurence's body, cleaned and laid out was on the stripped bed, covered with a sheet. On the table was a pile of bonds, credit notes and other documents. A guard, posted sentry at the door, saluted as Luke entered.

The officer drew back the sheet. 'Can you identify the body, sir?'

Luke looked. 'Yes,' he said after a long moment. His voice seemed to come from a long way away. 'It is my brother, Laurence Redbourn.' Laurence's face looked much younger and once again he could trace the little brother he had loved. 'God rest his soul.' He stooped and kissed Laurence's forehead. Laurence would hate this, Luke thought, but it was for Hester and for the small boy he'd lost so long ago.

The officer waited respectfully and then covered the body again. Luke straightened up.

'We've checked everything against the list you gave us, sir. It's all here. Though there's not much of the money left.' He pointed to about twenty guineas in two neat piles on the table.

Luke ran his hand through his hair. He suddenly felt

immensely tired. There was a chair by the table and he sank down onto it.

'If you'll just go through it with us, sir, and sign for it.'

'Yes, yes. Of course.' Luke tried to clear his head and concentrate.

It was all done eventually. The papers and money packed into a wooden box provided by the officer. Luke signed the forms and in return was given authorization to bury the body. 'I'll have it transferred to the mortuary, sir.'

'Thank you.'

'Sergeant Penge will get you a cab and go home with you.' The officer looked at Luke with concern.

'Cab?' said Luke vaguely.

'Go with him, Sergeant.'

Shock, thought the officer. He'd seen it before. The gentleman would be all right in a day or so. Nasty business though. Laurence Redbourn sounded like a rat, one better off dead. Still, he was the gentleman's brother when all was said and done. He saw Luke and the sergeant off the premises.

As the officer had thought, Luke quickly recovered the tone of his mind. There was much to do; the funeral to arrange, letters to write, and a discreet notice to be inserted in *The Morning Post* and *The Times. On Monday, September 21st, as the result of an accident, Laurence Redbourn, late of London. The funeral has taken place privately.*

For most of the next few days he was closeted with Walter and the clerks checking the returned documents and arranging for a new wall safe to be built. There was nothing now to prevent him setting the wheels for the annulment of his marriage in motion, but he took no steps. Perhaps it was just that he was overwhelmed by other business.

Hester was less resilient. The news of Laurence's death affected her profoundly and for some days she was unable to do anything but weep or sit stony-faced, eating nothing and barely able to speak. Minerva commandeered the parson's gig and came over to comfort her friend and persuade her to take some short drives for her health. Hester, like an automaton, did as she was told: it was simply less fatiguing to do as Minerva wished than to refuse and face the inevitable arguments.

All Anna could feel at first was an overwhelming relief. She had not realized how oppressive the burden had been until it was lifted. It was she who had written to Minerva informing her of Laurence's death and begging her to come and help Hester. She wrote to Tante Marie and Sir Robert too, giving what details she knew. (Sir Robert passed them on to Helen, now installed in a pretty cottage in Brompton. 'Serve him right,' was Helen's comment.) It was Anna who arranged for mourning clothes for herself and Hester and a black armband for Emmy. She didn't see why poor Emmy, who knew nothing of Laurence, should be taken out of her pretty prints.

If one burden had been lifted for Anna with Laurence's death, another remained. She did not know what was happening about her marriage. She didn't dare approach Luke on the subject. It had been a comfort to her to open her heart to Tante Marie. She now realized that Luke had not been so uninterested in her as she had thought. She had missed many small advances, at least, so Tante Marie had told her.

'A man like Monsieur Redbourn would never hint that he wanted a kiss unless he meant it, Anna,' she said. 'Do you mean to say that you never responded to any of these advances?'

'I scarcely recognized them,' confessed Anna. 'I thought he was just being kind. Or that I'd misinterpreted them.'

'And you a Frenchwoman!'

'But what can I do, Tante Marie?'

'You could try being a little more encouraging,' said Marie dryly.

But then Laurence had been killed and everything had become much more difficult. Anna couldn't believe that, once the first shock was over, Luke grieved overmuch for his brother. But all the same, so awful an ending must have had its effect. It would be grossly indelicate for her to start offering her affection now. Perhaps in a few weeks....

Even that hope was crushed by Luke saying diffidently one evening when Hester had gone to bed, 'Perhaps we should discuss your going home, Anna.'

'Going home?' echoed Anna, her heart sinking.

'I'm sure you must want to.' Luke's voice was strained.

'Want to?' All she wanted was here with her in this room in Ludgate Street.

Luke had turned away and she could not see his face as he said, 'I am, of course, ready to put in hand the annulment of our marriage. Laurence is dead. There is no more threat.'

Anna could say nothing. An ice-cold band seemed to have closed itself around her heart. The clock on the mantelpiece said half past nine. It would be frozen there for all eternity.

'But,' continued Luke, still not looking round, 'I'd be grateful if you would consider staying for a while. Perhaps until after your birthday. Hester is really in no state to be left alone.'

'Of course I'll stay.' Anna now knew how a condemned prisoner might feel, granted a reprieve. The clock moved on. Anna found she could breathe again.

Luke got up. 'Anna?' She looked up hopefully. 'Nothing. Not important.' He fiddled for a moment or two with a couple of cotton reels left out on the table and then left the room.

Anna's birthday fell on a Sunday and such was her general state of unhappiness that she had almost forgotten it, except as the date when she would lose Luke. So far as she was concerned, far from being the beginning of anything, it was the ending. The Friday before she had received a letter from Mr

Hargreaves asking Mr and Mrs Redbourn to call on Monday, October 5 at 11 a.m. when he would have something to Mrs Redbourn's material advantage to impart to her.

A letter from Child's Bank informed her that she was now the mistress of the sum of £500 left to her by her father, together with the interest accruing, and they awaited her instructions in the matter. Hester roused herself sufficiently to give her a fine silk shawl. There were greetings from Tante Marie and Luke presented her with an English-Italian dictionary.

'Rather dull, I'm afraid,' he said. 'But I thought it would be useful.'

'Thank you,' said Anna. 'I'm most grateful. They are not easy to come by, and I really needed one.' It was true. It was a thoughtful present, but hardly a romantic one.

The following day Anna and Luke set out for Gray's Inn. Their reception at Mr Hargreaves' this time was very different. As soon as Luke gave their names they were shown into the office. They were offered chairs. Mrs Redbourn was congratulated on attaining her majority. Mr Redbourn was offered condolences on the unhappy death of his brother.

Eventually the courtesies were over and Mr Hargreaves allowed himself to get on with the business in hand. 'First of all I am happy to inform you, Mrs Redbourn, that Mr Henry Ignatius left you the bulk of his fortune which amounts to ...' – he consulted his notes – 'something in the region of sixty thousand pounds.' He sat back smiling.

Anna went quite white. 'Sixty thousand!' she whispered. Luke will never want me now, she thought, and risk being labelled a fortune-hunter. 'But why me?'

'I suppose you might call it the payment of a debt. Mr Ignatius used your family emerald as collateral against a loan. It was that that enabled him to found his business empire. Mr Ignatius made his money in canals, you know.'

219

'But the emerald. Why did he not get in touch with my father?' Anna was still stunned.

'I do not know why he chose to do it this way. Guilt possibly. However, he was very specific when he came to me in 1801. He did not want to leave the money to your father. It was all to go to you when you were twenty-one. Of course, I had no idea that the emerald was not honestly come by.' He looked from Anna to Luke. 'But your husband will look after all this for you. Finance is not a lady's business.'

Anna opened her mouth and shut it again.

The lawyer unlocked a drawer and handed Anna a small parcel. 'This'll be more to your taste, I dare swear.'

The parcel was bulky and Anna knew what it was the moment she felt it. She opened it and there, wrapped in a roll of silk, was the cabochon emerald. Suddenly she was back in Tante Marie's kitchen in Paris, looking at it by the light of a guttering candle.

'I haven't seen this for fourteen years,' she breathed. She picked it up gently. It was even more beautiful than she had remembered: the gold filigree with its twinkling diamonds and rubies and the mysterious green stone with the fire in its heart. She turned to show it to Luke.

'It's lovely. I've never seen anything like it.'

'A fine piece,' agreed Mr Hargreaves. 'I remember Rundell and Bridge saying they'd rarely seen anything so fine of its type.'

When they left half an hour or so later. Mr Hargreaves himself came to the door to bow them out.

'Something of a change,' observed Luke.

'He's bowing out sixty thousand pounds,' said Anna cynically. She felt completely exhausted. All she wanted to do was crawl away and hibernate. Never had she felt so lonely or bereft.

They got into the cab. 'You can do what you like now,'

observed Luke heartily. 'A house in the best part of Town, your own carriage, a handsome duke, anything.'

Anna suddenly reached the end of her tether. 'I wish I'd never heard of that wretched fortune!' she found herself shouting. 'So far as I can see all it's going to bring me is misery. You're right, I'm sure. I can buy everything I want. Even, as you suggest, a husband. Wonderful! And what about me? Where do I fit into all this? Who's going to want to know me when I'm surrounded by this desirable golden glitter? I wish I were dead.' And that Luke, too, seemed to take for granted that this was what she wanted! Oblivious to everything else she burst into tears.

'Anna!' Luke tried to put an arm round her but she hunched herself away from him. She wouldn't speak for the rest of the journey home. Once inside she went straight up to her room and shut the door.

This behaviour was so unlike Anna that after luncheon, when she still hadn't appeared, Luke hailed a cab and went straight to Phoenix Street.

Marie was in the shop with Hercule sitting at her feet. There were a number of customers and Luke waited impatiently until she'd finished serving them. Marie grasped at once that this was something serious; she had never seen Luke look so concerned and pale. Had anything happened to Anna? She called to François to look after the shop and took Luke down to the kitchen.

Luke sat down heavily.

'You've been to see Mr Hargreaves, I expect?'

'Yes.' Luke gave her a brief run-down and then told her of Anna's outburst in the cab. 'I swear I had no idea she would take it like this,' he exclaimed. 'I thought she'd be pleased. God knows she's had enough to worry her the last few months.'

Englishmen! thought Marie. They knew all about horses or their wretched weather, but were baffled by a woman's heart. Did he really have no idea as to what was the matter?

'Perhaps I should get on with this annulment,' Luke was saying. 'Anna agreed to wait because my poor sister was in a state over my brother's death. Maybe it was selfish of me to ask her to stay....' His voice trailed away.

Marie took the bull by the horns. 'Do you want this annulment, Monsieur Redbourn?'

Luke looked at her and then looked away. 'I had hoped ...' he began and then stopped.

'I'm not convinced Anna wants it either.' She hoped she could say that without betraying Anna.

Luke looked dazed. 'Are you sure?'

'Why don't you ask her and see?'

The following afternoon Anna was alone. Luke and Walter were out somewhere on business and the clerks were shut up in the office. Hester had gone out with Minerva. They were going to a recital by Madame Catalini and Hester would not be back until late. Emmy was in the kitchen struggling to grate sugar from the sugar cone.

Anna wandered into the drawing-room and sank down. Ben jumped up onto her lap and idly she began to stroke him. What was the point in prolonging the agony, she thought? Sooner or later Hester would be willing and able to take up the reins of housekeeping again. Luke had already mentioned the annulment once. Now there was no more mystery about the will, doubtless he'd mention it again. Probably tonight after dinner.

She tried to contemplate her future and found that she couldn't think at all. Nothing occurred. The future she was facing was a dreary blank. Would Luke ever miss her? Or would he just be relieved that life had gone back to normal and in due course offer for Caroline Simpson?

Unable to bear the tenor of her thoughts Anna pushed Ben off her lap and went to see about dinner.

Mr and Mrs Redbourn ate their evening meal more or less in silence. Mr Redbourn congratulated his wife on her cooking. Mrs Redbourn hoped that her husband had had a successful day. Conversation languished. Emmy cleared away the plates. The Redbourns moved through to the drawing-room and sat down, one on each side of the fender. Luke picked up the paper, Anna her sewing.

Time passed. Emmy was heard clattering upstairs to bed. The clock struck half past nine. Anna got up to see to the tea.

Luke suddenly put down the paper. 'Anna, I think we must discuss the future.'

Anna sat down again. It has come, she thought, dully. This is it.

'I know we have agreed on an annulment....' Luke seemed to have some difficulty in continuing. 'But....'

'But?' whispered Anna, hardly daring to breathe.

Luke got up and walked to the window. 'Of course, if that is what you want I shall go ahead.'

'What do you want?' Anna's voice was scarcely audible.

Luke turned round. He walked over to where Anna was sitting and pulled her to her feet. 'Oh Anna, I'm afraid you won't like it, but I love you so much! All I want is to take you on a proper honeymoon....'

'But Luke,' Anna held his hands tightly. 'That is what I want, too!'

'Thank God!' Luke let go of her hands and pulled her into his arms. There was silence for some considerable time. At length Luke raised his head and said tenderly, 'Sweetheart, you are allowed to breathe!'

Anna took several gulps of air. 'It's just that I'm not used to this!'

'I should hope not,' said Luke virtuously. 'Here, let me show you....'

* * *

Hester got back from the recital at about half past ten. There was an oil 'peg' lamp lit in the hall as usual. She went through to the kitchen to check that all was well there and to her surprise found Ben sitting outside on the window ledge looking very disgruntled. She opened the window and let him in. He liked to sleep on one of the kitchen chairs and now had a drink of water and curled himself up and settled down. Odd, thought Hester. Surely Anna usually lets him in?

She picked up the lamp and went upstairs. In the drawing-room the tea things were sitting on their tray, unused. The room had the air of having been vacated suddenly: cushions were unplumped, chairs not pushed back into place.

Up on the top landing Anna's bedroom door was open. Mystified, Hester peeped inside. It was empty.

She looked across at Luke's room. The door was shut, but there, on the floor outside, was a rosette from one of Anna's shoes.